VIVIANA
VALENTINE
AND THE
TICKING CLOCK

ALSO AVAILABLE BY EMILY J. EDWARDS

THE GIRL FRIDAY MYSTERIES

Viviana Valentine Goes Up the River

Viviana Valentine Gets Her Man

VIVIANA VALENTINE AND THE TICKING CLOCK

A GIRL FRIDAY MYSTERY

Emily J. Edwards

CROOKED
LANE

NEW YORK

Published in the United States by Crooked Lane Books, an imprint of The Quick Brown Fox & Company LLC.

Crooked Lane Books and its logo are trademarks of The Quick Brown Fox & Company LLC.

Library of Congress Catalog-in-Publication data available upon request.

ISBN (hardcover): 978-1-63910-522-9
ISBN (ebook): 978-1-63910-523-6

Cover illustration by Rui Ricardo

Printed in the United States.

www.crookedlanebooks.com

Crooked Lane Books
34 West 27th St., 10th Floor
New York, NY 10001

First Edition: November 2023

10 9 8 7 6 5 4 3 2 1

For David, as always.

THE CHARACTERS

Viviana Valentine—a private investigator
Tommy Fortuna—a fiancé
Detective Jake Lawson—a cop
Herb Sabella—a reporter
Betty Wagner—a nurse
Dottie Robbins—a teacher
Mrs. Svitlana Kovalenko—a mother
Oleks Kovalenko—a son
Mr. Floristan—a victim
Mr. Bowen—a banker
Trevor Penhaligon—a missing man
Morty Lobel—a curious man
Rachel Blum—a bride-to-be
Sergiy Doroshenko—a homeowner
Thelma Thompkins—a photographer
Bill—a banker
Steve—a banker
Norma Ragazzo—a dancer
Rocío Luna—a math teacher
Peggy—a secretary
Frankie—a real piece of work

Marvin Girardi—a working man
Benjamin—a mystery
Henrik Fiskar—a tragedy
Tallulah Blackstone—a movie producer

NIGHT 1

Sunday, December 31st, 1950

"How many years in this city," I said, tagging after Tommy who was clipping down the sidewalk in his rubber-soled boots like a Clydesdale on a mission, "and I never *once* went down to the party."

"Well, the problem with New Year's Eve being in December is that it's freezing, it's snowing, and it's miserable," Tommy shouted back over his shoulder. Half of his words were lost to the wind whipping through the buildings towering over us as we approached the crowds, but it was his usual spiel, so I knew exactly how to fill in what I was missing.

"They should move it to May," I said in unison with him.

"You're right, Dollface," he said, stopping to wrap his arm around my waist and swing me toward him. "I need to stop my bitching."

"Ah, but then I might not like you anymore, ol' Tommy boy," I said, planting one on the two inches of exposed cheek between the brim of his hat and the top of his muffler, then wiggling away to continue on down the sidewalk. I wasn't missing the grand finale for anything in the world. Tommy hated the cold, and it was a testament to how much he liked *me* that, when our new secretary said it'd be a romantic night for us to go and see all the hullabaloo in Times Square for New Year's Eve, he played along and said *sure*.

"How are you so cheery?" Tommy asked, once again taking my hand and pulling me closer. He took a quick look 'round and spotted that, possibly for the first time in all of history, two people were alone on the sidewalks of New York City. He shuffled me toward a stoop, lifted me up, and planted my caboose on the hefty end of a fancy concrete railing leading up to a fancier private brownstone, and laid one right on me. "It's thirty degrees outside. We're about to go stand in a crowd of drunks for an hour to watch something we could hear about on the radio."

"There's a big difference," I said, rooting my frozen nose between his ear and his shoulder, eliciting a yelp as my cold flesh met his, hot and sweaty to the touch, "between hearing something and seeing it. But just once—*just this once*—I want to do this." I made the statement firmly, and because he was him and I was me, he knew better than to try to change my mind.

Ever since we got engaged around Thanksgiving, my landlady, Mrs. Svitlana Kovalenko, had not batted an eye if I didn't return home for dinner—or breakfast—every day. She was thrilled that we'd finally agreed to marry, and when Tommy was out of earshot, she frequently *harrumphed* that it was about damn time my boss had proposed, even though we'd never dated in the near-decade that I had worked for him.

Her brother, who owns the property she manages in Chelsea, arranged with Tommy to turn the top floor of the house into a real-life apartment for us to share, but Tommy felt strange staying the night at what was still an all-girls boarding house—especially because our secretary, Betty, lived downstairs. So it was a few nights a week at Tommy's apartment in Hell's Kitchen, just a few blocks north of our office, with plenty of locks on the doors and some neighbors who had enough on their own minds not to notice if Tommy and his new flame made a fair amount of noise. It's not like I was the first and only dame Tommy'd ever brought 'round.

"Fine, fine," Tommy said, pulling away from me. Without his body to block the wind, I was hit with a fire-extinguishing blast of cold. "But we better hurry if we want to see anything at all."

I hopped off the concrete and landed on the sidewalk, my feet slipping and Tommy's arm there to prop me up as I skidded like a cartoon character and laughed. If I planted my keister down in the snow, I wouldn't feel it for hours, that's for sure—I was frozen to the bone.

"I can only go as fast as my little feet will carry me through all of this ice," I said. "They need to make those kinds of rubber-soled boots for women, I tell you."

"We'll just get you ones for men," Tommy said. "Function over fashion, sometimes."

"You're still going to find me attractive if I'm thumping around in men's boots?" I said, poking him in the side.

"Viviana Valentine, I'd find you attractive in a potato sack," Tommy said. "But let's not put it to the test."

With every passing block, the crowds grew thicker, even though most of the partyers didn't seem to be heading toward the big show. Groups took to their stoops, singing Christmas carols and slugging hard liquor out of bottles, hidden from the law but not from knowing eyes, in paper bags.

"Happy Halloween!" A man in a holey sweater leaned over the railing of his porch to wave and throw confetti, and his friend grabbed him by the belt to keep him from landing in the junipers.

"And a merry Arbor Day to you, too, pal," I shouted back, waving.

"Stop encouraging them," Tommy grumbled.

"I promise to have you indoors and in bed as soon as possible, Mr. Fortuna," I said. "The second that ball hits the ground, we'll scram*ola* back to your place. You have my word."

Tommy nodded like I was making a blood oath. "Here, this'll cut through."

We shuffled through to an alleyway, and there were two more figures racing to the sidewalk near 9th Avenue, hurrying in the direction of the raucous crowds whose singing and jeers could be heard ricocheting off every building front. The man in front tripped and stumbled, and his companion caught him, slowly lowering him to the ground where he lay, his friend shaking him by the shoulders and trying to get him to come to.

"Is this much of a shortcut worth it?" I asked. "I can't see any of the schmutz beneath this snow and I am *not* stepping in garbage tonight. I don't want to smell like rotting shi—"

"Viv, stop." Tommy's hand jerked back and pushed me toward the side of the building. The force sent me flying on a sheet of ice and I slammed into some metal bins, making a clang. The crouching friend turned to look at us, his face obscured by his upturned coat collar. But he got up and ran off, leaving his companion near the downspout of the corner store.

"You check on the man on the ground," Tommy said. "Be careful."

Before I could even ask, Tommy was sprinting through the slush after the fleeing figure, and I was approaching the man who was left behind. His long, camel-colored coat was soaking through with blood near his hips, and his face was as pale as the snow around him and growing whiter by the second. There was a blood-covered knife next to his right hand, where it'd fallen by the wayside and clattered when his attacker ran off. I pulled open his coat and threw off my scarf, pressing it as hard as I could into his stomach wound. The scent of blood was everywhere, mixing with the light crispness of the snow and the stench of disturbed garbage.

I couldn't say a word. But my silence didn't stop the man whose life was coursing through my fingers from whispering his final words.

"Tell Frankie," he said, reaching for my hands, "it's okay."

It certainly was *not* okay, and I had mucus and tears rolling down my face as I only pressed harder into his gut, trying to stop the bleeding.

"I'm sorry," he said through his own tears.

And that was that.

All the noise of the party sounded like it was a million miles away, underwater, and like my ears were filled with cotton wool. What I could really hear was the pounding of my own heart and the sniffles of my involuntary need to keep the contents of my sinuses from further running down my face and onto a dead body. Not only was it disrespectful, but it'd also contaminate the crime scene. My fingers were frozen and my hands were shaking. Everything was Jell-O.

Tommy came back as I was searching through the dead man's pockets.

"All he has is cash," I said. "No ID, as far as I can tell. So this wasn't a robbery, or else the guy would've taken his money."

"You're right," Tommy said, trying to pull me away. But I wouldn't budge.

"I take it you didn't get him," I said without turning around. There was something light in the man's overcoat pocket, and I couldn't tell what it was through the thick, woolen fabric.

"No," Tommy said. "He knew where he was going. Made it to the fringes of the crowd then disappeared. No one's going to notice a man covered in blood on New Year's Eve. Half the crowd ends up in brawls."

"Did you call him yet?"

"Yeah, they said he'd be here as soon as he could."

"Thanks, Tommy," I said, pulling two matchbooks out of the man's pocket. They looked blank, except for a hint of gleaming white ink on the matte white paper of the book. Both match-books were brand new, and no matter how much I moved the cover in the light of the streets, I couldn't tell what was printed on it. "We'll just take the one, I guess. Leave the other for the cops."

"Generous of you, Viv," Tommy said. "Now get up."

"Let me keep checking his pockets!"

"Get *up*, Viviana." Tommy put his hands under my armpits and hoisted me like a toddler.

"Do not *ever* do that again, Tomasso Antonino Fortuna," I said, whipping around to stare into his eyes. "I know what I'm doing, and I don't like to be manhandled."

"I know you don't. But you are *covered* in blood, Dollface," Tommy said, pulling me in for a hug. I was shaking from the top of my head to my toes, and colder than I'd ever been before in my life, even when I was locked in an attic in Tarrytown in November. "And I need you to calm down before he gets here."

"Let me go for a sec," I muttered into his shoulder.

"You're freezing," Tommy whispered into the crook of my neck.

"Let me *go* for a sec!"

"No, Dollf . . ."

"I'm going to go heave into the trash."

"Right, there you go," Tommy said, releasing me. "That's the woman I fell in love with."

I raced to the side of the alley but couldn't get the cans open in time, upchucking a fair amount of Champagne onto the tops of several trash bins. "Oh God, I need to clean this up."

"There's a dead body on the sidewalk," Tommy said, pulling me away from my mess. "No one cares. You won't be the only person leaving a mess in an alley tonight. Besides, I see Lawson coming down this way. Look alive, Valentine."

I wiped my mouth with the back of my left hand and Tommy pushed my hair in place, but nothing was going to detract from the fact that my coat, hose, and shoes were soaked in a stranger's blood and guts. Detective Jake Lawson was coming down the alley to us, and in order to distract him from my mess, I walked as quick as I could to meet him halfway.

"Hey there, baby," he said, raising a hand for me to shake it. "Imagine my sadness when I heard you were off the market."

"I'm not going to shake your hand," I said, lifting my gloves for him to see the deep red stains. "I'd ruin your perfect outfit." Lawson was wearing a black topcoat in fine wool, a white silken scarf, black tuxedo pants, and shiny black shoes. "Where were you? The opera?"

"I was at my mother's," he said. "She's nearby."

"Jeez Louise," I said. "Does she demand you get in a penguin suit for holidays?"

"No." Lawson was terse, and his cheeks were reddening, but it may have been the wind.

"Regardless of why you're in that ridiculous getup," Tommy said, taking the detective's gloved hand in his own, "no woman with any self-respect goes out with a man who acts as though she's for sale."

"Funny you should say that on a night like tonight," Lawson added. "Plenty of girls in Times Square would beg to differ about whether or not they're for sale."

"They're providing a service," Tommy said, "not selling themselves."

"That's one way to look at it, Fortuna," Lawson said. "But let's stop arguing. There's a dead body on the sidewalk in case you haven't noticed."

There were three beat cops on the curb, attempting to shuffle drunken revelers away from the crime scene. The sidewalk was littered with footprints, garbage, and a new-falling snow. I didn't recognize any of the boys in blue, so I piped up to ask.

"Where's your little setter-dog, O'Malley? The short one I met over the summer."

Lawson stared at me hard, his face contorted. "What?"

"The little red-headed cop. He doesn't like blood, is that why you left him home?"

"He's not going anywhere," Lawson said. "I take it your little engagement is why you didn't read the papers."

"What?"

"K.I.A."

"*What?*"

"He tried to stop a hold-up off duty around Thanksgiving," Lawson said. "He tried to sneak up on a gang with a little Colt Detective he got without us knowing, but they beat the snot out of him. Head injury, right on the sidewalk."

"Good God."

"Shoulda called for on-duty officers and backup." Lawson shrugged. "Poor kid. We put together a collection to help with the funeral."

"He was what? Twenty-two?"

"If that."

"Did you get the guys who killed him?" Tommy grunted. He didn't know O'Malley from a hole in the wall, but Tommy wasn't a big fan of unsolved murder cases, considering what happened to his only brother.

"Probably not," Lawson said.

"You're a real piece of work." Tommy motioned toward the body in front of us on the sidewalk. "Now what about this guy?"

"I know you already took everything out of his clothes," Lawson said. "So . . ." He placed his leather-gloved hand out, and I deposited the cash and a matchbook. "That's it?"

"That's it. No ID, no keys, no nothing," I said. "The suspected murder weapon is by his hand."

"Yeah, we found it. Standard steak knife," Lawson said. "No logo, as far as we can tell from here. Could've come from anywhere—there's forty some-odd restaurants in a three-block radius, or it could've come from home. How long did it take him to bleed out?"

"A few minutes," I said. "They got him low, across the abdomen. I'm surprised his guts didn't fall out."

"He was in a seated position for most of it," Tommy added, "leaning back against the wall. Gravity did everyone a small favor there."

"Not sure if this guy would consider anything a favor," Lawson said, nudging him with a toe.

"At least have some respect, Lawson," I said. "I did the best I could trying to stop the blood."

"And you chased the other fella?" the detective asked, now turning to Tommy.

"He was headed straight for the crowd, knew exactly what to do to get lost," Tommy said. "He was a block ahead of me the whole time. My height, speedy fella, I couldn't get an idea of the build or his coloring because of the winter clothes. You can hide a lot under layers of wool. He could have been skinny as a bean pole under it all."

"It was a dark blue topcoat," I added. "Buttons same color—nothing shiny. No hat, gray slacks, black boots. Brown hair. No scarf or gloves, so there may be fingerprints."

"You're describing half the men out tonight in their soiled Sunday best," the detective said. "We'll try for prints, but unless we get lucky and someone files a missing person . . . we're up a creek and this guy is going in Potter's Field."

"That's the spirit I like out of my cops," I spat. "Futility. Hopelessness. Makes me feel awful safe."

"I'm just being realistic, Valentine," Lawson said. "But knowing you two, you're gonna chase it like hounds."

There was a ruckus out in the street, and the flatfoots waiting on the sidewalk turned their gaze away from the body and brought their mitts out of their pockets to lay 'em on a fella with a dark overcoat and a Kodak Pony.

"Tommy Fortuna, Tommy Fortuna!" The fellow was waving. "Can I get a statement?"

"What in the world . . ." My knees were shaking and I squinted to make out a face in the dark.

"Shit." Lawson turned his back to the bellowing man.

"Who's that?" I asked.

"Herb Sabella," Tommy muttered through gritted teeth. "Goddamn Herb Sabella."

I stared at the muckraker. "I thought he'd be taller."

"Nah, he's a sniveling, little, disrespectful piece of work," Lawson said. "And lucky for you, pal, he thinks this is *your* case." Lawson clapped Tommy on the shoulder and skittered further into the shadows of the alley.

"I'm taking Viv home to get her cleaned up," Tommy said with a sigh. "We'll be in touch."

"I have no doubt." Lawson tipped his hat in my direction and turned his back on us, just in time for two men in white coats with a canvas stretcher to arrive to collect our corpse.

"We better get back to your place, Tommy," I said. "I can't show up to Mrs. K's like this."

"No, you can't," he said. "But we're going to have to walk. No taxi is going to pick you up, neither."

It was a long, slow walk back through the blocks and up four flights of stairs to Tommy's bachelor apartment. I had to admit, it was a great place—a nice, cozy living room with a Victorian fireplace that still burned a few small pieces of coal at a time, a little kitchen, and a great big bedroom where Tommy had long ago placed a welcoming brass bed. I stood just inside the door while Tommy rummaged through his closet and emerged with the top part of his flannel night clothes and a pair of thick socks.

"They're a bit itchy," he said, "but Uncle Sam knows how to keep your tootsies warm."

"I'm just going to strip off right here," I said. "I don't want to track this all over."

"I appreciate that," Tommy said.

"Then I'm going to take a long, hot shower."

"Until the water runs out, I imagine," Tommy said. "And I will meet you in bed with some hot food."

"Thanks." I somehow hadn't gotten soaked to my slip, so I left all my outer clothes in a pile and went off to wash away the remaining gore of our mystery man. I heard the sound of a million people cheering reverberating off the white subway tile in Tommy's bathroom.

It was 1951 and we had a murder to solve.

DAY 2

Monday, January 1st, 1951

I pulled a frock out of Tommy's closet and dressed myself as well as I could out of what I'd left lying around in the past six weeks. I didn't have any clean stockings or a different coat; I had to shove bare feet into my boots, and the heel was rubbing something awful. There wasn't nearly enough to keep me warm for the mile-long walk back to Chelsea—even layered in three of Tommy's thickest sweaters—so he ran down the stairs and hailed a cab and whistled at me from the curb once he'd managed to rope one.

The driver gave me the eye as I slipped into the back seat next to Tommy, who decided that the day would best be spent in Mrs. K's warm dining room instead of his apartment with neighbors who were working through whatever substances they had partaken of the night before.

"Where to?" the cabbie leered.

"Thirty-fourth and 8th," Tommy said, taking control. "Mother-in-law is preparing a feast." Tommy took my hand, and we settled back against the frozen vinyl seat. There was frost on the inside and outside of the windows, and the heat from the car radiator smelled like dust and burning rubber.

"You got the matchbook?" I asked

"Right here," Tommy said, patting his breast pocket. "But don't worry about that right now. What's on the menu for today?"

"Well, she didn't get to celebrate much when she was back in the old country," I said. "The Soviets barred all celebration . . . for whatever reasons they had. So now that she's here, watch out. You're going to have to loosen that belt, ol' Tommy boy."

"You're leaving me in anticipation, Dollface," Tommy laughed.

"Listen, there's a lot of pickles, you're just going to have to deal with that," I said. "And I don't just mean pickled cukes. You'd never *think* of what they could pickle. Then there's the pork, and the cabbage in all sorts of forms, and caviar."

"You're joking," the cabbie piped in.

"Nope, her brother's a diamond dealer, and generous to boot," I said. "He sent over a great big basket with all the fixin's on the thirtieth and then we all stared at it, drooling. She promised we'd get to eat it on New Year's Day."

"You got any sisters?" the cabbie asked.

"Two, but they're real picky," I said, laughing as I imagined introducing Dottie, my housemate who was a happy spinster elementary school teacher, flirting with this rough-and-tumble fella who wanted an in for dinner.

"Ah, well, I'll just enjoy the sandwich my wife made me, as usual," he said, brandishing a hoagie wrapped in white paper. "You're here."

Tommy paid the man and tipped nicely, and we were greeted at the door by our secretary, Betty.

"Well, good morning, you two," she purred.

Betty had been harboring a not-at-all secret crush on Tommy the entire time I lived with her, but she didn't seem at all put out now that he was spoken for. She contended she always knew that we were an item, and I didn't know how to get her to grasp the truth that there had been no smoochin' on the desks at work . . . at least not until a few weeks ago. But 'round about the time that Tommy and I got hot and heavy, Betty had been fired from her position as an emergency room nurse and took the opportunity to work for us for a little while as our Girl Friday, since our last one moved to Los Angeles a few days after Turkey Day to become a movie producer. I didn't know what that meant, but Tally Blackstone assured me she had both the bucks for it and enough opinions to turn the whole of Hollywood on its head. And if anyone could turn a town upside down, it was her.

"Morning, Betty," I greeted her with a hug, already wiggling out of my boots. Tommy took his coat upstairs and was back down with my slippers in no time. "I know it's a holiday, but we might need your help a bit today."

"What happened?" Betty asked, leading me to the dining room, where Mrs. K's spread was already starting to overtake the table. "If this was an Agatha Christie novel, you guys would've been at the mayor's house last night, a priceless diamond necklace would have been stolen, and you'd be on the case."

"Much less glamorous than that," Tommy said. "God, this all smells so good. Where's Mrs. K? Sorry, Viv, I'm dropping you like a hot rock and marrying the landlady."

"Don't you go breaking Viv's heart," a deep voice came up from the stairs. Mrs. K's son Oleks was coming upstairs, and his biceps were flexing underneath the weight of a tray of dinner dishes, flatware, and glasses. Oleks had grown about an inch since Thanksgiving, and with his eighteenth birthday only a few weeks away, he was posturing like a peacock more and more around the house. "She's my favorite."

"Wouldn't dream of it, pal," Tommy said. He motioned to take the tray, but Oleks rebuffed him and carried his burden to the far end of the table. I couldn't tell if he was showing off or just doing his chores, but it didn't matter. There was a new tension between him and Tommy, and I was going to ignore it until I couldn't anymore.

"Don't give your mom all the details," I said to the teenage boy setting the table. "But we were front and center witnesses to a murder last night. A knifing, on our way to Times Square."

"There was nothing we could do to stop it," Tommy said. "We saw the victim go down, Viv tried to save him, I ran after the perp, but he got lost in the crowd."

"That's horrible," Dottie chimed in. The teacher had been quietly watching the goings-on from her usual seat at the table. I think she was used to schoolyard tiffs, and she had a little grin on her face as her eyes bounced between Oleks and Tommy. "Viv, that must've been difficult."

"I can't stop thinking about him," I said. "And I think I got most of his blood on my shoes and stockings."

"Ambulance drivers hate New Year's Eve," Betty said. "I've worked enough of the holidays to know how hard it is for anyone to get medical attention on days when the streets fill up. It's hard not to be a spoilsport when you know that people who could've been saved weren't, just because the streets were choked with people."

"I'm no expert, so I do wonder if this guy didn't have to die," I told Betty. "I tried my best, I really did."

"I'll call the medical examiner and see what I can dig up," our secretary said. "Let me run upstairs and grab a notebook, I can type everything up in the case file tomorrow when I get in."

"You don't mind giving up your holiday, listening to us chatter about the case?"

"Not at all," Betty said, peeking back into the dining room from the bottom stair. "I'm just happy you have a big case, finally. The last few weeks were crickets, just people making appointments for the new year." She ran full speed ahead, and Oleks took his empty tray back downstairs to reload, leaving me with Tommy and Dottie.

"Are you all right, though, Viviana?" Dottie asked. "It's quite affecting to have a man die under your care, I imagine."

"I'll feel a lot better once we get going on the case," I said, with tears starting to well up in my eyes. "I was sick after it all happened, but now my nerves are just steeled and I want to make sure whoever did this is caught."

"We're all here, as always," Dottie said, reaching out to squeeze my hand. She turned to Tommy. "I'm sorry you didn't catch the murderer."

"No more than me, Dorothy," Tommy said. "I ran as fast as I could, but he had a city block on us, and a plan."

"Do you think this was premeditated?" I asked Tommy.

"A bit—it wasn't a fight that got out of hand, the murderer led our vic down an alley, had a knife in his pocket, and knew exactly how to get lost in the crowd of overcoats out for New Year's Eve. He didn't do this on Christmas for a reason. Or today."

Betty slid back into her place with a stenographer's notebook and pencil. "Where'd he get stabbed?" she asked.

"An alley near 42nd and 9th," I said.

"No, I mean, where on his guts?" she asked, making slicing motions across her stomach.

"Oh! Below the belly button, I'd say," I responded.

"Do you think he was *aiming* below the belt?" She wagged her eyebrows at Tommy and the man winced.

"Ouch," Tommy seethed. "You have some dark thoughts for a secretary."

"I have realistic thoughts for a nurse," Betty said back. Tommy and I could be pretty cavalier about death, but nothing compared to Betty's detachment when discussing grievous bodily harm. "Fellas cut each other in some crazy places."

"Freud would have something to say about that," Dottie chimed in.

"It wasn't quite that low, but who knows what the guy was going for," I added. "But it was definitely a shove and a twist; the guy was bleeding like a stuck pig. Serrated knife, which should've hurt even more."

"Yikes," Betty said, writing it down. "But you said 42nd and 9th?"

"Thereabouts," Tommy agreed, picking up a slice of bread and buttering it.

"That's near the new Port Authority," Dottie pointed out. "Maybe they were out-of-towners."

"It's possible," I said. "Betty, can you call and get the schedule of when the last bus arrived on New Year's Eve?"

"Of course," she said. "But I imagine it was a lot earlier than near midnight. No one wants to drive in that mess."

"That's true," I said. "It was a little before eleven when it happened. We could've seen the ball drop if we hadn't gotten caught up in the murder and Lawson's investigation."

"Detective Lawson is on point for this?" Betty asked. "He's pretty dreamy."

"He's okay," I sighed.

"He was in rare form last night," Tommy added. "Showed up in black tie."

"That's pretty ritzy," Betty agreed. I think she was envisioning herself in an evening gown, with satin gloves pulled up to her elbows, and on Lawson's arm. She met him for the first time over the summer, when Tommy and I got caught up in a whole *different* murder investigation. But at least this one didn't frame Tommy.

"Not to burst your bubble, but he also delivered the news that one of the cops we met over the summer—the little ginger fella—was murdered recently too," I said. "But he didn't seem too shaken up about it. And said that the force was just basically going to let it slide."

"That's awful." Dottie looked stricken.

"But he questioned us about what we saw," I said. "He knows we're on the case, Betts, so maybe he'll be forthcoming with information. If he and his flatfoots even care to investigate."

Mrs. K bustled upstairs with the first meal of the day's main course. "Tomasso, glad to see your face," she beamed. "*Knyshi*, for the soon-to-be weds. For all the happiness in the world!" She put down her platter and came over to Tommy, thrusting his head to her bosom and planting a giant kiss on the top of his head. Tommy beamed.

"I'll need all the luck and good fortune you can give me, Lana," Tommy said, now helping himself to small *mlyntsi*, stuffed with cream cheese and mushrooms. "I hate to spoil the meal so early, but Viv and I witnessed a murder last night. I just want you to know, to hear it from me."

Mrs. K's eyes narrowed for the briefest moment. "But you all are safe?"

"We are," I assured her. "There's no way our heads can be on the chopping block for this, and the detective from the summer is the investigator in charge."

"I should warn everyone here, too," Tommy said. "We ran into Herb Sabella last night."

"Who's that?" Oleks said, giving Tommy the eye.

"Reporter for the *Daily Mirror*," I said. "He's a real piece of something, all right. He treats crime like Walter Winchell treats gossip. And he's not above reporting tattle, too."

"He's a little terrier when he sets his sights on someone," Tommy agreed. "And he noticed me at the crime scene last night. I'll threaten him good and proper if he's seen around these parts, just let me know."

"*I* can take care of this place," Oleks said, gripping his fork. "He better not show up on my doorstep."

"I am very sorry to hear that you saw this violence," Mrs. K said, cutting off her son's posturing. "This city. It is too dangerous. Getting worse every day."

"I don't know about that," Tommy said. "I've been here my whole life, and it's no more dangerous now than it was in the thirties."

"So, if this wasn't just a drunken street brawl," Oleks piped in, "what do you think it was?"

"I told Tommy once: it's always love, money, or politics," I said to Oleks. "Or some variation on the theme. The murderer didn't even pause to take the guy's wads of moolah, so I'm guessing it wasn't money."

"But with you and Tommy on his tail . . . ," Betty said.

"Did you realize it was an attack at first?" Dottie chimed in. "Mrs. Kovalenko, these blinis are your best yet."

"Thank you, dear," Mrs. K said, without even looking at Dottie. "Yes, Tomasso, did you know that the man was in peril?"

"No," Tommy admitted. "There were no shouts—or at least none we could hear over the nearby crowd and all that goddamn wind. And the man who committed the crime knelt over his victim for a moment before Viv and I could ascertain what was happening. I don't think it was a robbery. He had the time to commit one."

"Did you search the poor man?" Dottie asked. She had an uncanny knack for detective work, and despite Tommy's bald-faced attempts to hire every girl at Mrs. K's to work for him, she stuck with being a teacher.

"I did, indeed," I said. "That's how we know no one pilfered his cash. There wasn't much in his pockets—if he's in the city, he likely doesn't have a driver's license, and who takes their library card out on New Year's Eve?"

"Mine is just always in my purse," Dottie said. "But I admit, I am a special case."

"I find that rather charming," Tommy smiled.

"So it was cash, and what else?" Oleks asked, cutting Tommy off.

"Two matchbooks," I said, screwing up my face at Tommy and giving him a shrug. There was no need to start a tiff with the landlady's son, even if he seemed hell-bent on having one. Even Betty and Dottie's eyebrows were raised, but no one said a word.

Tommy swallowed a giggle. "I left one for the cops to catalogue, but Tommy has the other in his coat."

"We won't get it now," Tommy said to Mrs. K. "This has been enough talk of a murder investigation for a New Year's party. Svitlana, how long did it take you to *make* all of this?"

Mrs. K beamed as she jumped into telling us about each and every dish on the table for our luncheon.

Oleks was dutifully asked about his final semester of high school at Hughes, which he shrugged off, as I expected an ornery teenager surrounded by mother figures to do. Dottie expanded on her hopes for her little pupils, and Mrs. K said that she would love to come to the spring concert and recital.

"Are you applying for new nursing positions?" I asked Betty.

"Not really," she admitted. "I know that my secretary days are numbered . . ."

"They don't have to be," Tommy assured her. "You do a bang-up job."

"Thanks!" Betty said. "But the Nurses Association kind of makes sure we, um . . ."

"Get paid a lot better than an office secretary?" I asked.

"I wasn't gonna say it like that," Betty admitted. "But yes."

"Trust me, I know it's tight," I said, reaching across the table to squeeze Betty's hand. "But Tommy's right, it's great to have you."

"How is Tally?" Dottie asked.

"Oh, letters and calls are infrequent," I said. "But if the magazines are to be believed . . ."

"Yes, it seems she has a nice career in the Hollywood!" Mrs. K piped in. "I am very proud of her."

"We all are," I agreed.

"I hope she has found a nice girl," Mrs. K said, rearranging her flatware, but deviously raising an eyebrow.

Anyone could've knocked me over with a feather. "You knew?"

"Of course," Mrs. K said smiling. "I am a mother. I see all."

"You didn't say anything."

She gave a small half-shrug. "I love my girls."

"Now that dinner is away," Oleks said, butting in. "Viv—can we see those matchbooks?"

"Of course," I said. "But give me a minute. I'm full of pork kashi and my room is now on the third floor."

By the time I lumbered up the stairs and back down with the matchbook and Tommy's outerwear, dessert was on the table—clementines sat happily on everyone's plate, and then there were at least six different types of pies and cakes.

"Before you say anything," Tommy assured me, "these were purchased."

"I was gonna ask if you ever slept, Mrs. K," I said, tossing Oleks the matchbook. "Be careful with that, we only have the one."

"There's a glossy part to it," Oleks said, flicking the match-book cover in the yellow, overhead light. "Can you read it?"

"Haven't been able to yet," I said.

"Ah, well," Oleks said, passing the evidence to Dottie, who gave it a once-over and passed it around the table. "You'll get it, Viv."

"Thanks." I was into my second piece of tiramisu and my tummy was threatening to bust the button on my skirt. "I think I might head up. Tommy—see you at the office bright and early as usual, tomorrow morning?"

"Of course, Dollface." He got up and led me to the door, where he put on his overcoat and hat. Making sure we were out of the line of sight of the household, he pulled me in for a kiss. "Try to stay warm without me." He let me go and left into the night, whistling for a taxi as he ran down the front steps.

"Have you set a date yet?" Dottie asked.

I twiddled the two-carat Tiffany solitaire on my left hand. "Nah."

"Take your time, Viv," Betty said, skipping up the stairs. "He's not goin' anywhere."

"He waited nearly half a decade to even ask," Dottie agreed. "Don't worry about a thing."

DAY 3

Betty and I scrambled to the office together, surmounting snowbanks and sloshing through wet and disgusting slush. It was a warm enough day for early January, so we couldn't quite justify taking a cab for just the two of us.

"But when Tommy's upstairs with you," Betty said, "I bet you'll take a cab every day."

"Honestly, I'll bet we could run a significant portion of the work without even going in to the office," I said. "Only when we have meetings." I couldn't tell Betty, but I had my eyes peeled on every corner for the conniving little newspaper man, who I knew was going to pop up unwanted, at some point. The coast was clear at this time of day, so we skipped up the stoop and into the building.

"Mrs. K definitely won't want customers trodding through her whole house," Betty agreed, as we made our own way up to the middle floor of Tommy's office building. The stairs were rickety, and the railing was useless. I often wondered why the lawyer upstairs, Mr. McAllister, didn't ask the landlord to fix it up, considering he must've known all the tenant laws backwards and forwards, or at least could look them up no problem. But McAllister was an ambulance chaser by inclination, so I guessed he liked the thrill of being one wrong foot away from his own lawsuit.

The door to the office was unlocked; Tommy had beaten us
to the punch and already started a pot of coffee. "Mornin', Mr.
Fortuna!" Betty sang out into the office as she took off her coat.
"Thanks for the coffee."

Tommy came out of the back office with a smile. "Starting
the year off right, that's for sure. Two beautiful women in the
office, fresh pot of joe, got two meetings today."

"High-paying, by the sound of your voice," I said. "Just glad
people's New Year's resolutions seem to include hiring some
gumshoes."

"Viv, let's get situated. Betty, the first meeting of the day
should be here any minute. You know what to do."

Betty helped me out of my coat and swatted me on the
behind to shoo me into my office. "It's almost showtime, Boss."
She winked at me. I slipped into the room I shared with Tommy
and shut the door behind me.

"We're still going to look into the other night, right?" I asked,
settling into my desk across from Tommy's. I had my steno pad
right where I left it when I was last in the office, and a whole bouquet of freshly sharpened pencils on my desk. It felt strange not to
have the typewriter, but that was Betty's territory now. "Even if
no one is paying us?"

"Of course," Tommy said, leaning back in his chair. "Murder
is too important a crime to leave to the cops."

There was a knock at the door and Betty peeked it open.
"Detectives?"

A man pushed the door open the remainder of the way and
sneaked his way around Betty, who hadn't yet conveyed permission to enter the office. He was holding his hat in both mitts
and wringing the life out of the brim. "Speaking of crimes too
important to leave to the police . . ."

"I take it you're our nine o'clock," I said, standing and putting
myself between the man and the perturbed Tommy. Tommy had
a lot of rules about how we were to be treated by the no-goodniks

who came into our place, and the last time a man walked into our office like he owned it, we ended up hunting down a Soviet spy.

"Yes, yes, I'm sorry, I'm so nervous," the man said. He was short—five feet tall if he was an inch, stooped at the shoulders, and graying at the ring of hair that circled his head like a monk's haircut. His suit was black, but his shoulders were white with dandruff. Betty was giving him the once-over, and I saw her nurse's eye making diagnoses. I'd have to ask her once the man tittered his way back out the front door.

"Miss Valentine, Mr. Fortuna, this is Mr. Floristan," Betty finally said. "Will you need anything else before you begin?"

"No." Tommy's voice was curt, but it wasn't directed at Betty. She did a little curtsy dip and left, shutting the door behind her.

"Please settle down here, then, and tell us what the issues are." I nodded at one of Tommy's penitent wooden chairs and went to settle into my own plush, leather seat. It had taken me a few weeks to not feel bad that we made our clients sit in such uncomfortable chairs while I felt all nice and cozy, but Tommy had a policy to try to keep meetings down to half an hour or less, and the chairs were certainly part of the op.

"I'm so sorry, I'm terribly out of sorts, I don't know what to do," Mr. Floristan continued, using every single cliché in the book to tell us why he was now in our dim office.

"You're not the first," Tommy gruffed.

"Yes, well. Something of mine has gone missing," Mr. Floristan finally outed. "And I believe it's being held for ransom."

"You believe?" I asked. "It either is or isn't, isn't it?"

"Yes, well." Mr. Floristan shrugged. "I received a note but I think it's in code." He slipped a small, folded piece of paper out of his interior jacket pocket and handed it to Tommy, who looked it over, then handed it to me.

The paper was delicate and fraying at the creases. Either Mr. Floristan had had the note for several years or he was obsessed with it, opening and shutting it a million times a day, and depending on what was missing, that might be more likely the case. He was fidgeting, hopping in his seat and shaking. The note was type-written on an unmarked sheet of white paper you could buy from any Woolworths. We weren't going to glean much from anything but the message itself, that was for sure.

It read:

Dear Mr. Floristan—

p avvr doha pz fvbyz, huk fvb dpss dhua av whf mvy pa, p ruvd. h mvssvdpun apw dpss dhpa mvy fvb ha h mvva vm vby ovsf dvthu mvbuahpu, ha h obi vm vby whyr.

Sincerely,

Your Friend

"Yeah, well, that looks like a cipher, all right," Tommy said.

"May we copy it down?" I asked. "I'll return the original to you."

"That's very kind of you, miss," Mr. Floristan said, agitated that the paper was out of his hands while I scribbled it into my own notebook. It didn't make a lick of sense to me.

"When did you notice the ransomed item missing?" Tommy asked.

"I never did," our client admitted. "It's a . . ."

"We don't need to know what it is, specifically," Tommy assured. "Unless you think it might help us find the item or the perpetrator. Is it something that could be pawned or fenced easily for money?"

"No, it has very little value to anyone but me," Mr. Floristan said.

"And did this come with any kind of envelope or postage mark?" I asked.

"It's long gone," Mr. Floristan admitted. "I have a habit of opening my mail while standing in front of the fireplace and . . ."

whoosh. Right up with the logs." He made little wiggles with his fingers, which I assumed stood in for the flames. I looked at Tommy, and his eyebrow was cocked, which meant that he had made the same deduction I had—a wood-burning fireplace meant Mr. Floristan was likely in a house or a whole brownstone, not a dinky little apartment like Tommy's with its small coal burner. Floristan here had bucks.

"The only other thing I need to know is—is the item being held ransom something that may incriminate you, or be used to blackmail you?" Tommy asked. "Letters, journals, photographs, the like."

Mr. Floristan reddened at the ears. "What kind of man do you take me for?"

"A man who would pay a ransom, if he could only figure out how," Tommy shrugged. "We're very discreet, Mr. Floristan. Either you want our help or you don't."

"I want it, Mr. Fortuna, and I am prepared to double your usual rate."

"Very well, then," Tommy said, standing. "Our secretary will have the paperwork prepared for you in the outer office."

"Thank you, Mr. Fortuna, Miss Valentine," he said, standing and nodding in my direction as Tommy led him back out front.

Tommy was back lickety-split, but we waited until we heard Betty shout cheerfully, "Have a nice day!" before we started gossiping about the new client.

"I just cannot *wait* to find out what was snitched," I said, peering at the jumble of letters in my notebook. "I'll have Betty type this up with carbons so we can all have a copy and try to figure it out."

"That'll be good," Tommy agreed. "I wish we had that envelope."

"What good would it do, really, aside from tell us the general neighborhood where the ransomer lived?" I asked. "We can't just walk around Bed-Stuy going, 'Excuse me, sir, but are you extorting anyone for money?'"

"*Especially* not in Bed-Stuy," Tommy said, smiling. "I bet half of 'em would say yes."

"The puzzle is the case, then," I said. "Now how about that murder?"

"I think we start with the footwork there," Tommy said. "Did you bring your warmest clothes? I think we have to hoof it to the neighborhood and just canvas. Check local bars and smoke shops—anything that's open—to see if we can find the same matchbooks."

"Ah, we're lucky it's warm enough out today, then," I said, standing up and exiting out to Betty. "Hey, honey, can you type this up and make a few copies? We'll be back in a couple of hours."

"No prob, Boss," Betty said smiling. "Next appointment is at three."

"Plenty of time." Tommy and I slipped out the door, and he hailed a cab at the curb to take us to the outskirts of Times Square. We found the murder site no problem—someone had hosed down the bloodstained snow and left the alleyway with the only clear entrance for blocks. If they wanted to make the area unassuming, they had missed the mark completely. A clean New York City sidewalk lets everyone passing by know it's been cleaned. It would've been less conspicuous if they'd left the giant bloodstain.

"I'll walk south, you walk north," Tommy said. "Meet you back here in, say, two hours for lunch?"

"Sounds great, ol' Tommy boy," I said, giving him a smooch. "Stay safe."

"You too, Dollface." Tommy started crunching through the ice toward the next street, and I started out on my own course.

Most of the curbside businesses around Times Square had bright and flashy signage—and most of the ones geared toward nightlife were locked up tight and darker than a cave. It was too early yet for even clean-up crews to be in the clubs and bars, sweeping up the garbage from the past few nights and hosing off the latrines. The rambunctious excitement of New Year's Eve was long gone, even if the confetti still clogged the storm drains, and it was just any other Tuesday, midmorning in Midtown.

A tobacconist stood in the minuscule, horse-stall-like space in between a shoe shop and a deli on 9th Avenue. The front of the space was open to the cold, and the entire width of the store was split by a wooden shelf. Behind it stood a gentleman in a neatly pressed but garishly red suit, and stacks of cigarette boxes, rolling papers, and pouches of tobacco. The room smelled divine, and the man in the red suit fiddled with a space heater dangling from a rope in the rafters.

"Miss," the man turned and nodded at me. He was behaving like a salesman at Saks, quiet and deferential as if there was anything to peruse.

"Good morning," I said, approaching the clerk. "I met a man in this neighborhood the other evening, and—I guess like most girls who meet a gent on New Year's—he left me with a lot of questions." The man raised a penciled-in eyebrow, and I could tell he was dutifully intrigued.

"How can I help?" he asked. He leaned forward on his counter and picked up a cigarette in a long holder.

"Well, he told me to meet him at a club," I fibbed, "and handed me this matchbook as a reference point. I can tell there's something printed on it, but what, I have no idea. Have you ever seen anything like this before?"

"It's a blank matchbook," he said. "I've got cases of them in the back."

"No tricks?" I asked. "I just got the run-around from a guy on New Year's?"

"Seems like it, miss," he said, ready to toss the matchbook in the trash.

"Wait, I'll just keep it," I said, sticking out a gloved hand. The gentleman placed the matchbook in my palm. "The girls will get a laugh out of it later at the office."

"I'm sure. In the meantime, we have these new flavored cigarettes," the gentleman started, turning toward his boxes. "Vanilla, mint, clove . . . You name it."

"I'm so sorry, but I don't smoke," I said. "But thank you for your time."

Back through the stall door and into the wind whipping through the city, I paced a few more blocks, looking for any establishment that might be so secretive that it hid its own name and location on its give-away garbage. But I wasn't surprised to find nothing in the city's flashiest, busiest, most garish little neighborhood. I couldn't wait to get back to Hell's Kitchen.

I met Tommy at the alleyway and his face told me everything I needed to know. "So, what's for lunch?" I asked. "Do you want to eat here or head back to the quieter parts?"

"Quieter parts," Tommy grumbled, wrapping his arm around my waist. "There's a Chinese place on the way back, does that sound good?"

"Always." I leaned my head against his shoulder and we walked in lockstep down the major arteries, not even looking at the alleyways. I couldn't stomach another murder right now.

★ ★ ★

We called Betty from the restaurant and she joined us about ten minutes later.

"Thanks, you two," she said, digging into her chow mein. "I was starving."

"No problem," Tommy said. He was expertly picking up pieces of duck with his chopsticks and shoveling them into his mouth, and my smoked fish was delicious. "Why don't more people eat here?" he asked. The server just smiled.

"Because people are jerks," Betty said. "If it ain't meat and potatoes, they turn up their noses."

"We all lived through the thirties," Tommy harrumphed. "When we couldn't even get meat and potatoes together to save our lives."

"I'll be a happy girl if I never, ever eat navy bean soup ever again," Betty laughed. "Mr. Fortuna, would you mind if we got more of that wonton soup?"

"Help yourself, Betty," Tommy said. "Anyway, what did you make of Mr. Floristan this morning?"

"He sure was jumpy," I said. "Betty—medical reason for that, or just nerves?"

"Could be some kind of palsy, you're right," Betty said. "One combined with being a nervous Nelly."

"He did *not* appreciate Tommy insinuating he might be being blackmailed," I said. "Got mighty angry."

"Anyone can be blackmailed, just ask Tally," Betty said. "But my guess is that he's into collecting all sorts of strange little things, and someone is having a lark with him."

"Do you think he has enough friends, let alone the kind that play tricks?" Tommy asked.

"I'm sure he's very charming in the right situations," I equivocated. Betty giggled. "I bet he was a professor of some kind."

"Definitely a teacher," Betty agreed. "The kind that clapped boys on the knuckles with rulers when their hair met their collars."

"I had my fair share of those," Tommy said. "Look, I have a scar right here from when Mr. Tenshaw got me in geometry."

"I bet you were a hellraiser," I said.

"I was an *angel*," Tommy assured me. "Always on time, nails clean, yes sir, no sir, thank you, please, you're welcome."

"And then you'd steal the test answers when no one was looking and sell them on the playground for a nickel," Betty said through squinted eyes.

"Have you been calling my mother?" Tommy roared with laughter, tossing money on the table for the check. "All right, girls, let's get back to the office."

★ ★ ★

We passed the hours until our next appointment, each of us curled over the ransom note and trying to figure out the jumble. I was having absolutely no luck—none of the letters made even an ounce of sense, and I had to stop myself from tearing up the paper in frustration. Betty was drawn out of her concentration suddenly, judging by the loud "oh!" that came through our open door at exactly 2:59 PM.

"Miss Valentine, Mr. Fortuna," she repeated from that morning. "This is Mr. Bowen. He's your three o'clock." She slipped back out into the front office, shutting the door behind her.

"Mr. Bowen, nice to meet you," I said. "How can we help you today?"

"I need your help finding a man," he said, clearly and succinctly, as he sat down in his chair.

"Well, sir, I only just got engaged myself and Betty hasn't had a steady in ages . . . ," I joked, but Mr. Bowen clearly did not appreciate the lark.

"Has a man gone missing?" Tommy asked, ignoring me.

"Yes. A gentleman from my firm."

"Which firm is that?" I asked.

"Keller Bachmann Investments," he said flatly.

"And what does this missing man do at Keller Bachmann?" I asked, goading him for even more information. Blood from a stone came easier.

"He is pertinent to our daily business," Mr. Bowen said.

"Okeedokee," Tommy said, clapping his hands and making to stand up. "Thanks for coming by."

"Mr. Fortuna, I need to find this man."

"Can you tell us his name? General description? You came to us, Mr. Bowen, not the other way around," I said. My fish was repeating on me a little, and I was in no mood.

"I am terrified that our clients will learn that this man has not shown up for work," Mr. Bowen said. "It could have grave consequences for their future."

"Their future or your company's future?" I asked.

"It's their money, Miss Valentine," Mr. Bowen said. "Our clients don't care about anything but that."

"Why would anyone care about one employee?" Tommy asked. "Is he the president of the bank?"

"No," Mr. Bowen explained. "It's a very complicated system, investing, and I must admit that Trevor is much too small a cog for people on the outside to understand. But one cog out of sync, and the entire system falters."

"You're convincing me to keep my money in my mattress, Mr. Bowen," Tommy said. "But tell us more about Trevor."

"Trevor Penhaligon. Thick-necked little fellow, dark hair that goes to curl when he lets it grow," Mr. Bowen said. "He lives in Murray Hill, I believe, still with his mother and father."

"Young man, then?" Tommy asked. I was taking notes.

"Under thirty is all I can say for certain," Mr. Bowen said. "I haven't taken a gander at his employee files, myself."

"What measures have *you* taken to try to get this Mr. Penhaligon into the office?" I asked.

"I had my girl ask if there was a phone number on file for his residence, and there was not. I sent her with taxi fare to bang on his door, but no one answered."

"And if he had answered but didn't want to go?" I asked.

"I imagine Peggy would've taken him by the ear," Mr. Bowen said, cracking his first smile all day. "She has a way about her."

"Well, good for Trevor that he didn't get on the wrong side of Peggy, then," Tommy said. "Mr. Bowen, if we phone your office, will Commander Margaret give us all the information that she has on file for this missing man?"

"Who?"

"*Peggy*," I said. "It's a *nickname* for *Margaret*."

"I will instruct her to do so," Mr. Bowen said, not looking at me.

"Mr. Bowen, do you have any reason to believe that Trevor Penhaligon might be injured or deceased?" I asked. "Maybe he isn't showing up for work because he isn't able to."

Mr. Bowen looked surprised, smoothed the crease in his wool trousers and stood. "Miss Valentine, bodily injury is the only acceptable reason for Trevor to avoid his duty. Thank you both, but I must be off. I will leave my contact information with your girl."

He was out the door before either Tommy or I could shake his hand. Betty was bidding him goodbye in less than a minute.

"Well, I don't like *him*," she said as she came to lean against the door. "I'll take Mr. Floristan any day."

"I do hope that the missing Mister Trevor is fit as a fiddle and just decided to find a new job without giving his notice," I said, looking at Betty. "Between that yuk-a-minute and the abusive Miss Peggy, I'd probably want to just be a busboy or something."

"I wonder how many people work at the firm," Tommy said. "Betty, when you call this Peggy, can you try to suss that out? If it's a big bank, why one little guy going MIA is such a big deal is fishy."

"You bet, Tommy," Betty said, making a note, then glancing at her wristwatch. "Hell's Kitchen to Wall Street is a pretty hefty cab fare. Do you think he'll make it back to his office before five o'clock?"

"Nope, and I'm sure Peggy won't get notified of her orders until tomorrow morning," Tommy agreed. "Betty, head on out. Take a cab. I'm gonna take Viv out for the night."

"Thanks, Mr. Fortuna," Betty said. She had her coat on and was out the door before I could even ask what our plans were.

"Dinner and a movie?" Tommy asked.

"You hate movies," I pointed out. "You fall asleep every time."

"Dinner then, and we'll play it by ear."

"Sounds good to me," I said. "But it's four in the afternoon. That's a bit early for supper."

"Let's go for a stroll, then," Tommy said. "It's a nice enough day. In the opposite direction from Times Square. To the park. Anything. All the Christmas decorations are still up, it's not Epiphany yet."

"Works for me, ol' Tommy boy," I said. "A little bit of enchantment is nice sometimes."

NIGHT 3

Tuesday, January 2nd, 1951

Every shop window, from small mom-and-pop delis with red and green paper chains and scissor snowflakes to large department stores with live models in the displays cuddled up in furs, was still decked out for the holidays. We strolled through every block between 8th and 11th Avenues, and Tommy picked up some roasted chestnuts from a street vendor braving the winds off the water at Chelsea Park. We walked for hours, until it was well into dark, and slipped into a small Italian joint for dinner, somewhere in the borderlands between Chelsea and the West Village. The entire place stank of garlic and was illuminated by candles crammed into dusty Chianti bottles, swathed in marinara-splattered baskets.

It was perfect.

"Let's sit and eat and take as long as they'll let us," I said, sipping on my own glass of wine. "Happy New Year, ol' Tommy boy."

"Happy New Year, Dollface," Tommy said, clinking my glass. "At least we're starting out on the right foot of having new clients. But I won't rest easy until we really dig into the murder investigation."

"Same here," I agreed, tapping my nails on the bowl of the wine glass. "I wonder who Frankie is. The guy he was talking to as he bled out."

"Brother, friend, boyfriend," Tommy shrugged. "People dying say some crazy shit."

"You'd know better than me," I admitted.

"It's a lot easier to tamp down your feelings about watching a fella pass away in front of you when there are bullets whizzing overhead," Tommy said. "Not when there's snow falling and you can hear folks clanging through 'Auld Lang Syne' a quarter mile east."

"I swear to you, I couldn't even hear them," I admitted. "All I could hear was the blood pumping through my ears and you begging me to stand up."

"Adrenaline," Tommy pointed out. "It's what made you upchuck, too."

"I prefer my adrenaline rushes to come from the Cyclone, thank you," I said.

"Just the threat of death," Tommy said. "The way those boards rattle, *no* thank you."

"So you'd rather get your thrills on a frigate in the South Pacific?"

"I didn't say that," Tommy said. "But it was certainly warmer there than it is here."

"We should go someplace warm for our honeymoon," I mused. "None of this Niagara Falls nonsense, especially if we're getting hitched anytime soon. I'm not going *north* for the winter."

"Oh yeah? What do you have in mind?" Tommy asked. "The whole appeal of Niagara is that we don't leave the hotel room."

"As tempting as that is," I purred, "I've never been on a real vacation before. We have to see *something* interesting, or at least more interesting than the wallpaper."

"We could go to the mountains . . . ," Tommy offered.

"Still too cold. I know I'm supposed to want to go to the Poconos," I admitted, "but what about Key West? Hemingway always looked pleased as possum to be on his boat and fishing."

Tommy coughed into his glass. "You *fish*?"

"I do not," I said. "But I do sit on beaches in two-pieces rather wonderfully. I think."

"When you put it like that, I'll book the tickets tomorrow," Tommy said with a smile, just as a small older woman placed a tray of antipasti in front of him. Tommy plucked up an olive.

"I feel like I'm spoiled because I live in New York City," I said. "Is it terrible that I don't want to jet off to Paris?"

"Paris is still a heap of rubble," Tommy pointed out. "So is London. Rome . . . I'll bet it's gorgeous, but I don't feel like bribing policemen in order to pick up my own luggage at the airport."

"The way Lawson was talking, I'm not sure our coppers are much better."

"But at least I speak their language," Tommy said. "My Italian is rusty."

"Most of the Italian I know would get me arrested," I laughed.

"So Europe is out."

"Even if we could afford it, for sure. Besides, you can't book tickets yet. We need at least two days to get to the JP," I said. "Take that into consideration when you're calling PanAm."

"If we could leave ASAP, I'd be so happy," Tommy said. "But two new clients today. What do you think?"

"Mr. Bowen is being cagey," I said.

"Like a tiger in the zoo," Tommy agreed. "It's going to be juicy, whatever we find."

"I'll bet this Trevor fellow just quit," I said. "And if you just quit, would you answer the door for your boss?"

"Absolutely not," Tommy said. "I'd be happy if I never actually had to see anyone face-to-face at work."

"That's because you're an old grumpy Gus," I pointed out.

"And don't you forget it."

"Mr. Floristan is in an interesting predicament."

"That's a blackmail case if I ever saw one," Tommy said. "Not my favorite kind of case, but usually people will pay out the nose to make it stop."

"What do we do?"

"Solve the damned puzzle, first and foremost."

"And if we can't?"

"Then we don't get paid." Tommy shrugged.

"So let's hope we can solve the puzzle, huh?" I asked. "I'm about as good with brain teasers as fish are with bicycles, though. I just can't ferret those kinds of things out."

"But you can uncover Soviet spies," Tommy said. "Not a lot of people can do that."

"I can read people, not gibberish letters on a piece of carbon paper," I said.

"So tell me about Mr. Floristan."

"Well, he lives alone, I guarantee," I started. "Not even a housekeeper would let you out of the house with that much dandruff on your coat. She'd be mortified."

"True enough." Tommy picked up his fork to pierce a marinated artichoke heart.

"Educated as all get-out," I continued. "But not trustworthy one bit."

"I find people get less trustworthy the more degrees they get," Tommy laughed.

"Then start calling me Saint Viv," I laughed. "Because I can never tell a lie with only tenth grade under my belt."

"You know I can't call you Saint Viv for a whole *host* of reasons, Dollface."

"You dirty louse. But Floristan has some skeletons in his closet, and I just wish he'd told me what was stolen."

"What do you think his industry is?" Tommy asked.

"Collector of . . . rare Victorian undergarments." Tommy was caught off guard and barked out a laugh.

"Jesus, Mary. I wasn't expecting that."

"I know," I said. "That's why I said it. Try and top me."

"Buys and sells . . . fossilized dinosaur poop."

"Not bad, not bad," I admitted. "But not quite lurid enough."

"Anthologist of candid recollections on the mating habits of squid?"

"Better!"

"Thank you." Tommy made a small bow. "But you read him like a book. There's something beyond odd about him, and it's not just because he's so jumpy."

"Betty said it might be medical," I admitted. "So I'm just judging by the personality."

"He *did* have the shifty eyes of a Victorian underwear salesman," Tommy said. "You got that right."

"Read him like a book!" I chomped into a pepper I plucked off the platter, but it was a hot one and I immediately started coughing and tears streamed from my eyes.

"Need some more water?" Tommy asked as I caught my breath.

"No," I gasped. "But that'll teach me to do things for flourish." There were a few moments of silence while I dabbed at my eyes with my napkin and tried to regain composure.

"If there's one small relief, I'm glad it wasn't a dame," Tommy sighed. He changed the subject out of nowhere and it took me a minute to catch up.

"Who? The murder victim?"

"Yeah." Tommy stared down at the tablecloth. "That would've done me right in."

"You never struck me as the type that assumed we were all damsels," I said. "One of the only fellas in the world I ever met who treated me like regular people and not either his maid or his mother. It wouldn't be a bigger tragedy if the murdered person was a girl."

"Ah, I know, a man's still dead," Tommy shrugged. "But ever since you . . ." He glanced at my finger.

"One ring and now girls give you the heebie-jeebies?"

"Well, I've just gotten really aware," Tommy said. "Every time I see you and Betty walking up the street instead of in a cab,

I think about what could've happened to you between Mrs. K's and the office."

"Well, in June, a notorious gangster used well-placed cabbies to track me in an attempt to send you to the electric chair," I said. "And you didn't have these feelings for all the years I wasn't your girl, schlepping to the office?"

"I guess I did . . ."

"And it's not like you were a monk those years, neither, ol' Tommy boy," I laughed. "I wiped plenty of Helena Rubinstein Cherry Champagne off that kisser before meetings. Didn't waste a wink of sleep for any of those girls?"

"I'm just telling you how I feel," Tommy pouted.

The restaurant's resident *nonna* came by and poked Tommy in the shoulder. "What's the matter? Are you sick?" She motioned at his full plate of osso buco.

"Not sick, I promise," he said, smiling and picking up his fork. "My bride-to-be is just giving me a hard time."

She looked at me and beamed, so I showed off the rock. "Good for you, *stellina*! Tell him who is the boss." She shuffled back toward the kitchen, undoubtedly to tell her husband about the girl in the dining room giving her fiancé the what-for. I dug into my *cacio e pepe* and felt that glorious warmth of black pepper mixed with too much pecorino Romano. It wasn't much different from Mrs. K's bright orange macaroni and cheese, but it sure felt fancy.

"Neither one of us is boss, Tommy," I said, crunching down onto a large flake of freshly ground pepper. Between that and the pepperoncini, my face was going to melt off before the end of the meal. "Or at least I don't like to think of it that way."

"And that's why I can't wait to marry ya, Dollface," Tommy agreed. We finished off our meals and two minutes after our dishes were cleared, a plate of cannoli stood in front of us, one on its end with a lit sparkler stuck into the mascarpone.

"On the house," the resident *nonna* said. "For your engagement." Tommy stood up and gave her a kiss on both cheeks, so she whacked him with a dish towel and ran back to the kitchen, giggling, to brag to her husband.

After we stuffed ourselves silly, Tommy paid the check and we dipped back outside where the air was freezing and only hinted at the existence of garlic.

"Let's go to your place," I said, slipping my arm through Tommy's. "And let's walk. I need to burn off some of that cheese."

We started north back toward Hell's Kitchen.

"So," I started, kicking a lump of snow so hard it exploded into its own mini snowstorm. "Who was your first love?"

"Oh, Viv, that's a stupid question."

"No, it's not! I don't think I ever asked you before. And I don't mean to pour your heart out to me about all the ones that got away. I just mean, when you were a kid, who was the one that first got you all starry-eyed?"

"Well, then. Alma Bianchi. Junior high."

"And what was it about Alma Bianchi that just had your heart fluttering?"

"She hit my friend Joey so hard she knocked out a tooth," Tommy said, straightening up. "After that, it was love."

"What did Joey do to deserve losing an incisor?" I asked.

"Alma Bianchi's skirt had ridden up a little bit while she was sitting down in math class," Tommy said. "Joey leaned over with a pocket knife and sliced right through her garter. When she stood up, she realized there was nothing she could do to fix it, and there was Joey, laughing like a jackal in the corner. So she walked right up to him, reared back, and punched him square in the face."

"Was she wearing knuckle dusters? My God, she must've got him *good*."

"No, but she was bleeding something fierce after, and bruised her thumb good and proper because no one had told her not to wrap her fingers around it before going in for the hit. I took her to the nurse."

"So, did you ask her out for a date?"

"No, I was the one who got Joey to do it," Tommy shrugged. "But man. Alma. I wonder what she's up to nowadays."

"Are you going to think less of me because I've never hit a fella so hard I caused permanent damage?"

"You're young yet. Still plenty of time."

"See, that's what I like about you, ol' Tommy boy. Always thinking of my potential."

"Someone's got to, Dollface. Sometimes you sell yourself short! Sure, you haven't knocked out a man's teeth *yet*, but you're only in your twenties. There's a great big future ahead of you. Hell, one day, we might have to throw fists together. That's a tie that binds."

"You should teach me how to grapple a bit," I said.

"It's true," Tommy agreed. "Once we get a little time to ourselves, I'll show you some moves."

"What a honeymoon," I said, skipping up the front steps of Tommy's stoop. "Mai tais, two pieces, and fight training. You really are the perfect man."

"And from my vantage point," a strange voice said from out of the shadows, "you two are quite the couple. Hey, Fortuna, let me profile the both of ya."

I spun around and growled, but Tommy held my arm. A short man in an overcoat was standing at the foot of the steps, a camera dangling from his neck.

"Off-limits, Herb," Tommy said, descending the stairs. "My house. Viv's house. Anyone outside the office. You want a statement? Call me up. At work."

"Ah, but if I call you, you can hang up on me," Sabella shrugged. "Just tell me what you know. The lovebirds solving crime together, the public is gonna eat it up."

"We don't exist to sell more papers for Mr. Hearst," I said. "You heard Tommy. Get out of here. We have official channels for a reason, bub."

"Ooh, you're feisty, the women's pages are going to love you. What if I sent around Miss Devine to cover the nuptials?" He was fiddling with the lens cap of his Kodak, and Tommy advanced.

"Don't make me hit you, Herb," he said through gritted teeth. "I'd hate to damage a nice camera."

"Have it your way," the newsman shrugged. "I'll call on you soon. Ta-ta!" He disappeared again, and Tommy pushed me inside his front door, and I took his hand as we started upstairs.

"Gonna have to teach me to throw a punch sooner rather than later."

DAY 4

Wednesday, January 3rd, 1951

Tommy flung open the door of the office to a distracted and nervous Betty.

"There's a man here, Mr. Fortuna," she said loudly. "He doesn't have an appointment."

"They always need an appointment," Tommy responded. It was his most hard-and-fast rule—that anyone who couldn't bring themselves to book our time in advance didn't really have the guts for us to find out what they wanted us to find out. "If it's that lousy banker, I'm gonna . . ."

"I told him he needed an appointment, sir," Betty said, winking. She had good enough manners to call Tommy and me Mister and Miss while in the office in front of other folks, but the *sir* let us know she was doing it for show. "But he just won't leave."

"I'll handle it," Tommy said in a booming voice. He strode toward the open door of our inner office without taking off his overcoat and hat. His shoulders filled the entire doorway, so I couldn't get a look at who he was yelling at. "How *dare* you treat my secretary with such disrespect?"

Betty looked at me with a grin. "Oh, this is gonna be fun."

"Better get your med kit out," I told her. "When he gets like this, punches sometimes get thrown." Betty pulled a small leather case out of her top drawer.

"At the ready, Sarge."

"Atta girl," I said. "But I'm gonna go try to defuse the bomb."

As I approached Tommy, I saw that two arms were encircling him and I was ready to jump out of the way of a full-on wrestling match until I heard Tommy's voice change tone.

"Mort! As I live and breathe!" A hand was thumping Tommy on the back and the bomb didn't go off. "I need you to meet someone special."

Tommy and this Mort fella were back out in the front of the office, and I was greeted by the smiling face of a tall man with sharp cheekbones hovering over gaunt cheeks. He had dark, curly hair that was thinning at the crown, and a double-breasted charcoal suit that accentuated his skinny waist.

"Morty, this is Viviana Valentine, my fiancée and partner." I shook the man's hand and his long fingers practically wrapped all the way to my wrist.

"Nice to meet you, Mr. . . . ." I trailed off.

"Lobel," he said. "Mort Lobel, but just call me Mort, if you're marrying one of my greatest friends."

"Thanks, I guess, Mort," I blushed. "We are indeed getting married, at some point."

"Good, don't rush into it," Mort said. "Funny you should say fiancée, Tom, that's sort of why I'm here."

"Come on in," Tommy said. "Let's hear all about it." Tommy strode into his office and Mort went to shut the door behind himself until I stopped it with my foot.

"I'm co-investigator, Mr. Lobel," I said curtly. "That's what *partner* implies."

"Goodness, my apologies." Mr. Lobel reopened the door and Tommy pointed at the stiff-backed wooden chair for his friend to take a seat. I sat in my soft, leather desk chair and finally our unexpected guest got the picture.

"If you'd made an appointment like Betty told you to," Tommy said, "you would've known Viv and I are equals in this office. And Betty isn't here to be pushed around, either."

"I understand, Tommy, and I'm dreadfully sorry."

"Well, stay sorry. But why are you here? Last I heard, everything was fine and dandy."

"It was fine, as you said. The caterer is booked, she wants white roses on the chuppah, the whole thing is planned," our client said from his chair. But his face was changing. The cheer that had enlivened his face was gone, and now the deep-sunk eyes revealed a specter. "But Rachel—my intended bride, Rachel Blum—is acting strange. I'm afraid she's going to do something, call it off."

"Or do something that makes your mother tell *you* to call it off?"

"I would never want to," Mort said. "But family . . ."

"All families have that way about them," I agreed. "But how is your Rachel different than she was?"

"I hate to say this, but I can't think of a nicer way to put it," Mr. Lobel said. "I caught her in a lie."

"A . . . large one?" Tommy asked.

"Not especially . . ."

"Then who gives a crap, Morty?"

"She said she was having lunch with her friend Sarah every week," Mr. Lobel explained. "But we ran into Sarah recently and she said it'd been ages since she last saw Rachel."

"That's it?" I asked.

"Every week for months she wasn't spending hours with the woman she promised me she was seeing," he said. "That's quite a lot."

"So you want us to tail your fiancée," Tommy said, pinching his nose.

"That's the indelicate way of putting it," Mr. Lobel said. "But yes."

"That's fine," Tommy said. "I'm telling you off the bat that I don't like this one bit. And don't get mad at me if you hate what you asked me to find out."

"Wouldn't dream of it, Tom."

"Betty will have our standard contract waiting for you out front," Tommy said, standing up and leading his friend to the front of the office. "She'll ask you for a few preliminary details, and we'll have a report as soon as we can."

"Thanks." Mr. Lobel went to talk to Betty, and Tommy shut the door behind his friend.

"Oh, this is not going to be good," he whispered.

"Not in the least," I agreed. "Not in the least."

We heard the phone ring and it was a tantalizingly long few minutes before Betty came in, a smile on her face.

"Well, we'll open up *that* man's can o' worms in a moment," she said. "But first I'll tell you what the medical examiner's office had to say about our murder victim."

"Oh, this is exciting," Tommy said.

"To start off, the exact phrase the lady on the phone read from the notes was that the stab wound was *grotesquely unprofessional*," Betty said. "And they would know, I guess, they see a lot of stab wounds."

"More than I do, at least," I said.

"You know, I called the library, wondering if they had information on just how many people are stabbed in the city each year," Betty said. "They said they couldn't put an exact figure on it, but the girl did say that murder rates went down during the war, and the only reason anyone could figure was because all the menfolk were somewhere else."

"That's pretty damning," Tommy agreed.

"And then as soon as the war was over, bang! Zoom! Back to killin'," Betty said. "Numbers shot right back up."

"Horrifying," I admitted. "They didn't get it all out of their systems?"

"Or now every fella's got a taste for blood," Betty said menacingly. She had a tendency to read the pulpiest pulp novels available at the dime store and loved to pepper her new phrases into everyday conversation.

"What was so unprofessional about the wound?" Tommy asked.

"Well, it was pretty jagged," Betty explained. "Showed some hesitation, apparently, and the location, like we said before."

"Across the lower guts?" I asked.

"Yeah, I mean, it's unpleasant, but if you want a quick death, you go for somewhere in the neck," Betty explained, making a jabbing motion at the air in front of her, inching closer to the general vicinity of my jugular. "People always think it's the heart, but you gotta get in between the ribs for that to work right."

"See, I woulda shot for the left armpit," I said, lifting Betty's arm and smacking my hand into the side of her chest. "Lotta veins in there, close to the heart."

"If he'd gone for a gut wound, the smart thing would be to go for the liver, which is sort of in that spot where your ribs don't meet," Betty said, poking her fingers into my chest.

"Down in the intestines is pretty messy," I said. "Isn't there a big artery in the crotch?"

"There *is*!" Betty said. "If he was focused on down there, that would've been much more effective."

"You women are marvelous," Tommy beamed.

"So that's what they mean by unprofessional," Betty said. "Plenty of the pros know how to kill a man fast."

"That's nice, then," I agreed. "No mafia this time."

"Fingers crossed!" Betty grinned. "Just a good ol' fashioned alleyway stabbing."

"Could I have saved him, though, Betts? Be honest." I was girding myself for her answer.

"You? No."

"Thanks for the vote of confidence."

"I could've, but I had years of schooling, honey," she admitted. "Regular folk aren't meant to ever be elbow-deep in gore."

"I knew to put pressure on it," I said. "But that's as far as they got in Girl Scouts."

"That's the place to start, but with a gut wound, it's hard," Betty admitted. "Can't apply a tourniquet or anything. You said he was sitting upright?"

"Yup, leaning against a building."

"Next time," Betty said before realizing what she was saying, "*God forbid* there's a next time, get the fella on his back slightly and raise his legs. The heart was pumping like crazy 'cause the fella would've been in shock, and boy is there a lot of blood in your legs."

"And if you raise them . . ."

"I mean, it's not entirely correct, but the blood either can't get into 'em or drains back out of 'em," Betty said. "Gives you more time to get the blood to stop gushing out."

"Before the fella dies?"

"Before he dies, yes," Betty admitted. "Don't worry, Viv. Even doctors lose people, in the best of circumstances."

"You didn't kill the man through inaction," Tommy said sternly. "He was killed by the man who put a steak knife in his guts."

"I know that in my head," I said. "But my heart doesn't know it yet."

"It will, in time," Betty said, squeezing my arm.

I shook my head to try to loosen the imagery of a dead and dying man from my memory.

"I also called the bus station . . . ," Betty said, checking her notes.

"You're so on top of it!"

"I like filling in boxes," she said, shrugging. "Nursing is a lot of paperwork. What's the blood type, what's the heart rate, what's the glucose level . . . you need info, I'm happy to get it and fill in the blanks."

"And what'd the new chaps at the Port Authority have to say?" I asked.

"Well, I got a long-winded spiel about how they don't get passenger names for buses," she started. "I have a feeling they get a lot of angry calls from coppers wondering why they can't prove so-and-so was on the four fifteen from Canandaigua."

"Mean streets of Canandaigua, always spilling over into Manhattan. Practically can't step out the door without running into a man from Canandaigua, up to no good."

"Or Tonawanda," Tommy cut in.

"Personal fan of Quogue," Betty cut in. "New York State has the greatest town names."

"But you're telling us that we can't bark up that tree, aren't you?" I said.

"Pretty much. Last bus arrived before six PM, before the whole song-and-dance was shut down for the festivities," Betty said. "So unless he was sticking around in the same few blocks for five hours *and* we find a ticket stub somewhere in the alleyway, the bus terminal is not going to be a source of information for you two."

"Thanks for checking," Tommy said.

"Okay, Tommy," I said. "You need to spill: does this Morty fella have a history of being a pill?"

"Not at all," Tommy said. "Gentlest fella I ever got to know in this city. He survived Mauthausen. He had some family already here, then as soon as he was strong enough, got on a boat and joined them."

"What kind of camp was Mauthausen?" Betty asked.

"Slave labor. Austria," Tommy said. "Mostly tried to work them to death in quarries or factories. No food. There were gas chambers eventually, but they tried to get as much work out of the men as they could. I have absolutely no idea how Mort survived for as long as he did."

"Does he talk about it much?"

"Do any of the survivors?" Tommy asked. "I've pieced it together over the last few years, but that's all."

"Have you met these family members he's talking about?" I asked.

"No, not a one," Tommy admitted. "But I've known Mort for half a decade, and he's never mentioned them to be cruel before."

"That suit was pretty swanky—are they rich?" Betty asked.

"No, very modest," Tommy said. "Mort is in real estate, but not these high-rises or anything like that. Lives out in Bensonhurst, must've taken the train in."

"Have you met Rachel?" I asked

"No," Tommy admitted. "I knew they were serious, but I haven't met her. He hadn't met *you*."

"Good point," I marked. "Ahh, but you'd never, ever have me tailed like this, and if you did, I'd break it off completely, even if it meant I had to move back to Podunksville."

"I would too," Betty admitted. "If he wants to actually marry this girl, you two better tread lightly."

"I have half a mind to tell him to take a hike, ol' Tommy boy," I said. "I know he's a friend, but I'm not entirely comfortable with this. *The Continental Op* said 'no divorces,' and now I know why."

"Some divorces are fun, though, especially when we know her alimony checks are going to be fat. But it's okay, Viv, I'll try to do most of the legwork on this one," Tommy said. "So if it all blows up in his face, Mort will have to reckon with me."

"Thanks, Tommy," I said. "I get why he's upset, but people deserve to be able to keep their secrets until they want to share them."

"Oh!" Betty hopped up and scampered out of the office. She came running back in with a steno pad and threw it in front of Tommy. "Secrets!"

"Betty, did you crack that code in a *day*?" Tommy asked. He looked utterly bewildered.

"I'm not sure if you've ever seen a doctor's handwriting," Betty said, "but this was nothin' compared to terrible penmanship mixed with medical Latin."

"God bless."

"What does it *say*?" I said, hopping up to peer over his shoulder.

Tommy patted his pockets for his glasses, but nothing doing. "You read it," he said, tossing it to me.

I stood up in my most perfect posture and read. "I took what is yours, and you will want to pay for it, I know. A following tip will wait for you at a foot of our holy woman fountain, at a hub of our park." I read it again silently to myself. "So the blackmailer is foreign? 'Cause that ain't proper English."

"I think that's on purpose, Viv," Betty explained. "When you're doing the word jumbles in the newspaper, the first thing you do is look for the letter *E*, because that's the most commonly used letter in the alphabet. Read it again."

I did, ready to count my vowels. "There isn't an *E*."

"E-e-e-e-xactly," Betty said. "The stilted language is so he didn't have to use the most common vowel. That's what slowed me down solving it."

"Slowed you *down*?" Tommy asked.

"I like words." Betty shrugged. "The letter *P* appears by itself a few times, and I wracked my brain for single letter words that would make sense in a letter. All I could think of was *I*."

"But then how did you get the rest of the letters?" Tommy asked.

"I wrote out the alphabet in order, first," Betty said, grabbing the notebook from me and flipping back a page or two. "Then I put the letter *P* under the letter *I*, and continued singing the song, you know, putting the alphabet in order. Once I got to *Z* being under the letter *S*, I just started the alphabet at the beginning, with *A* under *T*."

I stared at her.

"It's a shift code," she said. "Pretty easy once you unlock it."

"I'll take your word for it," Tommy said.

"'Holy woman fountain' could be Mary, of course," I mused. "Or really any other lady saint."

"Are there a lot of religious statues in public parks, though?" Betty asked.

"There aren't even that many statues depicting *dames* in public parks," Tommy said. "There's that big Joan of Arc all the way uptown."

"The one off of Riverside Drive?" Betty asked. "God, that's a hop, skip, and a jump."

"But she was a pretty holy lady," Tommy pointed out.

"I wouldn't consider Riverside Park *our* park," I said. "But maybe it has a special meaning to the blackmailer and Mr. Floristan."

"It must," Tommy agreed.

"You're probably right," Betty agreed. "Viv, you gonna take a hike out there to check for the next clue?"

"Sounds like my afternoon is planned," I agreed. "I'll get my purse and be back as soon as I can."

"Take a cab, Viv," Tommy shouted as I left the front door. "We'll expense it back to Floristan."

★ ★ ★

There shouldn't've been that much traffic on a Wednesday midday, but I knew there was no giving logic to New York City traffic patterns. The three miles uptown took ages, in stop-and-go, bumper-to-bumper that made my stomach gurgle and my brain feel like I'd spent the entire ride spinning in my desk chair. As soon as the cabbie grumbled, "We're here, toots," I tossed him some bills, grabbed a receipt, and bolted from the car into the freezing cold park on the river.

Blessedly, there was no one around as I canvassed the area around the base of the statue. The figure itself was startling and impressive—Joan standing triumphant in a suit of armor, gazing toward heaven. The suit of armor somehow showed the curves of her chest, even though I didn't think they made suits of armor for girls back then when I couldn't even get rubber-soled boots for women this day and age. I knew Joan was just a little 'un when she launched her campaign, and her youth was depicted by the human figure being teeny-tiny compared to the horse she was mounted on. And that horse clearly knew what was up, I tell you that. His eyes were wild and nostrils flared, every single muscle in the beast's body tense and frightened. It wasn't fair to ride animals into battle like that, in my opinion, but a lot of people don't have much respect for the feelings of the critters in their lives, I knew that much. The statue was remarkable, and I'm glad I got to go and see it. I'd probably never be in this neck of the woods ever again.

But there wasn't a goddamn thing near it, on it, in it, or around it that looked like a package or clue from a blackmailer, unless the fella was getting creative with weather-beaten coffee cups and the ends of approximately six thousand hand-rolled cigarettes.

I nearly died of fright when I heard clip-clopping on the pavement behind me; the statue hadn't come to life to lend a hand, but a mounted cop on a chestnut mare was coming up the sidewalk to check in on the dame digging through the snowy bushes like a woman possessed.

"Do you . . . need any help, ma'am?"

"No, no. I dropped something on my walk to work this morning," I fibbed. "Piece of paper. I saw a bunch of garbage was blown in the bushes and thought I'd see if I got lucky enough for it to be here."

"It's probably in the Hudson," the man shrugged.

"That's my luck," I agreed. "Hey, I know this is probably a no-no but . . . can I pet your horse?"

"Usually I'd say no," the cop said, "but sure."

I approached the calm beast slowly, my hand outstretched for her nose. The poor thing didn't have a jacket on or anything, and her hot, moist breath made clouds around her nostrils. My mitten made contact with her long nose, and she did a little dance to show that she welcomed the little bit of love.

"Here." I looked away from the horse to see a carrot right in my line of sight. "She goes ape for 'em."

Sure enough, the carrot was barely in my hand before it was in the horse's teeth, and she was happily munching away on the vegetable, little orangey bits falling from her maw into the snow.

"She's wonderful," I said. "You're so lucky."

"That I am, ma'am," the cop said, patting the horse's neck. "She's a good friend, and on top of that, she gives off a fair amount of body heat."

"Must be nice if your usual beat is along the river."

"It is. Sorry you didn't get lucky finding your lost paper."

"It's okay, it was a long shot anyhow." I paused for a moment. "Hey, do you know if this is the only statue of a lady in all of New York?"

"I mean, the only one of a person lady I can think of," the cop said, sitting back in his saddle. "But there's the big angel in Central Park. Bethesda Terrace."

"Oh my God! You're right!" I squealed. "It said fountain!"

"What said fountain?"

"Nothing, nothing. Sorry! Gotta get back to work!" I hauled ass back to the main drive, waving my arms for a cab like a woman drowning at sea. A cabbie pulled over and I slid in the back.

"Where to?"

"Get me as close to Bethesda Terrace as you can," I explained.

"Ugh, I gotta go *through* the park?"

"Sorry you picked me up, bud," I said. "But step on it."

The driver hauled down Columbus, and just north of the Natural History Museum hooked a left and sped through the windy little road in the park, dipping in and out through tunnels, past the little castle, and popped out on 5th Avenue, heading south. He stopped at 72nd and yanked the meter. "That's the best I can do, toots."

"Are you all required by law to call girls *toots*?" I asked.

"Nah, but it's less offensive than *ma'am*," the cabbie explained.

"I assure you, it isn't," I said, leaving my payment and grabbing my receipt. "Thanks for the ride."

It felt like a mile's walk back into the park. "The blackmailer couldn't've struck in gee-dee *April*?" I asked, to the raised eyebrow of a man in a fedora and a beaver coat passing me by.

"Please, like that's the most surprising thing you've ever overheard in New York," I scoffed at his retreating back.

"Of all the cities in the world where I could've become a private investigator," I kept muttering as my feet clipped over the sidewalk. The snow was patchy, and a good portion of the blacktop was sheets of ice—I guess the parks department didn't pay the fellas to shovel when the visitor numbers were low. "Why couldn't I have chosen a city where it didn't snow? Los Angeles, I bet, is lovely this time of year. Miami, maybe."

Bethesda Terrace had its fair number of lookie-loos. I could spy the lady of the waters through the arcades, and I'm telling you, she was a stunner, but the colonnades were acting like wind tunnels, and the breeze nearly lifted me off my feet. The bowl around the angel was empty of water, but not of snow drifts; the pond behind the brick plaza was a frozen sheet of ice with countless Canada geese milling around, waiting for spring, honking and making a mess while doing so.

The only way to find a note, envelope, or package in a plaza the size of a small town was to be thorough; I started walking laps from the farthest edges of the brick-cobbled mall, slowly working my way closer and closer to the fountain. There were no benches or trash cans for hiding places, but with my luck, the crafty menace who was arranging this little cat and mouse game for

Mr. Floristan would've tucked the note in between two bricks, or do something equally hard to find. It took a few minutes—and more than a few times dodging a running, shrieking child or a tourist who needed to snap a photo with their Kodak Brownie from just this specific angle—but sure enough, after a quarter of an hour, I found myself shin-to-concrete at the basin of the fountain. And spied a little box wrapped in Christmas paper in a small nave behind the columns propping up the splendid statue.

"Well, goddamn." The sneaky little blackmailing bastard couldn't have hidden it somewhere where Mr. Floristan could've picked it up unnoticed. No, with God and several dozen tourists as my witness, I was going to have to tromp through some public art and climb it like a damn monkey.

I hiked up my skirt and ambled over the shallow concrete barrier at the edge of the pool with no problem. The snow was not all that deep, though as the basin dipped as I got closer to the fountain, a fair amount of that snow did end up in my boots and sogging right through my stockings. The part of the masonry that was usually below the water line—the parts with the drain suckers that brought water back into the fountain to shoot out the bowl—wasn't as tall as I thought, maybe just a few feet.

The issue was the icy, carved stone just above that, with intricate swirls of foliage. It was at a pretty steep angle, and I jumped up on it, my stomach taking the brunt of the cold surface. Lifting my right leg up and not caring who I flashed in the process, I hooked the toe of my boot into one of the curlicues and managed to leverage my body up the side of the fountain so that my arm could finally reach in between the carved stone pillars. My hand first met something cold, wet, and slimy, but with another grunt and grasp, I got the package in my mitts and slid back down into the fountain.

"Miss." A deep voice rumbled from behind me, and I turned to find two coppers shivering, ankle deep in the same snow I trudged through without a single tooth chattered.

"Howdy, officers," I said. "How can I help you?"

"Miss, why are you climbing that statue?"

"I'm so sorry," I blushed. "My beau is out of town for the holidays and he thought it'd be funny to have his friends set up a little scavenger hunt for me, to get my presents. I was stumped on the last one until today. I hope my gift wasn't damaged in the weather."

"It was left in the open like that and no one snitched it in ten whole days?" the cop on the left asked. "In New York?"

"I guess the angels were smiling down on silly little me," I said with a giggle. "Am I in trouble?"

"Nah, just tell loverboy to put the gift in the mail next time," the cop said, rolling his eyes.

"Will do, sir." I followed in one fella's footsteps back to the bricks and he lent me a hand scrambling over the edge of the pond. "Thanks."

Heading west toward the sunset, I made it to the edge of the park and headed south, back toward the office.

NIGHT 4

Wednesday, January 3rd, 1951

"Viv, good, you're back," Tommy said, as soon as I opened the door. He was wearing his outerwear and was clearly off to the races. "We gotta go see a man about a horse."

"Excuse me?" I couldn't feel my legs below the knee and my nose had run so far and fast I felt like a toddler with a head cold. "I already met a horse today, but I forgot to ask her name."

"Horses are shy," Tommy said. "They're generally pretty reticent about giving that kind of information to strangers."

"Give me five minutes to at least warm up. And clean up. Before you expect me back out there."

"Fine," Tommy said, tapping his toes.

"What do you have, anyhow?" I asked. Not for the first time, I was happy we had a sink with a tap just inside the office. I wet a towel and mopped my face, took off my shoes, and scrunched my toes, trying to get the blood moving again.

"Well, I was playing around with that matchbook," Tommy said. "And I wondered if the printed part of the matchbook—the glossy stuff we can't read to save our lives—might be more visible if it was darker."

"Oh, God, if you scribbled on the evidence . . ."

"I did not," Tommy said. "Though that was my first thought. No, I took a rubbing. And look!" He pulled a piece of paper from his pocket and on it, I saw a small square of pencil lead with the faint outline of a running stallion, flying mid-stride.

"Well, we do have to see a man about a horse, don't we."

"When you warm up, though, Dollface," Tommy said, taking off his hat. "I don't want to rush you, I was just excited."

"Thanks, ol' Tommy boy. Do we have anything to eat? I'm starving."

"Betty's out for sandwiches. Roast beef for you."

"I love you, you're perfect, be mine forever."

"I thought that was a given with the Tiffany on your finger."

"It was a good start, but you really sealed the deal with sandwiches."

"Thank goodness." Tommy was grinning like a fool, came over, and swept me off my feet. "Let's make out like kids until she gets back."

"Sorry to ruin what sounds like a great time," Betty said from the door. "But I've got food."

"You're a saint, Betts," I said, wiggling out of Tommy's arms and running for the bag. "We can smooch later, Tommy, but I need a full stomach first."

"We should dine and dash," Tommy agreed. "Sorry, Betty. But I want to get out before all the clubs and everything open up. I want to see all of who's coming and going through the evening."

"No skin off my nose," Betty said, plopping down at her desk with a tuna melt. "You two are adorable."

"Thanks, Betty," Tommy said through a mouthful of pastrami.

"He's right, you know."

"Who?"

Betty pulled out a copy of that day's *Mirror*. "Sabella. He wrote a little something that the headline says is about the murder, but really it's about you two."

"That son of a—" Tommy growled.

"Let me read it first before you get too angry," I said, putting aside the sandwich. It smelled so good I was mad that I had to do anything but chew. I took a minute to scan the two column inches. "Betty's right, it's supposedly about the murder, but he spends forty of his ninety words talking about us. Apparently, I'm quite the glamorpuss, even when covered in blood."

Tommy took an angry bite and continued raging. "He's gonna throw a wrench in this whole investigation!"

"Calm down, you're gonna choke on the slaw," I said, swallowing my own giant bite. "Whatever we're looking for will be there, we just gotta get there alive."

"Right." Tommy swallowed. "Hurry up."

"I'm going as fast as I can," I assured him, with a mouth full of food. "You've got the table manners of a Viking."

★　★　★

With Tommy breathing down my neck, I managed to glom down my sandwich in a matter of minutes, and we were already on the hoof to the fated alleyway faster than you could say Jack Robinson. Thankfully, whoever cleared the sidewalk heaped more snow into the spot that was vacant just the day before. There was no more police presence, and if you didn't know any better, there was no sign a man had died there only a few nights ago. Which I guess is a good thing, if you owned the dry cleaners across the way.

"So what are we looking for?" I asked Tommy, shuddering a bit as the sun hid behind the buildings.

"Not sure," he responded. "You'll know it when you see it."

"That's the kind of confidence I like," I said, turning about in a circle. It's New York, and it was past the holiday, so everyone was back at work, and there were people of all sorts rushing up and down the sidewalk, from men in pristine overcoats to women in furs and shivering fellas whose coveralls were fit for the June heat but not the January freeze. "I'm sure it'll be subtle, whatever it is. No neon signs, even though that's the usual 'round these parts."

"Yeah, think a brass plaque next to the door, or an image on a light fixture," Tommy said, taking me by the arm as we strolled. "Whoever this is doesn't want to advertise."

"Are you a member of any secret clubs I should know about?" I asked. "Masons? Elks? Rotary? I need to know."

"Dollface, are you asking me if I have mob ties?" Tommy laughed.

"I know you don't, 'cause I think you've tangoed with every family from Boston to Hackensack," I said, laughing. "I just want to make sure you're never going to go sneaking off into the night to enjoy drinks with the fellas and get up to no good."

"I do like drinks with the fellas," Tommy said, pulling me in close and landing a kiss on my temple. "But I don't sneak. And any no good I'm up to is for work. You'll always know when I'm going and where I'll be, and I will *always* come back to you."

"Don't make promises you can't keep, Tommy Fortuna," I said, tears welling up in my eyes a bit. "This is a dangerous business."

"You having second thoughts about marrying a gumshoe?"

"Never," I said. "But I've been in this business long enough, too, to know the reality of it."

"If I get stuck in the guts, my love, I will crawl from Bushwick and beyond to die in your arms," Tommy said.

"You're goddamn right you will."

"I simply expect you to stay in Sicilian widow's weeds for the rest of your life," Tommy said.

"Is that like a real *rest of your life*, or like a life sentence in prison—a couple of decades before I can petition for parole?" I asked.

"Praying to your dead husband for parole!" Tommy laughed so hard he nearly slipped on the sidewalk.

"Watch it, ol' Tommy boy," I said, steadying him. "Don't crack your head on the pave—wait a second."

"Wait a what, why?"

"Look up."

Tommy gave a pirouette in place and started scanning the sky. "No, you goof," I said, stopping him. "The arch over the door."

Chiseled into the limestone arch over a basement doorway was a faint outline of a running stallion.

"How did you *see* that?" Tommy asked. "There's no light or anything."

"I have no idea, but I'm glad I did," I admitted. "Now what?"

"Now we watch," Tommy said. "There's a diner across the street, let's get some coffee and scope the place out."

We hurried to the diner and took our perches at the counter in the large, plate glass window. Tommy ordered a slice of cherry pie, and even though I was stuffed from my deli sandwich, I had to admit it was mighty tempting.

For the first hour, it was nothing but commuters—no one even glanced at the nondescript little door as they hurried through the frozen twilight. Our evening was much more pleasant, even if I did get blasted with cold gusts every time someone opened the door to come and grab their own plate of dinner. Tommy polished off his pie, and three cups of coffee, with a relish that was only going to lead to indigestion as soon as he lay down in bed.

"Maybe they're not open today," I said, finally grabbing the attention of the waitress and opting for apple instead of cherry. The girl in the pale blue uniform turned to grab my dessert, but Tommy touched her lightly on the elbow to get her attention.

"Hey, hon," he said as she turned. "You ever notice anything strange happen across the street?"

"It's New York," she said back, cracking a smile. "You're going to have to be more specific than that."

"The place with the horse over the door," I said. "Down the little stairs."

Her eyes got real narrow. "Why?"

"We're private investigators," Tommy said, reaching for his wallet to show that he could pay the bill, as well as his typed-out license from the state of New York.

"Something fishy is happening there, and it's related to a crime," I added. "A serious one."

"I can't tell you for certain, as I've never gone in myself," she said, chewing on the end of her pencil. "But I'll tell you, it's more gents than ladies that go in, ten to one."

"No one here's ever tried to go in, just for larks?" I asked.

"You don't slip into places like that without anyone noticing, girlie," the waitress said back. "Not when you smell like fried onions no matter how much you wash."

"Thanks, hon," Tommy said. "We'll take our check with the slice of apple, too."

"No prob."

Tommy was antsy as I took slow, deliberate, polite, and lady-like forkfuls of dessert. "Why the hell did you wait til I ordered to make your plan?" I asked.

"Sorry, Dollface," he said, but didn't relax.

"It's fine." The last bit of crust was consumed and Tommy was up, plucking my coat off the hook by the door and holding it for me to slip into. "So what are we going to say?"

"I don't know yet," Tommy replied, putting on his hat. "I guess we just play it by ear."

"Exciting."

We scurried across the street and Tommy led the way down the short length of stairs to the door. He went to knock, but I spied a gleaming brass doorbell and pushed it. I felt like I was trick-or-treating.

After what felt like ages, the gleaming black door opened, and all I could see was a glowing white shirt collar and cuffs emerging from a black livery suit. The entrance was lit only by candles—the light bounced off of mirrors and gleaming wood—and the warm air smelled like cigars and furniture polish inside. A shadowed face coughed and asked pointedly, "May I help you?"

"Here for the evening festivities," Tommy said back, straightening up.

"You have the wrong club, sir," the shadow murmured back. And the door slammed in our faces. Rather than wait for the man to reconsider, we skipped back up to the sidewalk before chatting.

"Well, we're in the right place," Tommy said. "We'll figure out how to break into Troy, don't worry."

"I'm not worried," I said. "Should we tell the detective about this? I mean, it's going to eventually be his case, we can't arrest someone for murder."

"I hate the fact that we always have to bring in the fuzz when it gets to the end of a case," Tommy huffed. "Let him do his own dirty work."

"He's one of the better ones, but even on New Year's, Lawson was resolved to calling this unsolved and putting that poor man in a plain pine box."

"What does he want?" Tommy grouched. "A million bucks a year?"

"Judging by that penguin suit he showed up in, I bet he wants to be commissioner and then maybe mayor," I said.

"That's not the kind of gig you get by working up the ranks, Viv. Those are the kinds of gigs you get by paying off the right person, good and proper."

"You're right, and I bet he knows that. But hey, maybe he figures he'll be the first one yet."

"Sounds exhausting," Tommy said. "I'd rather just work for fun and profit."

"When does the profit kick in?" I teased him, and he swatted my arm. "But I can tell you—just the detecting bit of the job is exhausting."

"Ain't that the truth. Even without all the politics."

"I don't know . . ." I linked my arm into his and stared wistfully at the people running around the city, not paying attention to the souls around them. "Tally showed me that everything is politics, even if we don't want it to be."

"How do you figure?"

"Well, you and I just had a five cent piece of pie at a diner," I pointed out. "While fellas in there—and more fellas than dames, remember—were probably eating twenty-five dollar steaks. Nothing good happens in a joint filled with men and expensive meat."

"They're not strategizing the war in a gentleman's club, Viv."

"Maybe not, but they are talking about city councilmen and the fact that they don't like stepping over bums on the sidewalk on the way to church," I said. "That's politics."

"You're right."

"They talk about how high their taxes are, their wives' brothers fighting in Korea, and where they think the next war is going to be," I said. "That's politics."

"You think there's already a next war?"

"There's always a next war," I said. "Even if 'the next war' is a fight to keep certain people out of their favorite restaurants, or who's going to be the next mayor."

"And whoever's mayor of New York City is on a national political stage," Tommy said. "You're a smart cookie, Dollface."

"Just a nervous one," I said. "Your place?"

"No problem." Tommy stepped toward the curb and gave a piercing whistle and frantic wave. The cabbie at the end of the block gunned it and screeched to a halt at his feet.

"How do you do that?" I asked, sliding across the leather bench seat in back.

"Do what?"

"Always get what you want."

"Magic." Tommy gave his address, and it was a matter of minutes before we were in bed, warm, and asleep.

DAY 5

Tommy was shaving with his electric Norelco when I finally pulled myself from the covers. "What's on the docket for today, Boss?" I asked, traipsing my way to the shower.

"Today is Rachel's usual day to go to 'lunch,'" Tommy said, waggling his eyebrows. "So I have to follow her."

I stepped behind the curtain and grimaced. "I'm sorry," I shouted through the steam.

"I just wish I still had my Polaroid," Tommy said back. "Gotta take regular film."

Bacon and eggs were ready by the time I was done getting ready for the day. "Do you think you'll ever get another instant camera?" I asked, plucking the bacon from the plate.

"Sure," Tommy said, thinking. "I think if Mort's case goes on for more than a few days, I'll have extra cash and can zip back up to Boston and get another."

"That's good, they're so much more convenient."

"You head in to the office and meet up with Betty," Tommy said, "and one of you can take the roll to my developer later in the day, see what I see with Mort's girl."

"Aye, aye," I said, giving him a smooch on the cheek. "I'll lock up here."

"And take a damn cab to work," Tommy said, slipping on his overcoat.

"I will." And with that he was out the door. I finished my breakfast at a slow pace—it felt nice to know that I could arrive at the office on my own schedule—washed the dishes, dried them, put them up, arranged the bed linens, sorted the laundry, dusted the living room, and opened the curtains for the first time all day. It was my preferred morning routine, but I couldn't help but wonder if it occurred to Tommy at all that his shirts shouldn't go in the same bin as the kitchen towels that needed a wash.

★   ★   ★

Tommy's apartment being closer to the office than Mrs. K's meant that I did not take a cab to work. The morning was bright and sunshiny, and the blocks between there and his place were mostly residential, filled with hollerin' children mad as the dickens that they were already heading back to school. Behind a chain-link fence, kids skittered through an icy, paved playground playing tag before the bells rang and they had to be in their seats. One boy took a spectacular nosedive into the pavement and seemed ready to wail until his machismo got the better of him and he waved to his friend who had just arrived inside the gate. He had a nasty scrape on his cheekbone, and I did not envy whichever woman was going to have to focus all of that pent-up energy on algebra instead of action.

The sun was just barely high enough to show itself above the buildings across the street when I skipped up the stairs to the office. The door was unlocked, and the beautiful scent of brew was already emanating from the room. Our secretary was at her desk with her feet up, a donut, the paper, and a cup of joe by the time I joined her. "Well, aloha, Miss Betty," I said, tossing my coat on the rack. "How are you this fine morning?"

"Fine and dandy!" She was chipper as a chipmunk.

"Anything good in the rags today?"

"Herb Sabella caught CiCi somewhere she probably shouldn't be, near a seedy part of town," Betty explained about one of the city's more avant-garde girls, one who was more into art galleries than society balls. "He's supposedly on the crime desk, but he sure likes takin' pictures of dames on the public sidewalk."

"Looks like she's the one inheriting all of Tally's column inches," I said. "Poor thing. Or lucky thing, depending on who you ask."

"Where's our hunky private detective?" Betty asked.

"Trailing after that poor man's fiancée lady," I said. "God, I hope she's not up to something."

"Me too, honey."

"I can't help but be glad that no one is that concerned about me and Tommy getting hitched," I admitted, pouring myself some coffee in a ceramic mug hopelessly stained brown on the inside, no matter how much I scrubbed. I hovered over the box of donuts and chose a powdered before settling down with my rump on the windowsill to jaw with my friend. "My mama said congratulations and that was that. I'm sure they'll try to make it for the wedding, but money's tight."

"I know Tommy said the fella was modest, but that was some nice suit he was wearing," Betty admitted, dusting her own sugary fingers on her skirt. "Weddings can get pricey, and folks have gotta think you're up to something real dicey to threaten to cancel one at the last minute."

"And I guess it's a good thing they have the propriety of not living together yet," I pointed out. "The logistics of separating stuff must be a nightmare."

"How is it going with you spending so much time at Tommy's?" Betty asked. "He strikes me as the kind that likes being a bachelor."

"He does, that's for sure," I said. "He's got a nice place—real furniture, real curtains, the whole nine yards. He takes pride in where he lives. But . . ."

"It's okay, I'm your friend right now, not your secretary," Betty assured.

"I really hope it all goes through in moving into Mrs. K's," I said. "I'm going to need the support of having a landlady that at least cooks meals for us if we need them. If I had to be a fully working detective *and* do all the work of a housewife, I'd probably lose my marbles."

"It's true," Betty said. "I don't know that many girls who didn't work before they got hitched up, but the pressure of keeping a house *and* a job is an awful lot."

"I know some women do it and make it look easy."

"And I know a lot of women who do it and they look like they're an inch from death's door every time I see 'em," Betty shot back. "Lots of the nurses had wee ones, too. And not a single father could learn how to change a diaper, it seems."

"How do they get away with it?" I asked.

"They think 'cause they pay for more it absolves them," Betty said, ready to snap her pencil in two.

"Is that why they don't pay us diddly?" I howled, laughing. "Ugh, no, don't get the wrong idea about Tommy, honey."

"I don't, but I think you're having regular nerves," Betty assured me. "Lots of men—more men than not—treat their girls a whole lot different after that marriage license is signed. It's normal to be scared, I think."

"Scared is a bit strong," I said. "Maybe just nervous. Dottie has the right idea . . ."

"Don't you dare drop that dreamboat man and become a Dottie," Betty said. "It suits her, she likes her life. It won't suit you one bit."

"I won't, I won't," I said. "Besides, he's a mean cook. That's a fine exchange for making the bed."

"But you should ask him, point blank," Betty said. "Make sure he knows that you're not going to be the only one scrubbin' toilets just 'cause you're now the Mrs. instead of the mistress."

"Damn right."

"*Damn* right."

Our meeting of the She-Woman Man Hater's Club came to a swift end as the phone rang. Betty swooped to pick it up.

"Fortuna and Valentine," she said. The caller responded and she handed me the receiver. "Detective Lawson."

I stuck my tongue out at the phone while taking it from my secretary. "Viviana. What have you got for me?"

"What have I got for *you*?" The detective groaned. "This isn't your case, Valentine."

"Sure it is, the man bled in my boots, Lawson."

"So I take it you're high and dry too."

"I wouldn't go that far," I said. "But I don't have anything to convict anyone just yet, so rather than have you go and slap some bracelets on an innocent man, I'm keeping my mouth shut and throwing away the key."

"More women should do that," Lawson bit.

"Normally you try to sweet-talk me more," I said. "Some girl break your heart on New Year's?"

"You, Viv," he said sarcastically. "Engaged to that lousy Fortuna."

"You had years to beat him to the punch, Lawson," I explained. "And in cases and romance, he always beats you to the line. Goodbye, Detective Lawson. I know just how to reach you when I need you."

I hung up.

"So what are we doing in the meantime?" Betty asked, picking up her nail file.

"I don't even know," I admitted. "I suppose we have that package I found at the fountain yesterday, but I was trying to hold off opening it until we all were here."

"Oh, just do it," Betty said. "We can clue Tommy in on what we find when he gets here, he won't mind one bit."

I scrambled into the back office and plucked the small parcel off my desk. Peeling off the paper as I returned, I tossed the ball of wrapping into the trash after I revealed a small, wooden cube beneath.

"Oh." Betty's face scrunched up.

"It's a block."

"Hand it here," Betty said. "It's not solid. I'll get it in a jiffy."

I tossed the wood her way and she set about poking and prodding at it.

"I hate these damn things," she muttered.

"What is it?"

"Another infernal puzzle," she said. "I did some time in my rotations in a head trauma ward, they just love handing these things to people and watching 'em struggle."

"That sounds awful."

"It's supposed to help with trans-spatial orientation, concentration, and short-term memory," Betty continued to mutter. "But I think some doctors just like to make people mad."

"I don't even have any trauma and I think that would drive me bananas," I admitted. "Are there some people who just can't do puzzles?"

"Of course there are," Betty said laughing, as the blocks clicked open and fell apart on her desk. "People like you."

"What's people like me?" I asked as Betty pulled a small piece of paper out of a cavity in the wood.

"You go like a scent hound," Betty diagnosed as she handed the paper over. "You're a woman of action, by and large."

"I don't like fiddly things," I admitted.

"Which is why you are not a nurse," Betty said.

"Things like that just make me so angry," I said. "Taking more than ten seconds to open a box with something inside? Absolutely not. The box would be out the window and on the sidewalk already if it was up to me."

"I know, I've seen you try to untie a knot in the laces of your boots, don't you recall," Betty said. "And heard it when you threw them against the wall when the knot wouldn't let go. What does the letter say?"

I cracked the wax seal on the paper and almost immediately got dizzy. "'Nother code," I said. And it looked way more complicated than the last.

There's no SECRET here!
Ildee sscnw I AFbesllonn ptan e sy
IkZidr m beyy'AAkg euyi
y'In ys'Ir!,ddastldtwaonee'iuuu
eol pnouetl nrrp.!an
Happy New Year!

"Is that . . . Welsh?" Betty asked as she pored over the paper.

"I have no idea," I admitted. "But look, it's not addressed to anyone, like the last one."

"I think it's on the same paper, though, from what I recall."

"Typewritten."

"Yup," Betty admitted. "So no handwriting analysis."

"Good thing you read all those books," I said, poking her in the ribs. "You know exactly what to consider next."

"I didn't think real-life PI work was anything like those novels," she admitted.

"It's not, by and large," I admitted. "You just showed up at the right time."

"Should I make a few copies of this?" Betty asked, already swinging her chair toward the typewriter.

"Yeah, and make sure you get the spacing and capitalization right, too," I said. "It might have something to do with the actual brain teaser."

"Aye, aye, Captain."

I left Betty to her clacking keys and went back to my desk in the office. It felt strange—I was no help here. If Tommy needed someone confronted or clues picked up from a scene, I was the girl. But our current Girl Friday was running circles around me on this case, and I couldn't help but feel jealous, even if Tommy wasn't here to see it firsthand.

I had several calls to make—the FBI still needed information and notes from our case in November—and I knew I also had to make one that would set Tommy off if he ever knew about it. I spun the dial for the operator and waited for her to pick up.

"Get me the office of the *Daily Mirror*," I said. "Please."

The girl at the other end sighed. "Thanks for saying please."

"Least I could do." The switchboard girl at the newspaper picked up and I was patched in to the crime desk.

"Sabella." The small man had a powerful voice over the line.

"It's Viviana Valentine," I purred. "Thanks for the nice words in the paper, but you could've saved yourself twenty and not described my legs so much."

"Dames and their legs sell papers."

"Dead bodies don't?"

"Of course they do, but I sell the most papers when it's a dame who's dead."

"Sorry to disappoint," I murmured. "But listen: you scratch my back and I'll scratch yours, *comprende*?" I had no intentions of scratching anyone, but I didn't need to make any enemies, the way Tommy seemed to be hell-bent on doing.

"Sure, I believe ya," Herb muttered. "But my claws are filed down as we speak. I ain't heard nothin'."

"Well, that's a shame," I said. "I got no tit if you got no tat."

"Well, even under that coat I could tell you got ti—"

"Good night, Mr. Sabella." I slammed down the receiver.

★ ★ ★

It was well past dark when Tommy returned from his day of trailing the poor but infamous Rachel. He slipped into the office just as I hung up on a lady trying her damnedest to sell me a subscription for encyclopedias, and flopped down in his chair, the camera in his mitts tumbling onto his desk blotter.

"That good, huh?" I asked, picking up the camera and making sure it wasn't damaged.

"Don't worry about that old thing," Tommy said. "You could drop it off the Chrysler building and it'd survive."

"I don't want to expose the film."

"I do, sort of."

"Oh no."

"Well, she's meeting with a man, I can tell you that much," Tommy said. "Didn't see anything incriminating with my own two eyes, but they disappeared for a while in a department store."

"Well, that could be anything," I said.

"Have you frequently gone shopping with male acquaintances?" Tommy asked.

"I don't have too many male acquaintances," I admitted. "I live in an all-girls boarding house. I just know the mugs you bring around here."

"Well, that's good for me, then," Tommy said. "I know all their faces. But let me get that film out without damaging it; you can take it to the developer tomorrow after we trail Mr. Bowen's missing man."

"Have I *mentioned* how much I hope he just quit and got a new job?" I asked.

"You have." Tommy was fiddling with the winding mechanism on the camera and held his breath as he flipped open the back panel to reveal that the film was safely and fully protected from the light. "*Phew.*"

"Another benefit of the instant camera," I said. "I hope we get another one, stat."

"Here, toss this in your bag," Tommy said, flinging me the film canister. "Let's go home."

"Betty! Grab your purse!" I hollered. "We're going home!"

Betty met us in the front office, fully prepared for the winter weather. She was a bubblegum confection in a bright pink overcoat with white rabbit at the collar and cuffs, a knit white hat, and fuzzy mittens. She'd traded in her indoor shoes for white, patent-leather boots. Betty was just a few years younger than me, but her taste leaned toward the twelve-year-old. With her bottle blond hair and rouged cheeks, the whole look worked on her, but I wondered how much longer she'd try it once she was on the dark side of twenty-five, or engaged to be married herself. She caught me studying her and stuck out her tongue, then slipped us each a folded-up note.

"It's the new puzzle," she explained to Tommy. "Came wrapped up in one of those wooden block brain teasers."

"God, I hate those," Tommy said. "They made me do 'em all in the hospital, to make sure my thinker was still on straight after I got clocked at sea."

"And they still let you out?" I said, howling as I ran out the door.

"Betty, will you marry me?" I heard Tommy say as Betty giggled.

"Absolutely not, you brute," she said as she skipped down the stairs behind me. Tommy was giggling as he locked the door behind us, and the architect on the first floor, Mr. De Lancey, slipped his head out of his door to shush us all before slithering back into his office and slamming the door. Without skipping a beat, we each flipped off his door and tumbled out of the office building to the street.

Tommy whistled for a cab, and within minutes we were back at Mrs. K's.

NIGHT 5

Thursday, January 4th, 1951

Oleks was on the front stoop in a coat, hat, and gloves as we all three ambled up the front steps.

"You okay, honey?" Betty asked. "You're turning blue. Why are you outside?"

"I'm supposed to be studying for a chemistry exam," the boy admitted, giving Tommy a death glare. "But I can't think over all the noise."

"What's happening?" I asked.

"They're starting work on the apartment," Oleks said. "They have to do things in the basement to make sure everything works right upstairs, with the kitchen and everything. It's a mess, and I can't think straight."

"I'm sorry, kid," Tommy said. "I really hope it won't take too long."

"Don't 'kid' me, old man," Oleks shot back. "I'm going to the library. Tell Mom I'll be home later."

Oleks got up and shot down the steps before any of us could talk him out of leaving.

"He's going to miss dinner," I said.

"He also wasn't carrying any books," Tommy pointed out.

"So much for studying," Betty said. "Come on, it's cold and I'm starving."

We went single file in the front door, left our mucky boots and coats in the vestibule, and entered the dining room to find Dottie setting the table. She hadn't missed a word of what transpired on the stoop.

"I think we might be able to chalk some of that up to teenage hormones, at least," she said, placing down five plates. Tommy slipped by her to the sideboard to grab cloth napkins and flatware. Betty skittered downstairs for glasses and to deliver the news to Mrs. K that her son wouldn't be home for dinner.

"But do you think most of it is me and Tommy?" I asked. "I know Oleks and I get along, but . . ."

"He's probably had a crush his whole waking life," Tommy shrugged. "But never thought about it all that much until I started showing my ugly mug around the place more and more."

"And I must tell you, the noise really is rather grating," Dottie said. "I've been staying at school later and later to avoid coming home to grade papers and such. It's dreadfully difficult to concentrate."

"God, I'm so sorry," I said, removing all the garbage of life from the center of the table. It was at least four of Betty's paperbacks, half-opened mail, and Oleks's chemistry book, held together with industrial masking tape.

Dottie shrugged. "It's temporary."

Tommy went downstairs to bring up platters of food for our landlady. "What do you think they're doing?" I asked.

"I believe it has something to do with the gas mains, and also types of drains from kitchen plumbing," Dottie said. "I admit, I started to glaze over as Oleks explained it. But he seemed rather interested in how all the processes worked."

"The gas I understand for a stove top," I said. "But plumbing? There's already a bathroom on the third floor."

"Beats me," Dottie said. Betty emerged at the top of the stairs from the basement, holding the door open for Mrs. K and Tommy, who were laden with dishes—an enormous tuna noodle casserole that would take up half the table, a mountain of fresh-made biscuits, and a green salad smothered in so much Italian dressing you could smell the vinegar a mile away. My mouth watered.

"We will let my son have his feelings," Mrs. K scolded. "He is almost a man, he will do what he does. As long as he comes home safely." She gazed out the front window, where the streetlights were already illuminating the pavement.

"He'll be fine," I said. "He knows these streets like the back of his hand. The neighborhood's been the same since he was a baby."

"And he's obviously no baby anymore," Betty said. "He's taller than Tommy."

Mrs. K sniffed and smiled. "He is *so* big," she admitted. "But he is still *so* young."

"Is he nervous about the draft?" I asked.

Mrs. K flinched. "I do not believe he has considered it much."

"It's different when your friends start leaving town," Tommy said. "That's when it sinks in."

"Oleks is the eldest of his friend group," Mrs. K said. "But three doors down, Mrs. Czinege. Her boy has gone."

"All the way to Korea or just boot camp?"

"All the way. The letters take their time."

"During the war, Chelsea felt so *empty*," Betty said. "Quiet. Kind of eerie sometimes."

"Were you always in Hell's Kitchen, Thomas?" Dottie asked.

"Goodness, no. My youth was spent avoiding scrapes in the north Bronx," he said, making his borough accent thicker and thicker with every word. "I didn't move into Manhattan until I got knocked out of the war."

"And what? You chose the worst neighborhood you could find?" I teased.

"I chose the best neighborhood I could afford!" Tommy howled, and we all got caught up in the laugh. I'll say this for Tommy—he might be causing some tension between me and Oleks, but he sure could diffuse it in most situations.

Both Tommy and I went back for seconds and thirds of the casserole while Betty picked at a few helpings of salad and bread. By the time we all finished our meal, we were nodding off, and Mrs. K was debating bringing up an apple pie before Tommy stopped her. "Of *course* we want pie. But wait a few minutes, Lana—we're all adults here, let me nip out for a good brandy to enjoy with dessert."

She smiled and, within minutes, Tommy was out the door with his hat on, and Betty was swooning. Mrs. K went downstairs to warm the pie.

"That's thoughtful," Betty said, blushing. "Should we find something good on the radio?"

"You flick through channels, I'll take the dirty dishes downstairs," I said. A newsreel was informing us about the Chinese forces in Korea, but I couldn't concentrate on what they were saying before there was a hum of static and the dining room filled with some slow jazz.

"Let's not let Mrs. K hear any of *that*," I heard Betty whisper to herself.

I carried a tray of plates and platters back downstairs for the landlady, and her entire apartment was in boxes.

"Mrs. K, what gives?" I said, plunking the load next to the sink.

"Oh, the workmen," she waved me away. "They need to reach services."

"Is that all this is?" I asked, my eyes narrowing.

"Yes, pretty girl. I assure you."

I didn't believe her.

"But tell me you're charging us more for the apartment than for rooms," I said. "This is too much trouble. We can just find a new pla—"

"No."

"Apartments are easy to come by, Mrs. K. Married couples move in 'em every day."

"No."

"Are you sure?"

She didn't quite answer, but pulled the pie out of the warm oven and pointed at the ice box with a tilt of her head. "Whipped cream on the second shelf, pretty girl. Bring it up with you." And with that, I knew the conversation was over.

Tommy had returned with his fresh bottle of brandy and was in his chair by the time I came back up with the whipped cream. Dottie, Betty, and Mrs. K were all relaxed but clearly waiting for my arrival.

"What a perfect evening," I said, scooping huge dollops on top or on the side of warm pies, as directed by each one of my friends.

"Do you think you'll turn one of the bedrooms into a proper sitting room upstairs?" Betty asked. "You can have your own little parties."

"Who the hell am I throwing parties for if not the likes of you?"

"I have friends, Viv," Tommy said. There was an edge to the statement, but a smile on his face nonetheless.

"Oh! Of course. *Ha!*" There was no covering up my embarrassment, but Betty and Dottie had seen me step in it enough over the years that they just pushed on with the conversation.

"Oh, I think I see Oleks coming up the sidewalk," Betty peeped before the door flung open and the boy entered.

"Glad you are home safe," his mother called out to him. "There are leftovers downstairs."

The response would only politely be called a grunt as Oleks slammed through the dining room and downstairs to his mother's apartment.

"Why didn't he just use the outside door?" I asked.

"The theatrics are part of it," Dottie explained. "This is why I don't teach junior high and older."

"Do you have any idea what he is planning on doing after he leaves high school?" Betty pressed on. Mrs. K beamed.

"Sergiy wishes to open up his own shop," she said, referencing her brother who owned the brownstone we were all living in. "Not just dealing diamonds to other men, but having his own jewelry business. He says he needs Oleks to run the store, his own boys are too young."

"Stepan is, what, sixteen?" I asked. "Sergiy didn't want to wait?"

"Stepan will go into the wholesale," Mrs. K said. I think this was her polite way of saying that the business her brother was already in was the money train, and the shop might just be another favor for his nephew, whose father had died when he was just a boy.

"Well, I think that's just lovely," Dottie said, sipping her brandy in the smallest little bits to accommodate her temperate tastes. "This is very nice, Thomas. Thank you for the treat."

"Not a problem, Dorothy," Tommy said back. "How's school going, anyhow?"

Dottie launched into a monologue about reading goals and state educational assessments and Tommy did his best to uphold our half of the conversation.

"How do you know so much about elementary school?" Betty asked.

"Oh, you know—one of my sisters is a teacher like Dorothy here, and she and the other two have whole brigades of little ones," Tommy explained. "You just pick it up over time. But none of them have hit their teens yet, so I'm not sure what to do with the man downstairs." He shrugged and took a glug of his liquor.

"Same thing as you've always done," Mrs. K said, standing and picking up our dirty dessert dishes. "Love them and keep them safe." She disappeared behind the swinging door that led to her downstairs apartment, and Tommy stood up too.

"See you gals bright and early in the morning?" he addressed Betty and me. "Dorothy, a pleasure." He nodded and traipsed to the front door, and I followed.

"Surely you're not going home to an empty apartment and a cold bed at this hour," I said, checking my watch. "It's not even ten."

"No, I'm going to go have a trek past the missing Mr. Penhaligon's apartment in Murray Hill," he said, eyeing the block for a taxi. "See if he might be more active in the evening hours than the daylight."

"Do you want company?"

"Nah," Tommy said, donning his hat and leaning over for a kiss. "Get your beauty sleep. I'll fill you in in the morning."

"Night, ol' Tommy boy."

"Night, Dollface."

Returning to the dining room, I found Dottie and Betty were waiting for details. "It's the missing banker," I explained to Betty. "Tommy's just going to case out his house for a little while, see if he's up for any late-night errands."

"What do you think is happening?" Dottie asked.

"What I *think* is happening and what I *hope* is happening are different," I said. "I hope he just got a new job and left his bosses dangling on a string. What I think is happening is the bosses are afraid of him not coming back."

"What do you mean?"

"Maybe he was whacked for something," I said, making Dottie jump. "I don't think for one second that bankers and mobsters are all that different on the inside. A buck is a buck. But a killing would make them look awful, if the body is ever found. Bankers are as thick as thieves, and when you're dealing with that much moolah, you have to at least have the appearance of your nose being clean. And after last month, my eyes are peeled for spies and infiltrators."

"What's the likelihood you'll be on two Soviet spy cases in the span of sixty days?" Betty asked.

"Well, judging by the way that the news men talk, apparently very likely!" I said, laughing. "But that just has to be propaganda, right? Like all them posters during the war. 'Careless talk costs lives' and all that hooey."

"They wouldn't'a made posters if it was hooey," Betty said solemnly. Dottie suppressed a giggle.

"I suppose that's true," I said. Betty was a real believer in truth, justice, and the American way, and sometimes I didn't feel like arguing. "Listen, I'm going to bring the rest of the dinner dishes downstairs and help Mrs. K with the washing up. It's the least I can do, I think. You girls have a good night."

I grabbed the brandy glasses and the sticky flatware and tumbled down the stairs to Mrs. K's, knocking on the door of the basement apartment at the foot of the stairs. "Come in," I heard a deep voice say, and it took me a moment to remember Oleks was home and that his voice now had the deep roll of a kettle drum.

I slipped into the apartment, and he didn't remove his head from the icebox. "Just chuck it in the sink, I'll get to it."

"No, it's okay," I said, approaching the large, porcelain vessel. It took up almost the entire wall of the tiny kitchen, with a deep, singular basin so large you could wash a bloodhound in it, and drainboards on each side spreading out like wings on a gull. "I can help."

"I said I would get to it," Oleks said to the eggs, trying desperately not to look at me.

"Well, thanks then." I tossed the silverware in the sink, laid the glasses along the side, and beat feet out of the basement and up three flights of stairs. Both Betty's and Dottie's bedroom doors were closed on the second floor, and I was alone on the third, with no one to distract me from my messy thoughts.

Tommy had three sisters? After ten years of working in the same office, he'd only mentioned his poor brother, never sisters, with nieces and nephews and all those types of relationships. I'd seen him slip out with dames on his arm and come back to the office, bleary and stinkin', after nights out with the fellas, but family was mostly verboten—until there was a rock on my finger. Made me start wondering where the family seat was in the Bronx exactly—were we talking Arthur Avenue, or right up there near that women's college? Were these sisters going to like me one bit—were they older or younger than Tommy, closer to my age? Would I be expected to be friends, help out with the kids, and talk about treatments for diaper rash? I was in over my head, and terrified of the in-laws to whom I hadn't yet been introduced.

The twin bed I'd slept on for a decade had gone back into the windowless room downstairs, squashed between the stairs and the bathroom. Upstairs, Tally had insisted on a plush double mattress, and left it here for me to spread out on. It was the most luxuriant thing I'd ever owned, even softer than Tommy's brass bed at his apartment. There were satin touches on the sheets, four bed pillows, satin throw pillows, two bedside tables, each with its own lamp. And best yet, a window out which I could watch for planes in the sky, hoping for a night dark enough to see a star.

The brownstone across the way was inhabited by a singular, extended Italian family, and it was nice to watch things settle in before the curtains closed for the night. Two men were playing dominoes on the dining room table; the floor above, a toddler swaddled only in her cloth diaper streaked into her bedroom from her bath, her mother following behind with a fuzzy pink towel and laughing. Each little burst of life made me smile. Even if they carved up Mrs. K's into a billion apartments, I'd still be able to have dinner with Dottie and Betty, talk about our days, and what we hoped happened tomorrow.

Wouldn't I?

DAY 6

The phone was ringing downstairs and I heard Betty lumber out of bed to pick it up. I was halfway down from the third floor when I heard her sleepily mutter, "Sure, Tommy, I'll tell her," and hang up.

"Good, you're already up," she said, talking through her yawns. "I hate waking you. You get violent. Tommy wants you to meet him in Murray Hill to scope out the missing banker, as soon as you can."

"I guess it's a morning of breakfast on the hoof," I said, turning around to get myself ready and out the door. "I guess I'll see you when I see you at the office, Betts."

"Sounds good, Boss," she said, slipping back into her room. "But by the smell of it, Mrs. K is making bacon. Sorry you're missing out."

I was out the door before Dottie and Betty even made it downstairs for their plates of bacon and eggs.

The street was empty of cabs, and even though it was warm enough to not freeze entirely to my bones, there was a drizzle that made me resent the three-mile, northeast walk that was now staring me in the face until I slipped down the cold, stinking stairwell on 8th. Each concrete step was its own unique trap—slushy damp piles on one stair might hide a half-asleep rat; the surface of another, a patch of black ice that could send you flying. Picking my way down the endless shaft, I found my way to the subway. I didn't have to transfer to a different line—the IND would get me close enough—but the subway always made me feel claustrophobic and a little bit like I was going to catch a cold just by bein' on it, what with every car being filled to the brim with sniffling, sneezing, coughing, and generally unhappy commuters. But it was muggy and warm beneath the surface of the streets, and the squealing steel wheels along the track woke me up faster than a cup of weak, streetside coffee ever could. It was less than an hour since Tommy's call to the boarding house and I met him on the sidewalk outside of the mark's house. Or his parents' house, at least.

"Dollface," Tommy said, leaning in for a smooch. "You find a cab?"

"Nah, I took the train," I admitted. "And I really wish I'd remembered an umbrella."

"By the looks of it, it'll stop soon," Tommy said. "But I'm already soaked. Here, let's get under the awning and I'll catch you up."

A shoeshine boy's bench was conveniently placed under a ripped, green awning and no one was waiting for service—the boy was nowhere to be seen, knowing full well only a crazy person would ask for a buff on a day when the sidewalks were covered in squelching snow and mud. Tommy pulled a squashed bagel wrapped in soggy paper out of his coat pocket and handed it to me.

"Breakfast, and don't say I don't ever do nothin' for ya," he said with a giggle.

"Who says romance is dead?" I asked, feeling the cracks between my teeth fill with poppy seeds. "So what did you rustle up last night?"

"They're either early risers or have shipped out entirely," Tommy said. "They should be in that building, right there," he said pointing at a white brick building with fancy corbels at the roof line. "On the second and third floors . . ."

"Ooh, a duplex," I interrupted.

"But they ain't there. Or they can see in the dark."

"The roller shades are down," I said, squinting at the front of the building. "Did you buzz?"

"Nah, got here too late last night and too early this morning," Tommy said. "And I may be a no-good private investigator, but I still like to have some manners. It's after eight now—you want to try it?"

"Of course." I dusted the poppy seeds off my lap and stood, tossing the crumpled white wrapper into a trash can. "Do I got seeds in my teeth?" I asked, grinning like a fool at Tommy.

"Yeah, but it's not too bad," he said, eyeing the traffic for a break so he could scurry across the street. "Now, Viv, after this bus." The light was still green but I ran to keep after him, jay-walking as fast as I could across the five lanes of concrete.

"At least the name is on the buzzer," I said, pressing the white, pearlescent circle on the front panel. I could hear an obnoxious bell ring through the building—the apartment was empty, not even furniture was in there to muffle the sound of the call button.

"Well, that's the pits," Tommy said. "Mr. Bowen isn't going to like that."

"Wait a click," I said. "Look at the mailboxes."

"What? They didn't file a change of address form."

"*Exactly.*" I started tugging at the mail protruding from the slot.

"It's a federal crime to tamper with someone's mail, Dollface."

"I won't tell if you won't." The brass door to the mail slot was being pushed open by mountains of junk that had been shoved in by the postal carrier, who didn't seem to give the slightest fig that there wasn't someone there to collect all the general delivery leaflets and fliers. I shoved my fingertips into the small crack created by the force and yanked. The latch broke and out came reams of paper, all of which I picked up and forced into my handbag. "We'll sort it out in the office, away from the scene of the crime."

Tommy got to the curb and spied a yellow cab coming in hot down the avenue. He placed two fingers in his mouth, let out a piercing whistle, and waved it over to the curb, giving the address for the office as he slid across the seat. "I hope there's more in that pile than phone bills and ads for shoe repair," he said, throwing his head back to stare at the ceiling. "Or that banker's case is kaput."

"I can't read in the car," I said, "or I'll throw up. So now we just wait with bated breath until we get back, have a nice, hot cup of coffee, and sort through it all."

Betty had her head in her hands and was poring over her typewritten sheet with the latest code on it from Mr. Floristan's case when we strode through the door, pulling handfuls of crumpled-up paper out of my purse and tossing it on the floor in the center of the office.

"What smells like a barnyard?" she asked, curling up her nose.

"About sixty layers of wet wool between the two of us," I said. "We'll hang everything on the radiator to dry in just a second. Look!"

"What'd you do?" she asked, eying the pile, "Snitch a garbage can?"

"Close," I said, collapsing to the floor before I even took off my coat, and pulling out the obvious junk. There was no way that plumbers were pulling in enough business from these fliers to warrant the printing costs—and, not to mention, the ink was running like a bat out of hell from all the moisture and rain the leaflets had been exposed to for however long they were sitting in a leaky mailbox. My fingers were getting dyed.

"Well, they're overdue on the gas bill, but this is strange." I pulled a postcard out of the pile and showed it 'round.

"Where is that?" Betty asked. The front of the postcard featured a blurry photo of a stone statue, which resembled a great big bird, with hulking shoulders and a tiny little head. Next to it was a nondescript little evergreen shrub, which offered absolutely no hint as to where this eagle could reside.

"No clue," I admitted.

"Does it have anything on the back?" Tommy asked, excitedly grabbing the postcard out of my fingertips and flipping it over. "Nothing printed about what this could be a picture of. But the writing says '*1 pm. Daily. Until we meet.*'"

"It sounds like a love letter," Betty said.

"Or an open-ended invitation," Tommy said.

"Well, hopefully that hasn't been in the mailbox since Labor Day," I grumped. "'Cause whoever sent it would have run out of patience by now."

"It says January 2nd on the postmark," Betty said, squinting at the back of the card as Tommy analyzed the photo. "Do you think it's to someone specific?"

"I'm not sure," Tommy waffled. "Can any of you tell what this is?"

"No clue," Betty admitted.

"Are we sure it's even in America?" I asked.

"Where else could it be?" Betty asked.

"Ever since the Nazis used an eagle for their stuff, American eagles on everything make me do a double take."

"They are pretty similar, now that you mention it," Tommy said. "But American eagle insignia are rarely holding swastikas."

"*Rarely.* I'm not going to think about that too hard right now." I squinted back down at the postcard. "Well, I'm also not going to Berlin to solve a case, no matter how much Mr. Bowen is paying."

"But it looks kinda touristy, and it's still intact, so it isn't Berlin. Stuff for regular folks in any city doesn't have that much detail," Betty said. "The fancy carving only comes out when someone donates it and wants to feel special."

"Well, have a good pore over it," Tommy said. "Viv—will you take that roll of film from yesterday to the developer's for me? I have a meeting with Morty."

"A meeting?" I asked. "You don't even have the film yet!"

"More of a lunch date," he admitted. "And Morty knows all the best places to eat."

"Well, lucky you," I said, fishing around in my purse to make sure I still had the goods. "Gimme the address, and when I'm done running your errand, Betty and I are getting steaks."

★   ★   ★

The address Tommy gave me was on Amsterdam Avenue, near West 63rd, right near Mr. Moses's project for the great big, new music center. The streets were all torn up and filled with the sounds of banging, clanging, and men shouting; wide-open lots stood with piles of bricks in the center, and it took me a minute to realize those bricks were once buildings. A wrecking ball hung next to a four-story with a big chunk taken out of it, and right two doors down was the address for Tommy's friend. I rang the buzzer and was immediately granted access. Up two flights of stairs filled with the sounds of saxophones and music in Spanish, I found a door propped open. I knocked lightly and heard a high-pitched voice shout, "Come on in!"

"How do you even think with all that racket?" I asked the disembodied voice.

"First time in San Juan Hill?" A petite backside pushed open a closed closet door, and a girl with curves in all the right places emerged from a dark closet wearing men's sailor trousers and a form-fitting tennis sweater with a nice hole in the elbow. Her tightly curled hair was wrapped in a vibrant silk scarf; her dark skin was luminous. "You must be Tommy's new girl." She didn't offer a hand but leaned against the doorjamb and appraised me like I was a yearling at the county fair.

"I'm Viv!" I said, too enthusiastically. "Nice to meet you!" I guess my brains thought the best way to cover up the nerves in my stomach was to be as peppy as a cheerleader. The girl was amused.

"Aren't you just."

I didn't know what that meant.

"I'm sorry, ol' Tommy boy didn't give me your name."

"Thelma Thompkins," she said. "Pleased to make your acquaintance."

"Nice to meet you, Ms. Thompkins," I said. "Tommy asked me to drop off some film for him—he said you could develop it?"

"Of course I can." She flipped her hand at the small strip of counterspace in between her two-burner gas stove top and her sink. "Leave 'er there."

"You have a whole film lab in this joint?" The entire apartment was larger than my old room with no window at Mrs. K's, but barely. By the sound of a flush down the hall, I gathered Ms. Thompkins here had a communal toilet, and her kitchen area didn't amount to much. But the rest of the apartment was filled with shelves, which were in turn filled with boxes, books, gadgets, and supplies. Behind an easel, there was a small twin mattress on a low bedframe covered in blankets, and a large tuxedo cat.

"A whole film lab and usually no one to bother me," she said.

"When can I come pick it up?" I asked, on my way out the door.

"When I call you and tell you," the tiny woman said. "Leave the door open on your way out."

★   ★   ★

I stalked the ten or so blocks back to Tommy's, stomped up each and every step to the mezzanine office, burst open the office door, and only gave Betty a grumpy wave before I stamped back down the stairs to wait for her in the vestibule of the building.

She skipped to keep up after me as I flew up the sidewalk to the southern edge of the park.

"There has to be something good around here," I said, whipping my eyes past every storefront, looking for any place that looked like it'd serve me an expensive cut of meat.

"What's got into you?" Betty said, pulling me into some joint that had a black awning and white letters that just said *Bar and Grille*, that extra *E* letting us know we were in for something fancy. We were seated by the gent up front and Betty ordered two martinis before I grunted out the words.

"A stunning number named Thelma Thompkins, that's what." I gave a gulp to the martini and Betty had to stop me before I swallowed the olive, toothpick and all.

"So what?" Betty asked. "Tommy's got a past. So do you. You've met most of 'em."

"But I never once met Thelma," I said. "Which meant she was something special."

"What's the logic there?"

"You only introduce girls who don't got reason to get jealous to your secretary," I said, and Betty had the decency to nod along like I was speaking the God's honest.

"She was that pretty, huh?"

"Betty, when I tell you she was a knockout," I said, laughing. "And my complete opposite. Petite and curves that don't quit. She was a doll, I tell you. A *doll*. She takes pictures but she could be in 'em, no sweat."

"Ah, don't get hard on yourself, sweetheart," Betty said, patting my hand. The waiter came over and we each ordered a T-bone steak with baked potatoes. "You should see the way that man makes eyes at you."

"But I got stuck with this honker," I said, pointing at my Sicilian nose. "And I'm almost tall enough to look Tommy in the eye when I'm flat-footed. I got blessed with every feature the magazines say men *don't* want. She was cute as a *button*."

"And there's a reason they're not together anymore."

"She was kind of a cold fish," I said. "Wouldn't shake my hand, only gave me her name when I prodded for it. I asked her when I could pick up the developed images and she said 'When I call you.' Now how's that for something."

"She's got other work!" Betty said. "It may not be a slight one bit."

"I hope not," I said. "I don't like being in competition with anyone, especially if someone thinks the prize is a man. I'd rather get a new job."

"It's hardly competition when you're the one with the Tiffany diamond on your hand. Most girls would say you already won."

"I won't consider it a done deal til we're in front of the JP," I said. I didn't mean to, but I went about attacking my steak with a gusto that made Betty skootch a bit away from the table.

"It's already dead, Viv," she said. "And you're making me nervous with that steak knife."

I put down the cutlery and tried to regain composure by sipping the rest of my drink. "He at least coulda given me some warning."

"That's true," Betty said. "And worth mentioning. To him. Calmly. Perhaps in his apartment. Away from convenient stabbing implements."

"Why don't fellas think these things through?" I asked.

"For all you know, they don't have a history," Betty pointed out.

"It was just something about the way she dismissed me, is all," I said, thinking over dessert and, recalling Thelma's petite figure, I turned down an apple pie, despite the hankering in my angry stomach.

"You sick?" Betty asked as I shook my head at the waiter. She ordered cheesecake and stared at me hard.

"No, just mad."

"I'm not gonna try to talk you out of a mood anymore," Betty said. "Just try to resolve it before you get back to the office tomorrow."

"Yes'm." I reached over with my fork and stole a bit of Betty's whipped cream.

"What do you want me to focus on this afternoon?" she asked. "No new clients are coming in."

"That's good, because we're up to our eyeballs in the current ones."

"Any momentum?"

"Definitely not on Mr. Floristan—that new puzzle is a doozy. We're stuck on Morty at the moment, until we get those pictures back, and the banker fella . . . unless that postcard from this morning is a major break, I don't know what's doing."

"And the murder?"

My stomach heaved a little as I remembered the feeling of warm blood sticking to my stockings. "I have to ask Tommy about that," I said. "That feels like one we have to do as a team."

"Well, then let's get you back to your partner," Betty said, scraping her fork in the leftover cream cheese on her plate. "That was delish. You missed out."

"It's okay." I slipped a ten dollar bill into the fold for lunch plus tip, and Betty whistled. "I'm going to have to earn that back, that's for sure."

"Business is good, but it's not *that* good," Betty agreed.

"You have to be thinkin' nurses' whites are better than our little show by now, huh?" I asked. We slipped out the door into a city that already felt like the sun was going down, even though it was barely two o'clock.

"I'll go back eventually," Betty agreed. "But not emergency again. I'm not getting any younger."

"Betty, you're twenty-four."

"My bones are achin', Viv," she laughed. "Let me daydream about being the attending at a nice podiatrist's office."

"What's that?"

"Foot doctor."

"Oh, gross, no thank-a-you," I said.

"I imagine it's mostly just shaving corns and fitting people for orthopedics," Betty mused. "Usually nothing but old folks and listening to them gripe about their aches and pains."

"You listen to me and Tommy gripe plenty," I said. "So you're well prepared."

"You are such a *Nörglin!*" Betty squealed. "I better not hurt as much as you in three years."

"When you're lookin' down the avenue at thirty, Betty," I said, yanking open the door to the office building, "you'll change your tune."

I ran face first into Tommy, who lifted me up and swung me round right into the vestibule. "Now a woman lookin' down the avenue at thirty is just what I want in this world," he said, dipping me. "A woman who knows what she likes. Stands up for herself."

"Howdy, ol' Tommy boy," I said, giving him a kiss on the nose as he lifted me. "We just spent too much money on lunch."

"Can't take it with ya, Dollface."

"You sure you don't have any more brothers?" Betty asked.

"Only the sisters, I'm afraid," Tommy smiled. "Betty, we're steppin' out. I got a lead on something I need to sniff out with my girl, here. Lock the door behind you once we're out of the office, since we have no meetings on the docket. Call Midtown North if someone comes knockin'."

"No prob, Boss," she said. "See you for dinner?"

"We'll try our best," I fibbed. If Tommy was taking me out of the office in the afternoon—that usually meant another dinner on the town. Maybe we could try that Greek place on 59th.

We skipped on down the stoop and Tommy made a quick beeline in the direction of Times Square. "So, how was lunch with Morty?" I asked.

"Productive," Tommy responded. "He had an in at The Turn Out."

"What's that?"

"The club with the horse matchbooks, Dollface," Tommy explained. "It's quite the joint."

"Places that are 'quite the joint' inside don't usually let dames in the door," I pointed out. "Did he take you there on his own volition?"

"Nah, I asked him about it, just in case he knew," Tommy said. "Morty knows all the best places, like I said, so if he didn't know where I was talking about, then he could call up a fellow and find out. He said he could use a friend's connection to get us in."

"He knows all this from Bensonhurst?"

"Morty's a hell of a guy."

"And Rachel is fine with him knowing all of these places in the five boroughs?"

"I don't think he spends much time in Staten Island."

"Who does, really," I snorted. "So why are you taking me with you?"

"Because the cocktail waitress I spoke to agreed to meet with me after hours," Tommy said. "I'm bringing you so that she knows there's no funny business."

"Or she'll think it's real funny business," I said.

"As long as you got your license, she'll figure it out."

"And what makes you think the bird will sing?"

"She looked like a girl who hasn't stopped cryin' in ages," Tommy said, slipping into the darkness of an alley. I glanced around quickly to get my bearings and realized this was the staff entrance and exit to the fancy club. A fella in a dishwater-stained sweater was out back, eating a sandwich straight out of the white paper, standing on the grate that led to the club's basement storerooms and kitchen. As soon as we started hovering, he went back inside, not even swallowing the bite in his mouth. "Not much longer, I don't think."

Tommy busied himself lighting up cigarettes, smoking them to his fingertips, and tossing the butts into a planter while I leaned back against the building, eyes to the upper windows across the alley, waiting for something interesting to happen and thinking about how to bring up Tommy's ex after dinner. Betty was right that I needed to say something about entering someone else's territory without any advance warning, but she was also right to say that I couldn't get mad at Tommy for having an ex to begin with. Lord knows I do too, though at least one of 'em was currently out of the picture in Sing Sing.

A loud, ear-piercing squeak emanated from a metal door behind the planter and a petite bottle blond moused her way into the open, searching left and right for someone through puffy eyes that no number of cucumber slices were going to cure. Tommy stepped into her line of sight and she looked both relieved and extra scared.

Tommy opened his mouth, but she shook her head and motioned to the end of the alley. We let her get halfway down before we started following, then followed her for three blocks until we found a newsstand filled with men waiting for the evening post. It was freezing in the shadows, and our girl eyed a brown bag of M&Ms. Tommy tossed the newsboy a nickel, and she snatched it up, tearing off the corner and funneling the candy right into her mouth.

"Sorry," she said as she chewed. "They don't feed us."

"How long is your shift, hon?" I asked.

"It's a two-parter," she said, giving me an eye but answering anyway. "First is eleven o'clock to five, second is ten to four."

"You work twelve hours a day, spread out over two shifts?" I asked. "Until four AM? That's bonkers."

"It's what pays the bills," the blond shrugged. "Besides, in between I can grab a meal and a nap if I need it."

"Where do you normally go for food?" Tommy asked. "My treat."

"What's with the dame?"

"That's my partner, Viviana."

"Partner in what?"

"We're both private investigators, Norma."

"What are you talking to me for, then?" She backed away from us and skittered a little on something slippery.

"We're talkin' to you because on the night of December 31ˢᵗ we witnessed a murder," I explained, trying to keep my voice low. "And the only clues I found in the victim's pockets were a wad of cash and two matchbooks."

"Plenty of places got matchbooks." This Norma girl was now walking down the street and away from us, beating feet to put some distance between us and her. But the way she kept glancing over her shoulder . . . I was reading her language and scurried to keep up. "What makes you think that I got something to do with whatever malarky you're caught up in?" she hollered.

Norma jaywalked across the street but stopped at the next corner. She gave me a little wave with her mittened hand. I had to wait until the light turned before I could make it across and join her. She reached up to give me a friendly hug goodbye. "I got tomorrow off from the club," she whispered in my ear. "Meet me at my other job, afternoon." She slipped something into my pocket and disappeared inside of a diner. I knew better than to follow.

I hailed a cab and fell into the back seat. "Wait for that fella running up to join me," I said. "He's my husband, don't worry."

The cabbie started the meter, and Tommy came hurtling through the door, slamming it behind him, giving the driver Mrs. K's address.

"No, can we go back . . . home?" I didn't want to say *your place*—it sounded so unseemly.

"Sure." Tommy shrugged and updated the new address with the cabbie.

"What'd she leave you with?" Tommy said, eyeing my pocket.

"Feels like a card," I said, fishing it out. "Oh God, don't let the girls see this." The piece of cardboard was a shocking pink with bold, black lettering and a silhouette of a girl leaning down one side, showing off all that God and the illustrator gave her. "Looks like we're going back to Times Square."

"*Monsieur Baiser et ses filles du péché*," Tommy read, laughing. "Good grief."

"What does that mean?"

"Forgive my . . . actual French . . . ," Tommy said to the taxi driver, steeling his nerves. "It means Mister Fuck and his girls of sin."

"Just rolls right off the tongue, really," I howled. "Well, at least there's no confusion of what line of work she's in."

"Just think about how the supper club must treat her if she wants us to meet her *there*," Tommy pointed out.

"I bet Monsieur Baiser is a pretty easygoing guy."

"Those types rarely are." Tommy sighed and his head fell back against the seat. "But I think we can guess that Lawson hasn't found her yet. And he hasn't found the club."

"No, if she'd spoken to the cops, she would just deny, deny, deny."

"But deny what, exactly?" Tommy said. "What they do at the club?"

"Her other line of work?"

"Could be the same line of work," Tommy suggested. "Just a different venue."

I took a deep, deep breath. "Does it always feel this hopeless?"

"Yeah, when there's no real reason why," Tommy said. "Until you find the reason why, it's going to feel like you're drowning."

"And if we don't find out?"

"Save your brain power for the case." The cabbie pulled as close to Tommy's building as he could, and we both got out of the car. Tommy leaned back in through the front window and paid the man, while I stood on the sidewalk, my teeth chattering in the wind.

"Get her a good supper," the man said and motioned at me with his chin. "And tell her you love her."

"Can and will do."

NIGHT 6

Tommy led the way to the front door, unlocked the three bolts, traipsed up the stairs to the fourth floor, and unlocked four more bolts on the door to his apartment. I scurried in and he redid the locks behind us. The trip in, up, and in was serenaded by two knock-down, drag-outs, at least three screaming babies, and someone listening to a record, of what I could only rationalize as a Klan rally caught on wax, at top volume.

"What a joint this place is," I said, tossing my coat on the hook on the back of the door. "I can't wait until our place at Mrs. K's is done."

"It's a tough place for a dame," Tommy agreed. "But I can't come live with you until that place is finished."

"I doubt she'd mind so much."

"*I* mind. Even if we *are* married before it's finished. It'd feel too much like shacking up with a bunch of single girls, and I don't care for it."

I spied that day's copy of the *Mirror* on Tommy's coffee table. "Making sure we aren't fit to print?"

"He's been quiet since that little piece about your legs," Tommy said. "But he'll come back. We have to be careful."

"I'll watch my six," I said, paging through. "That Brooklyn bookie thinks his bail should be reduced."

"He was running a twenty-million-dollar racket and everyone knows it," Tommy shrugged. "Good luck on that."

"There's a new picture out," I said, squinting at the small print in the dull light. "*The Killer That Stalked New York*. Says it's about a diamond smuggler who's killin' folks."

"That's a little too close to home," Tommy said, shivering.

"Oh, but she's doing it with smallpox, not bookends," I said. "Never mind."

"Oh rats, so we can't sue anyone," Tommy said. He opened the door to the icebox and examined what was inside. "I could do chicken piccata?"

"Can we go out?"

"Sure. Let's just figure out a place."

"Well, considering we can't even decide when we're going to get married . . ." I meant it as a joke, but it came out as a jab.

"Have we even really talked about it?" Tommy pulled out a phone book and started looking through the restaurants section. "We could always do Chinese again."

"I could do Chinese." I stood up to peer over his shoulder. "No, we haven't. I know we want to keep it small."

"Who says?" Tommy asked. "I wonder if the pierogi lady is still in business."

"I says," I said. "Pierogi are too heavy right now. I can do Chinese."

"I keep thinking we should have a massive church 'do,'" Tommy said. "Just take it to the nines. But I'm not sure if I want duck again."

"You can order something other than the duck," I said. "And we don't go to church, why would we have a big ol' church service? Jesus'll smite me in my off-white dress the second I make it up the front steps."

"The chicken is white meat there, it has no flavor, they use the dark meat for the soup," Tommy said. "And my mother will want a church wedding. All three of my sisters had church weddings. Where do you have a wedding otherwise?"

"Where is she again?" I asked. "Your mother. And you like the pork ribs there, there's always pork ribs."

"That's awfully expensive for just a Friday night. The Bronx. Well, Bronxville."

"A man who wants a big wedding doesn't want pork ribs?"

"I always *want* pork ribs, I just don't have the cash on me right now. That don't mean I won't have cash for the wedding."

"What's the difference between the Bronx and Bronxville?" I asked. "And do you have the spare dime for egg rolls?"

"Are you going to ask me cash on hand every time we eat?" Tommy asked, now giving me a hard stare. "And the difference is one's a borough and one's not. Bronxville is a town in Westchester."

"You're mother's in Westchester?" I was surprised. "That's fancy digs. And I just don't want to get to the restaurant and be short, it's no worry."

"That's why I'd make you chicken piccata here," Tommy said. "And it's just a cottage."

"A cottage in Westchester? She owns it?" I asked. "And fine, the chicken sounds fine."

"Of course she owns it. And it's not Westchester the *city*, it's Westchester the *county*. I'll make the piccata."

"I can make it."

"No, you can't." Tommy was in the kitchen in front of the gas burner, and I could see him waffling on what to say next. He took a deep breath and let it out. "This is a tiny kitchen and things aren't in logical spots."

"But once we get married, you'll want me to cook," I said. "Let me make it."

"No, like I said, it's the kitchen in this joint. Don't worry about it."

"You'll expect me to cook at some point. Once we have kids."

"Who says we're having kids? And we won't be here when we do."

"I just assumed we were having kids. And of course we won't be here, we'll be at Mrs. K's, but I have to get my practice in some time."

"We won't be at Mrs. K's either," he said. "It's too small. And you'll have to practice a lot. When was the last time you made anything?"

"Never. But every man expects his wife to cook."

"I'm not every man. I like to cook, in my upside-down, goofy kitchen where there's ingredients hidden in the coffee table. The place is small. I'll have to sell it."

"You own this apartment?"

"Of course I do." Tommy turned his back to me to get a pan and missed my jaw falling to the floor.

"Tommy, how much money do you have?"

"Enough."

"That's not an answer," I said, picking up my purse. "That's an evasion."

"I just wasn't prepared for the question, Dollface."

"I know what I have in my sock drawer, my purse, and my bank account to the last dime," I said. "I *have* to."

"It's a bit screwy with the business and investments and stuff."

"Investments?" I gasped. "You have money enough to buy a stock or a bond?"

"More than one," Tommy said. "It'll half be yours by the end of the year."

"I don't want it!"

"I want you to have it, though. We just talk to the lawyer about it."

"McAllister, upstairs at the office?"

"God, no. He's an ambulance chaser and a drunk. I have a lawyer up in Bronxville."

"You have a *lawyer*?"

"You do too, technically. He works for the firm."

"This is making me all shaky," I said. "You only need a lawyer if you do something wrong and want to stay out of jail."

"There's more to law than just criminal law, Dollface."

"But it's all crimes!"

"No, there's plenty of law that just keeps you out of trouble, protects you from things. Trial law and criminal law is sad law. Wills and trusts are happy law."

"No such thing as happy law," I said. "Wills and trusts only exist because everybody fights when people *die*."

"I just like my Is dotted and my Ts crossed. That's it. You'll like him, he's a good guy."

"I don't think I want any chicken, after all. I think I want to go home. I'm not feeling well." I bustled to the door and threw my coat over my arm as I twisted at the locks but somehow couldn't find the right combination of movements to free me from the apartment. "I need to sleep in my own bed for a night, Tommy. Let me out of here."

Tommy brushed by me and flicked the last lock to open the door. "Call me when you're home."

"Fine."

I struggled to get my coat on as I tumbled down the stairs, past the closed doors of the other anonymous apartments that held any number of strangers, some of 'em violent, some of 'em bigots, and at least one of 'em a violent bigot. I was so steamed that I didn't even hail a cab as I slipped down the concrete stoop and onto the sidewalk, barely catching myself before my shoes shot out from under me and I hit the pavement. I marched in the direction of Mrs. K's fit to be tied.

I was somewhere near Birdland and all the mishigas that goes with the jazz club scene when I heard hard footsteps fall in behind me. Plenty of people coming and going on a sidewalk on a Friday evening, even in early January, so I just kept my ears tuned to it for a ways, then darted a quick right on 46th Street just to see what was doing. The footsteps kept up, so I turned around, swinging.

"What's the big idea?" I yelled, my voice ringing off the cement building sides. "You want what's in my purse? Well, it's a whole lotta nothin'! If I had a dime, I'd at least hail a cab to see how far it'd take me!"

The lug slunk back like a hit dog but didn't quite take off yet.

"What are you waiting for, huh? Leave a dame alone! You want my lipstick? It's three seasons out of fashion," I reached into my bag and pulled out the tube, launching it at the fella's head as he ducked away. "I can yell louder than this, ya bozo, lay off!" I swung my handbag on the strap, making like I was ready to beat him to death with two pounds of patent leather. He ran off into the shadows, down off the curb so fast he almost got taken out at the knees by a Checker cab.

The cabbie spotted me. "You okay, sugar?" I just waved him on and righted course. Nothing, not even a real-life concerned citizen, was going to get between me and my landlady's Friday night meal.

★   ★   ★

I opened up my own front door with just the one deadbolt and slammed the door behind me. Four heads peered into the front entryway from the dining room.

"No Thomas tonight?" Mrs. K asked sweetly.

"No." I kicked off my shoes at the dented wall next to the doorway and tossed my purse and coat on the rack next to the door. "What's for supper?"

"Veal parmigiana," Oleks said with a stuffed mouth. "Just in case *Tommy* was here."

"He ain't," I said, flopping into my chair and grabbing the spaghetti bowl.

"You two split up?" Oleks asked.

"No, just having words," I said. I was going to have to handle this with kid gloves.

"He's a real piece of something," Oleks said.

"*Son*." Mrs. K shot a death glare down the table, while picking up the platter of veal cutlets to hand to me.

"It's fine," I said. "He's not going anywhere."

"Why not?" Oleks asked. "He's messing everything up."

"How do you mean?"

"The whole house!" Oleks said, his fork slinging spaghetti sauce down the front of his T-shirt. "It's a mess!"

"It's temporary," Betty said, shrugging.

"It's not *your* house," Oleks barked.

"I've lived here for years!" Betty squeaked.

"It's the home of everyone who is a tenant," Mrs. K said sternly. "*Zamovkny.*"

"I will not be quiet," Oleks responded. "What gives them the right to make all these changes to the house? Shouldn't I get a say in who lives here?"

"Is the problem with the changes to the building, or is the problem with who is going to be living in the building?" I asked. "Because the changes can still be made, if your uncle wants them, and Tommy and I can move out."

The suggestion hung in the air, silent.

"No one wants you to move out, pretty girl," Mrs. K whispered.

"Where is Tommy this evening, Viv?" Dottie asked.

"His place," I said. "He dropped a bit of a bombshell on me."

"What happened?"

"Oh, nothing I want to discuss just yet," I said. "I just feel like the man I've known for a decade may not be the man I'm marrying."

"He have a whole second family on Long Island?" Oleks asked. "I wouldn't put it past him."

"No, no, no," I said, forcing a laugh. "Most people would consider it a good surprise, but still a surprise."

Oleks made a grunt and picked up his plate, descending back into his mother's apartment to wash his dish.

"What's eating him?" I asked Mrs. K.

"He does not like the change." The woman shrugged and stood with her own plate. "Can anyone help me downstairs?"

"I will." Betty was smarting from Oleks's remarks, and if I knew Betty, she was going to try to prove her worth to the house for the next two weeks. "Viv, why don't you go call Tommy to tell him you're home safe."

"In a minute." I wanted to chat with Dottie, who always gave level-headed advice, even when I didn't want it.

"He's going to worry."

"Let him, for a minute more."

Betty and Mrs. K shrugged and thumped the tray of dirty dishes down the stairs to wash them.

"He should worry," I told Dottie. "I think I was almost mugged on the way home."

"Viviana! Are you all right?"

"I'm fine," I sighed, letting the anger leave my shoulders. "I'm always fine."

"You may not be," Dottie said. "Dear Oleks is very angry."

"Over the summer, he didn't seem to mind having the mysteries come home with me."

"But over the summer, the house was not being changed into an apartment building."

"Just the top floor, though."

"And the basement, where Oleks already lives, is a rentable apartment," Dottie pointed out. "Nothing's to say that Mr. Doroshenko won't do the same to the middle floor, and this floor as well, and it will no longer be a boarding house."

"Could they do that to you and Betty?"

"There is nothing legally prohibiting it."

"That would be so rotten."

"I would not be pleased, no."

"I'm sorry."

"You didn't have the conversation with Mr. Doroshenko," Dottie pointed out. "And that could be why Oleks is quite angry with your Tommy."

"He told me this evening that his mother owns a house in Westchester," I said. "And he owns his apartment in Hell's Kitchen. He's loaded, Dottie."

"Well, I think Tally was what we would call *loaded*. Tommy just sounds comfortable."

"Then why was he paying me peanuts all those years?" I asked. "Why is Betty not making any money now that she's got my old job?"

"Family money and business money are two separate things to most people," Dottie shrugged. "Though I agree it doesn't seem fair."

"It was all so silly. He wanted to make dinner at home, I suggested Chinese. He said he didn't have enough cash on him for it, and I just exploded."

"The banks are closed, he couldn't cash a check, it happens."

"So then I stomped home and in all my tizzy, I didn't think I had enough money for a cab, and almost got into a scuffle around 49th Street," I said. "All because I was feeling grim about money."

"All of these are normal, regular problems that are confronted during courtships, Viviana," Dottie said. "But you and Tommy sort of skipped that part."

"But I've known him for so long!" I whined.

"But you were his secretary then," Dottie said, getting up. "Not his fiancée."

I sat in silence, scowling at the wood grain of the table.

"I'm going to go grade papers," Dottie said. "Call your husband-to-be, missy."

Dottie always knew when to break out her teacher voice, and I couldn't help but smile.

"Yes, ma'am."

I let Dottie get a head start to her room on the second floor before I started upstairs to the phone on the landing. I spun for the operator and within a minute she was ringing for Tommy. The receiver was snatched out of the cradle, and I heard his voice come down the wire.

"Viv?"

"Yeah, I'm fine, I just finished up dinner." I was trying to sound cool and casual, like I hadn't been purposefully trying to make him wait and squirm like a worm on the hook.

"I can't believe you just walked out on me."

"I'm fine, ol' Tommy boy. There's nothing this city can throw at me that I can't handle."

"Why'd you say that?"

"I fell into a confrontation 'round the jazz clubs, it's fine."

"It isn't fine! Mrs. K was right," Tommy said. "This city's getting too dangerous."

"Six months ago I was stalked by a murderous gangster," I pointed out. "A purse-snatcher is nothing."

"You're too cavalier."

"I'm a grown woman who doesn't want to move from her home, Tommy." I let out a sigh. "I am never, ever leaving Manhattan. You know that, right?"

"We'll discuss it some other time," Tommy said. "I'm just so relieved that you're home safe. I love the hell outta you, Dollface."

"Good night, Tommy." The phone was hung up before I realized I hadn't said *I love you* back.

DAY 7

Saturday, January 6th, 1951

Betty and I sat at the breakfast table staring at the latest puzzle in Mr. Floristan's blackmail case well into the morning before Tommy showed up.

"I stopped by Telly's," he said, tossing an envelope, fat with photos, at me. "That jumbled mess hasn't changed in years but she had to show me around the whole place."

His ears turned pink as he discussed his ex-girlfriend's apartment in front of his current fiancée, and a fiancée that was plenty steamed up at him, to boot.

"It is pretty sloppy," I agreed. "How does she get any work done?"

"She finds a way—she really only took the place because there's a huge closet that she can use as a darkroom. It used to be the landing for a stairwell, far as I can tell. But then the buildings got rejiggered in the thirties and now she's got a whole, huge space with no windows." He thought for a moment. "I wonder how she's gonna get all that junk out of there."

"Where's she going?"

"Don't know yet, that's part of the problem," Tommy said. "But that louse Moses has the building set to be torn down as soon as possible."

"I noticed that when I went to drop off the roll. The wrecking balls are awful scary. Just swaying in the breeze like someone's forgotten laundry."

"Do you think Mrs. K might let her take your old room, just on a weekly basis?"

"*What?*"

"She can put most things in storage, I guess." I'm not sure if he knew quite the implications of what he was saying, but Betty sure did. She was poking me in the side, and when I turned to look at her, her eyes were wide. Betty didn't want Tommy's old flame as a housemate any more than I did.

"I certainly hope that's a last resort for poor, uh, *Telly*," I said. "Tommy, have you looked at the snaps yet?"

"Nah," he said, patting all his pockets. "I left my cheaters at my place, so I'm not sure how many details I'd see anyway. Why don't you girls take a gander at them here? I'm going to run back home and grab my glasses." He slipped out of the house again and Betty opened the envelope.

"He *is* acting like he owns the place," she muttered.

"She will live in our house over my dead body."

"I hope he's just thinking of how to help," Betty said, always giving someone the benefit of the doubt. "And not that we'd welcome her with open arms for any long period of time. I don't mean to be cruel, but that's a strange predicament for everyone. Even Telly." I peeled the masking tape off the flap of the envelope and set about arranging the rectangular prints on the table.

"Was Tommy missing his glasses when he took these?" I asked. "My God, it's like he took them all through two steamed-up windows."

Every one of the thirty-odd snaps laid on the table was of two people—but which two people, absolutely no one but God himself could be sure. Two people hugging, two people linking arms, two people walking into a shop. Two people exiting a shop, two people hugging again, two people going their separate ways in a crowd. You'd have to want it to be Rachel for it to be any dame in specific.

"These are lousy," Betty agreed. "We're going to have to send someone to follow that poor girl again."

"I don't like this one bit," I said. "Unless they were shopping for housewares for the life they're going to have when she runs away from Morty, these two blobs are just having a normal day out."

We pondered the photos for an hour, squinting and rearranging the images until our eyeballs hurt.

Betty let out a deep sigh. "This is a whole lotta nothing, but she is lying about where she's going."

"That's if Morty is telling us the truth."

"He doesn't have a reason to lie to me," Tommy said, as he came back into the house without knocking, his big, Coke-bottle glasses in his gloved paw.

"There's nothing usable here in these photos, Tom," I said. "Maybe someone who sees twenty-twenty should take the next round of snaps."

"Fine, then you're on the case when she hits the town again," Tommy said, grumbling. "But I know what I saw. She was with a gent who wasn't Morty."

"That doesn't mean a damn thing, and you know it," I reasoned. "Just this morning, you were with your 'Telly' and I don't for one second think that you were having an affair."

"Oh, well, thank heavens for that," Tommy said. "I'm gonna get Morty on the horn and give him an update. Then we have to go see a girl in Times Square, remember? I'm going to give my regards to Lana." He pushed through the door to the basement and we heard him thump down the stairs to say hello to the landlady.

"Before you even say anything, I'll talk to him," I told Betty, who was gathering up the pictures and stuffing them back into the envelope.

"But don't you say you're sorry," she whispered. "He knows your whole history—you have no surprises. Or if you do, fess up fast."

"Nope—he can see my bank statements if he wants to," I laughed. "I got nothing to hide." He already knew about my filching days as a juvenile delinquent, but Betty sure didn't need to.

Tommy emerged with his coat and hat still on. "Ready to roll?" he asked, picking my coat up off the stand by the door.

"Sure." I shimmied into my jacket and looked at Betty. "We're going to be a while."

"Okay, Boss." Betty settled back down into her chair. "I'm going to keep staring at this puzzle."

"Thanks, Betts."

I followed Tommy out the door. Down the stairs and onto the sidewalk, I tugged at his sleeve to make him slow down and fall into step with me. The tension between us eased as he did so, but neither one of us made the motion to apologize.

"I won't suggest Telly take the room at Mrs. K's unless she's still in her place when the ball starts swingin'," Tommy said. "She's messy as all get-out and she can keep artists' hours. The last person who should be living at the boarding house. She'd drive everyone mad."

He paused for a second before continuing. "This isn't because she's Black, is it?"

"Of course not. You brought around plenty of girls over the years who weren't Italian, Irish, or what have you. And I never want to see any girl tossed out on her keister," I said. "Mrs. K never kept anyone out of her house, even before Telly. But Telly also hasn't asked for your help, and I know I'd be fit to be tied if some ex of mine swooped in trying to save the day when I didn't want him to. She's a grown adult woman, she'll ask for help if she wants it."

"I have a tendency to like women who don't mince their words, I guess."

"Besides," I pointed out, "who's to say she doesn't have a current fella ready to solve some problems with her?"

Tommy just grunted as he led me in the direction of a seedy row of shops. "Here we are."

The club on the outskirts of Times Square looked awful. The exterior was painted a lurid shade of green, and the sign above the door had blinking lights—though most of them were on the fritz. A downspout from the roof managed to cover one wall with a wicked brown slime.

"What's a cute couple like you doing in a joint like this?" a voice called from behind us.

"Herb, I swear on my mother's grave." Tommy turned around and the newspaper man was behind us, smiling like a little fink.

"Your mother isn't dead," Sabella said, quickly lifting his camera to his eye and snapping a photo of us. "But this picture might kill her, huh?" He laughed and took a giant step away from Tommy, who looked ready to take a swing.

"We're just talking to a girl," I said. Tommy shushed me.

"Oh! Well *then*," Herb Sabella said. "A crime of love and passion? A fight over the love of a wayward daughter?"

"Sniff around all you want, Herb," Tommy said. "You'll get nothing out of us."

"That's what you think!" Herb sang as he waved us goodbye.

Tommy breathed slowly out his nose. "*Dammit.*"

I waited for Tommy to open the door for me, less out of chivalry and more out of my desire to not touch anything. Or maybe his desire to get a pane of glass in between Herb Sabella and my big mouth.

Inside, pinups and girlie photos lined the walls. The photos left a bit to be desired, but the illustrations of girls were in bright Technicolor, with cherry-red lips and other anatomy painted to draw your eye. To one side of the shop was a long counter

manned by a gent dressed all in black with an oiled goatee, looking like a real slick cartoon of the devil. He gave Tommy a raised
eyebrow and me the ol' up-and-down.

"Show is in the back," he said. "Hope you got nickels."

"We're here to meet Norma," I said. "She's expecting us."

"Whatever she wants to do on her own time," he shrugged.
"I'll go get her." The man hopped off his stool and slid out from
behind the counter to go and find our girl. He returned a few
moments later, with Norma in a short red wig, white bustier, and
black patent-leather heels. I decided right then and there to keep
my coat on; Norma wouldn't take me seriously at all if she saw I
was wearing a soft blue angora cardigan with daisies on the pockets.

"I'm going to take my lunch now, Marv," she said. "You two
can come in the back with me." She led us single file behind a
large bookshelf filled with magazines into a room that held a few
armchairs, a radio, and had a small window out to the back alley.
It looked like something out of *Homemaker* magazine.

"You guys want some coffee?" Norma put on a pink, fuzzy
bathrobe that was graying around the neck and cuffs and poured
herself a cup out of a large electric coffee urn.

"No, thank you," Tommy said. "We don't want to take your
whole lunch break."

"I'm just relieved you're here," Norma said. "I need to know
someone—anyone—is looking into what happened to Henry."

"Have you spoken with the police?" I asked.

Norma gave me a glare. "Girls in my line of work don't talk
to the fuzz if we can help it."

"What were you going to do if Tommy and I never came
around asking questions?"

"Pray and remember." She took a long sip of her coffee and
turned to Tommy. "Henry is a bartender. Hasn't shown up for
his shifts for a week, but that's not unusual in our line of work.
People move on, skip town, or worse, all the time. No one was
going to ask around for any of us."

I watched as Tommy nodded, but I couldn't bring myself to react. Norma seemed so sure that this Henry was all but forgotten by anyone who wasn't her. It made me wonder just how many souls the likes of Detective Lawson sent to nameless graves in Potter's Field every year.

"Was anything bothering him?" I asked. "Did he seem preoccupied or distant?"

"No *thing* would bother Henry," Norma said. "He was the nicest, calmest man alive. Capable, that's the word I would use for him. Stepped into any situation to make it better. He was a good, good man. Not many of those in the world."

"Were there any bad, bad men at the club? Anyone who would want to make things harder for Henry?" I asked.

"Of course."

"We need you to be more specific," Tommy said gently. "If you can."

"I'm just a waitress there, and there are a few of us. We aren't in with the dancers," Norma said. "And as far as I know, no one at the club is full-service for the patrons. That's the most delicate way I can say it."

"What gives fellas the impression that it might be a full-service establishment?" I asked.

"Nothing *we* do, I can tell you that," Norma said firmly. "And most of the time when you tell a fella that you're not available for what they're ordering, they'll accept it or try to ask you out on a real date. But some fellas don't quite catch on."

"Or they don't take no for an answer," I said, giving Norma a gentle smile.

"And that's where Henry stepped in. It wasn't his official job, but he did it so well," Norma explained.

"Was there anyone at the club whose official job it was?" I asked.

"No. No one was able to help if someone tried to order off-menu, if Henry wasn't there, or if they tried to order off-menu from Henry."

"Did that happen often?" Tommy asked.

"Of course. And normally it was just fine because he had a way of making the whole place just *go* with a smile."

"It must be awful to get that kind of question," I said. "Can you remember the last time this happened to Henry?"

"Of course. It'd been happening daily, with the same girl, since at least Christmas."

"A girl was allowed in?" Tommy asked.

"Girls with chinchillas and that much lettuce go wherever they want."

"Would the club have a record of who she was?"

"Not officially." Norma was resolute in that. "We're all cash, reservations are taken under membership numbers, not names. She stuck to the shadows."

"Well, that makes things harder on us, I guess," I said. "If she was that persistent, any chance she, or someone in her employment, followed him after hours or between shifts?"

"Without a doubt," Norma said. "I heard him talk about 'Frankie' a bunch of times, but that's probably a fella who frequented. I don't like to know their names—makes it too personal."

"What was Henry's full name?" Tommy asked.

"Henrik Fiskar. Not a German, his people were from one of them cold countries up north."

"Anything else you'd like to let us know?" I asked.

"That's all I have, but I'll find you if I need to."

"You need anything from us? We can help in many different ways," I asked, my eyebrow arched as I beckoned toward the front, where we'd left the slick Marv.

"Nope," Norma said, knocking back the rest of her coffee. "And don't get the wrong idea, missy. I love my jobs. Don't you approach any more of us with that tone you put on with me."

Norma took off her bathrobe, straightened her wig, swiped on some new lipstick, and went back to her post in the girlie show.

"I had a tone?"

"A bit," Tommy said. "Come on, let's get out of here."

We were silent on the sidewalk as Tommy started hoofing us east.

"I can't help it, I feel bad for her," I said, scurrying to keep up.

"Why? She said she likes it, who are you to argue?"

"But . . ."

"You were raised to think it was wrong, but that's how society wants you to think. How does Viviana Valentine think? The woman who spent her youth as a petty thief and is currently a private investigator? Not exactly women's work approved by priests and old ladies at church."

"There's nothing *petty* about stealing Rolexes and Cartier, I'll have you know."

"I'm just saying, in our line of work, not everyone needs rescuing," Tommy said. "And even fewer people need moralizing."

"I didn't even realize I was doing it," I said. "Should I go back and apologize?"

"No, let Norma have the last word. She deserves it."

"What are we going to do about Henry?"

"Everything we can."

"Wait just a gosh darn minute." I stopped on the sidewalk. "I'm supposed to be investigating whether this Rachel dame is stepping out on Morty, but Morty's got an in to a club where you can do all *that*?"

Tommy turned pink in the ears and changed the subject. "No one was dancing at lunch time, I assure you, but I'll ask him about it. Come grab drinks with me at some place near Lenox Hill. We're digging into the missing banker."

Ten more minutes of walking and the park was in sight. Tommy pulled me under an ornate iron and glass awning.

"This isn't *some place*, Tommy. This is *the Plaza*."

"Don't worry, the fellas are paying, they already promised."

"Who are *the fellas*?" I asked, tugging on his coat pocket again. "Did you make a meeting with someone without telling me?"

"Slipped my mind."

"It slipped your mind to tell me that we're going to the fanciest bar in the city to talk to two people about one of *our* cases," I seethed. "I'm not dressed right."

"You're dressed fine," he sighed. He put his arm around my lower back and pushed me into a dark and whispery lounge. "Now *git* along, li'l do—"

"If you call me 'li'l doggie' I will wash your mouth out with a bar of soap."

"It's a turn of phrase." He giggled and made eye contact with the coat check girl, and she stared at the counter while my cheeks turned red.

"It's not funny."

Tommy was urging me out of my coat and hat so he could hand both to the check girl, who now looked up. "If I'd told you where we were going, you would've bugged out somehow."

"Hey!"

"You know you're allowed in here, right?" Tommy pulled me to the side of the foyer before we entered the bar. "No one's going to stop you."

"Sometimes it feels like they want to."

"Well, there's no laws on the books that says they can keep out broke white girls, but they can kick you out if you continue making a scene," Tommy said through gritted teeth. "You don't have to like it, and I guess I now know better than to treat you like a girl who goes to the Plaza, but this is for a case. So buck up. And for the record, the *fellas* called *me*."

Tommy strode into the bar and left me by the coat check girl, who was staring at the furs behind her like she hadn't just heard my husband-to-be scold me like a child.

The rage was coursing through me like water out of a broken hydrant. Tommy knew full well that I was born and raised in a two-room shack with no running water just a few years before bozos like the two good-for-nothing suits we were meeting at this highfalutin' bar exploded the entire stock market and sent the entire world's savings down the shitter. He could forgive *me* if that wasn't a good enough reason to treat these sons of guns with a little bit of contempt. Not every one of us managed to keep the heat on in a cottage in Westchester County—some of us had baby cousins who starved to death for lack of even navy bean soup and had to listen to our aunties wail as the babes got buried in pauper's graves through the charity of the Church. I couldn't help it if everyone around me—everyone I had thought I was equal to for the past ten years—had it better off than I did until the war. Betty and her bunny fur cuffs and Tommy with his cocktails at fancy hotels.

If Tommy wanted to marry a girl who was comfortable at the Plaza, he could have that ring back.

But if there's one thing a reformed reprobate like myself knew, it was this: if a job needed to get done to keep the lights on, I knew I sure as hell could do it. I straightened my skirt, adjusted my hat, and strode into the Plaza like I owned the place. Or at least like I could afford one night upstairs.

Tommy was at the bar and not so patiently waiting. He asked the bartender for the location of his party and two sidecar cocktails. Once the orange twists were arranged just *so* on the rims of the glasses, Tommy snapped up the coupes and beelined for two men sitting in a corner booth. Each wore the uniform of a man of town in relaxation—flannel pants, a long-sleeve button-down shirt, tie, and a cashmere sweater over top.

"Bill. Steve." Tommy nodded and the two men nodded in turn. "This is my partner, Viviana." I slid into the booth after Tommy and noted that neither Bill nor Steve could be over twenty-three years old. Their faces were boyish and lineless, cheeks chubby, and their eyes nervous.

"Hello, gentlemen. Thank you for calling to meet with us today," I said, and offered my hand. They took my fingertips instead of giving my paw an actual shake. "Like he said, I'm Tommy's *business* partner, I appreciate your time."

"We're just happy someone wants to talk about Trevor," Bill said, sipping his Gibson.

"We understand Bowen hired you to find him?" Steve asked.

"He did," Tommy said.

"We like the old chum quite a bit." Bill looked sad. "It's not like him to leave a loose end. We got your information out of Peggy, Bowen's girl. Every little bit of information helps, no?"

"Was there a reason you shouldn't've liked him?" I asked. "Seems like a strange thing to say off the bat."

"He is somewhat of an odd fellow, really," Steve said. "Doesn't mix well."

"Meaning? Off-color?" Tommy goaded. "Terrible body odor? We need specifics here, fellas."

"Just . . . strange. He's not very good at small talk," Steve said. "The usual 'How's the wife?' 'Did you go golfing this weekend?' chatter."

"He panics a little, stammers a bit, then hides in his office at his earliest convenience," Bill added. "Most took to teasing him behind his back about it, but I assume he is just painfully shy."

"He's a fellow who likes rules, and I think that conversation like that is too open-ended," Steve said. "If you have a question about work, he has an answer. But if it's a question that's not procedural, God help him."

"He's been trying for ages to streamline the office," Bill added.

"That's what Peggy says," Steve added. "We've only been there a few months."

"There's a lot of turnover, it's a tough business," Bill blustered.

"I suppose military precision wore off on him," Steve explained, "even though he wasn't in the service for long. This type of document has this color folder, this record goes in this particular bin."

"Military precision. Everything has a place and everything in its place," I said. "I find that rather calming, and good for business as well."

"She chaps my ass about it quite frequently," Tommy said. Bill and Steve were taken aback by Tommy's crassness and laughed into their drinks.

"If a piece of paperwork does go missing, my goodness, how he steams," Steve added. "He'd been bullying for a Thermofax machine."

"What's that?" I asked.

"It's a new product that makes an exact replica of a document," Steve said. "All the rage. It uses heat. Don't ask me how it works."

"But golly, can Trevor tell you," Bill added. "You'd think it was turning water into wine the way he evangelized about it. Bowen finally broke down and purchased one so Trever would keep quiet."

"Cost Bowen a pretty penny, I must say," added Steve. "Trevor played with it for hours. No one else can figure out how to use it."

"Has he ever had a long illness before?" I asked. "Or taken a long vacation?"

"No, he's not the kind," Bill said.

Steve agreed. "He won't take a sick day unless he's sent home from the office. Would rather make a mess of the men's toilets than admit he has a stomach virus."

"And a vacation? Who would he go with, his parents?" Bill asked.

"No one at the office has ever asked him out for drinks? Over for a cookout?"

"He doesn't leave Manhattan," Bill said. "He likes the streets."

"The grid?" Tommy asked.

"Orderly." Bill thumped the table to stress the key hallmark of the city. "He bought that duplex in Murray Hill."

"He *bought* it?" I asked. "Two apartments?"

"Trevor is *exceptional* with money," Bill said. "As great with investing as he is terrible with people."

"If anyone asked him somewhere, it would have been Peggy," Steve said.

"Mr. Bowen's secretary?" I asked.

"She's not sweet on him," Bill assured me. "But she's kind to him. He makes her work so much easier, you know. With the bins and the colors and the filing. She sticks up for him when the ribbing gets to be too much."

"Or too loud, and he can certainly hear it in his office," Steve said.

"Did they create the system together?" I asked.

"No, it was made after many years of Peggy griping about Mr. Bowen's messes," Bill said. "He looks the part of a banker, and a good one at that, but he can be careless. All of his paperwork is a mess, you can't make heads or tails of it."

"He didn't go to a good school," Steve said. "Not like us, where order is drilled into you at every step."

"I've been told at happy hours and industry mixers that he can't keep a staff for very long," Bill added. "His mess makes everyone's job too hard."

"He looked orderly to me," I said. "And Peggy and Trevor have both been there quite a while."

"Someone that mad about an employee walking off the job sure likes his ducks in a row," Tommy agreed.

"Perhaps over the years Trev rubbed off on him," Bill shrugged.

"I've found myself making sure all of my pens are capped by the end of the day, and in the correct segment of my desk drawer," Steve agreed. "My wife likes that I've managed to keep my socks in order lately, too. She wants to meet this Trevor and thank him."

Tommy spent an hour getting more details about our singing canaries—both in the same year at Andover, London School of Economics, now back in the States for a career in high finance. Steve moved to Cos Cob with his wife, Nancy, while Bill was enjoying Greenwich with Bridget. Both had a boy and a girl. It took all my might not to ask how the missuses would feel when they came home on a Saturday afternoon reeking of gin.

True to their promises, they put our drinks on their tab and Tommy and I departed the Plaza. He hailed a taxi and put me in it to get back to Mrs. K's for dinner.

Alone.

NIGHT 7

Saturday, January 6ᵗʰ, 1951

Saturday, January 6th, 1951

"Dottie's got a lead." Betty was hovering at the door, waiting for Tommy and me, and was clearly shocked to find me by my lonesome. She was practically hopping back and forth in her knitted socks and pink flannel housecoat, her hair tied up in rags to get a curl. She looked just like a little kid who had a secret. Or one who needed to use the facilities.

"What kind of lead?" I managed to find a pair of slippers in the pile of shoes by the door that weren't yet covered in mud and street gunk, and slipped them on. "Someone wanting to confess all? Please tell me it's someone who wants to confess all."

"Unfortunately, no," Dottie's voice carried in from the dining room table. "I do understand that I'm not on this case in an official capacity. But I couldn't help but chat with Betty today about what she was working on, and I wanted to invite my friend from school, Miss Luna, to come and help."

I followed the voice of my housemate—and the scent of chicken and dumplings—into the dining room, where a short woman with glossy black curls sat next to Dottie. They looked a pair, both in brown oxfords, tweed skirts, and cream-colored, cable-knit sweaters. But Miss Luna's clothing was a bit better fitted, a bit closer to the body, and she somehow managed to make boring brown wool into a chic little outfit. Maybe it was the red satin neckerchief tied *just so.*

"Hi, I'm Rocío," she said, standing up to shake my hand. "It's nice to meet you."

"Nice to meet you too!" I said plopping into a chair. "Sorry Tommy had to bug out. We're the private investigators with the case."

"Such exciting work," our guest said. "Not that watching a child unlock the secret of long division isn't thrilling in its own way."

"So far, I've found that being a private investigator mostly means walking all over the city and asking rude people questions," I said.

"So, just like being a sixth grade math teacher," our guest laughed.

"Pretty close."

"Dottie said, though, that you were having a tough time with a puzzle?" she asked. "I have a way with them, you could say, so she called me and asked me to dinner, to see if I could take a look."

"Be my guest," I said, and Betty handed over her worksheet.

"Oh, this is something."

Dottie pulled a pencil out of her bun and handed it to her companion, who barely looked up.

"It's not a Caesar cipher or a double substitution," she muttered, scribbling lines of letters along the margin.

"Boy, you seem to know a lot about codes," I said pointedly, shoveling a bit of chicken into my mouth. "This is delicious, Mrs. K."

"Thank you," Mrs. K said with a smile. "Oleks, you're barely eating."

Her son was holding his arm up in the air, in line with his sight. "I'm timing her," he said, motioning toward his cheap watch with a laugh, and his eyes went straight back to Rocío.

"I'm not going to get it that quickly, hon," she said, looking up. "I'm sorry, I'm being rude."

"No, not in the least," I said. "This has a tendency to happen when there's an interesting case."

"I'm tapping out, kid," she winked at the landlady's son. "Is it okay if I take this home and use some, uh, tips I have from the olden days?"

"Of course," I said. "I have a question, actually."

"Shoot," Rocío said, taking a bite of her dinner with a smile.

"When he was medically discharged, Tommy was a seaman. If he were here, would he be saluting a superior officer?"

Rocío laughed. "Yes, I think he might. But I let it slide in casual situations."

Oleks grinned. "What did you do?"

"I am not at liberty to say."

"*Cool.*" Oleks dumped another scoop of casserole on his plate and reached halfway down the table for the steamed broccoli.

"Son, you may *ask* for someone to pass you the vegetable," his mother chided.

"Next time, I promise."

"So, what you aren't at liberty to talk about," I said, pulling apart a lovely homemade biscuit. "How'd you get that gig?"

"As it turns out, when you're a girl at Rensselaer studying mathematics who speaks fluent Spanish, Italian, and English," Rocío said, "certain people hear about you."

I looked at Oleks. "And you speak . . . ?"

"Ukrainian, Russian, English . . ." He ticked off on his fingers. "And ninth grade Spanish."

"Better than nothing, kid," Rocío nodded approvingly. "You could be pretty useful this day and age. How's your math?"

"Terrible," Oleks admitted.

"We could fix that, you know."

Mrs. K laughed, and Oleks shot her a look. "I do my best, Ma."

"I love talking about something that isn't crime," I said, taking a big bite of my chicken. "I am crimed out. No more bad guys. Nothing nefarious. I really need a breather."

"I went to the library this afternoon," Dottie began. "I had every intention of doing my annual reread of *The Tenant of Wildfell Hall*, but they had to request it from another branch."

"You left the library empty handed?" Betty teased.

"Of course not," Dottie said, blushing. "But now that I mention it, I realize that this story violates Viviana's no crime edict."

"What did you get?" Rocío asked.

"Patricia Highsmith's *Strangers on a Train*," Dottie said. "Have you all heard of it?"

"No," Oleks said. "Is it good?"

"It depends on your definition of good," Dottie admitted. "Gripping writing, but the plot is rather unseemly."

"Unseemly is practically my middle name now," I said. "Spill the beans."

"Well," Dottie said, settling in and pulling her napkin off of her lap and placing it next to her plate. "Two men meet on a train."

"Do they . . . know each other beforehand?" Oleks asked.

"Of course not, it's called *Stra* . . ." Dottie realized she'd gotten set up, and shot him daggers. Rocío stifled a laugh.

"You did that all by your lonesome," she told Dottie, patting her hand.

"You're right, I did." Dottie smiled at Oleks. "Somehow—I admit, in a way that was not contrived but completely unlikely—they began opening up to each other about their hardships and admitted each one had fantasies of murdering someone in their lives."

"That's not normally first date conversation," I said.

"No, but somehow it works here," Dottie said. "Then the less scrupulous man suggests to the other that they trade murders, in an effort to evade detection."

"Goodness," Mrs. K said. "That is appalling."

"It is, I have to admit," Dottie said. "And Highsmith writes everything so well, it's chilling. A very different book altogether from a murder mystery like Christie's *Crooked House*."

"Would that work, though?" Oleks asked.

"It'd slow investigators down, that's for sure," I said. "Violent crimes are rarely committed against strangers."

"I suppose that's comforting," Betty said.

"There are some real sickos, though, who kill with means and opportunity, without real motive," I said. "You're too young to recall everyone shaking in their boots about Leopold and Loeb."

"That's what you think is gonna happen if we stay in the city, huh, Mom?" Oleks asked his mother. "That some fella with a Tommy gun is just going spray Woolworths with bullets and take us all out because he's crazy?"

"Not too many of them on the street anymore after the National Firearms Act," I said. "Signed right after you were born."

"In my experience," Mrs. K said, growing grave, "there is no such thing as a crazy man who murders. There is always a motive, even if the motive is just anger. Anger at the world."

"Once again, when you're right, you're right," I said. "I think movies always make us think people kill someone because of a dust-up or greed or love."

"Don't say things like that to her," Oleks grouched at me. "She's going to try to make us leave New York."

"Too crowded," Mrs. K said again, shaking her head. "Too many bad men."

"And women!" I added in chirpily. Oleks shook his head to let me know I was *not* helping.

"I love it here," Betty said. "Especially this time of year. But it always makes me sad when the Christmas decorations come down."

"They do add a lot of light and life to the streets," I agreed. "But Valentine's is right around the corner."

"And I can imagine you're partial to that," Rocío said.

"I don't like sappy romance, but I love all the big, bright colors and giant boxes of cheap chocolates," I said laughing.

"Should we be taking notes for the fiancé?" Rocío teased. I forced a weak smile.

"I've always been of the mind that a dinner at home and just listening to a record would be ideal," Dottie said.

Rocío tapped her own temple and winked at me, while Betty kicked me under the table.

"That's probably second on my list," I agreed with Dottie. "One year, I saw a skywriter over Chelsea Piers flipping and zipping and writing out a proposal, and I thought it'd be awful to be that girl, whoever she was."

"Imagine if she took two minutes to adjust her girdle at the wrong time," Betty said laughing.

"Fella's probably still waiting for an answer . . . ," Oleks said.

"It is best not to mince words," Mrs. K said.

"How did Oleks's father propose?" I asked.

"In the old country, it is more that the families come to terms," Mrs. K said. "But I was very lucky that Grygoriy and I had been sweethearts since we were small."

"There was no one else my father would have even looked at," Oleks said.

"There's something to be said for finding your soulmate early," I said. "But this day and age, we all have to do a little shopping around."

"Betty—how's your browsing going?" Dottie said. "Viviana—perhaps Tommy knows of someone . . . ?"

"I can't set Betty up with Monty Bonito," I laughed. I'd met one of Tommy's ne'er-do-well connections over Thanksgiving, who was adept at picking locks and had a soft spot in his heart for zoo animals. Within a week of knowing him, I'd also found out that he was known to the FBI, and why.

"Like I said, I love this time of year, but it's slim pickings for finding a paramour," Betty said. "You'd think romance was in the air, but when it's cold as the dickens, you don't spend too much time out on the town and trying to find your one true love. Everyone's just scurrying home on slippery sidewalks."

"And you couldn't pick a one of 'em out of a lineup once they get their hats, scarves, coats, and mittens off," I said.

"Ain't that the truth," Betty agreed. "So maybe dating's on hold until it starts to warm up."

"What's on the agenda for everyone tomorrow?" I asked. "Don't anyone dare say *working*."

"I was going to go to the Central Park Zoo," Rocío said. "The animals *love* the cold. They frolic around so much, they have a great time."

"Oh! Would you like some company?" Dottie asked.

"I will make you a thermos of hot chocolate," Mrs. K said. "Very fun day."

"That would be swell, Mrs. Kovalenko," Rocío said. "Thank you."

"My pleasure." Mrs. K was beaming.

"I have to go to the hairdresser's," Betty said. "My coif is getting a little copper." I tried not to stare at Betty's bottle blond to assess its shade, and just nodded.

"Even though it is sad, today is Epiphany and the decorations must come down," Mrs. K said.

"I guess I'm helping with that," Oleks grumped.

"And you two?" Dottie asked, staring over her spectacles.

"I don't want to say it," I whined.

"You don't have to *say* it, but the answer is the same as today, I assume," Dottie said.

"Well observed," I said. "But yes. The city's gumshoes never sleep."

"I'll take a look at this puzzle tonight," Rocío said. "I think I know what it is, but I want to call a friend and have their input."

"We would be forever in your debt," I said. "We can compensate you for your time."

"No need," Rocío said. "It's good practice for stretching muscles that haven't been stretched in a while."

"How long is 'a while'?" Oleks asked with a wink.

"Since about 1944," she said.

Oleks cleared our plates and helped his mother bring up some pineapple upside-down cake.

"Well, now you're making me daydream about a vacation," I said.

"You should go visit Tally in Los Angeles," Betty said. "Maybe she can take you to Hawai'i."

"I've never been out of the country," I said.

"You've more than earned the time off in the past year," Oleks said.

Dottie turned to Rocío. "She helped get Tommy's name cleared for a murder charge in June."

"And was thrown down the stairs by a mobster," Oleks said. "Had to go to the hospital and everything."

"Was stalked by his entire organization," Mrs. K reminded them.

"Then she caught a handful of Soviet spies over Thanksgiving," Betty added.

"It was only the one spy," I said.

Rocío raised an eyebrow at me and smiled. "Am I sure I want to continue to make your acquaintance?"

"Eh, I'm harmless," I laughed. "But I am really tired."

"Then it's settled," Betty said. "I'll telegram Tally and let her know you'll be out to visit as soon as you finish up your current caseload. She'll have a whole month of activities planned."

"I'll probably end up more tired at the end of vacation than I am now."

"I bet she'll have you meeting Cary Grant!" Betty swooned.

"Well, when you put it like that . . . ," I said. "Let's hurry up and get this all finished, everyone."

Rocío stretched and tossed her napkin on the table. "I have to say, this was one of the best nights I've had in ages. But I should go home and get some sleep before our day tomorrow. Meet you around ten at the gates, Dottie?"

"I will be there with bells on," my housemate agreed. "Let me walk you out."

Dottie slipped out to the sidewalk with Rocío to try to help her catch a cab. After a few minutes, we saw brake lights slipping away from the curb, and Dottie came back into the dining room.

"Well, she's nothing short of dynamite," Betty said.

"I have never been so excited to go to the zoo," Dottie agreed.

"Well, you better go get your beauty sleep," I said.

"Goodnight, girls. I'm glad you like her." Dottie exited up the stairs and I heard her shut her door behind her.

"Well, that explains the no boyfriends thing," Betty said.

"She did swoon pretty hard over Detective Lawson over the summer, though," I pointed out. "Or at least, that was the hardest I'd ever seen her swoon before."

"But not like this!" Betty giggled. "Maybe she just likes the person, not the packaging."

"She was *beaming*," I whispered. "I've never seen her so happy."

"Can't wait to hear how she likes the zoo," Betty agreed.

"Selfishly, though, I hope Rocío gets that puzzle solved," I said. "But I'll feel like a chump if she gets it in one night."

Oleks sat down at the table with a hot cup of an herbal drink he called *sbiten*. "I don't know," he said. "I don't think it's fair to compare your skills to a professional military code breaker."

"Fair point."

"What do you think it says?" Betty asked.

"I hope it says the thief's name, address, blood type, and daily schedule," I said. "But it'll probably just lead to another headache."

"It probably will." Betty yawned. "Okay, I'm following Dottie up. You going up too?"

"You bet. I'm bushed."

We piled the remaining dishes from dinner in the center of the table for Oleks and traipsed upstairs.

"Next week, we'll take you out," I assured Betty as I headed up to the third floor.

"We'll see if we make it that far," Betty whispered to the dark. "Good night."

Day 8

The phone was blasting off the hook downstairs and I shot to the second floor to silence it before it woke Mrs. K. It was dark and freezing, and polite society—which at the moment included a bunch of girls in a Chelsea boarding house—would consider it the middle of the night.

"Hello? Who's dead?" I whispered into the receiver.

"No one who wasn't dead yesterday," Tommy said back. "Or at least that we know of."

"Thank God for that."

"I need you to get dressed and meet me at the diner at the end of your block," Tommy said. "I have someone here who needs to talk."

"Be there as soon as I can," I said. "And have Miklos get me a cup of his special coffee."

★   ★   ★

Faster than you could spit, I was sliding into a booth next to Tommy and across from a man in a moth-eaten coat and holey skullcap, wolfing down a full breakfast of bacon, eggs, and sausages. Tommy kept his eyes on the man and greeted me with a grunt.

"What time *is* it, exactly?" I asked, as the owner of the diner, a small Greek man named Miklos, shoved a white mug in front of me. "*Efcharistó*, Miklos."

"*Parakaló.*"

"Where'd you learn to speak Greek?" the mystery man asked, food tumbling out of his mouth.

"I tried to learn *please* and *thank you* in as many languages as I could when I moved here," I said. "It's not that hard."

"It would be for me," he said, slurping up his own black coffee but motioning to my smaller white cup. "What's so special about that?"

"It's Greek coffee. They make it different from Americans. They boil the grounds in a thing, add a ton of sugar, it foams up, it's a whole production."

"Neat."

"Not to be rude, but I'd love to know your name," I said. "And why this fella here dragged me out of bed in the small hours to make your acquaintance."

"Joe Green," he said, thrusting out a chin.

"Like hell it is."

"That's what it says on my unemployment card, so that's what I'm sticking to."

"Fine."

"I found Giuseppi Verdi here standing on the corner by Times Square," Tommy said. "Layin' down a bouquet of flowers."

"I wouldn't call it a whole bouquet," Joe said. "It was a rose."

"And baby's breath."

"I don't even consider that a flower," Joe said. "It's like parsley on a dinner plate."

"Regardless," I cut in, "why the flowers?"

"The man who was killed," Joe said. "He meant a great deal to me."

"That's sweet," Tommy said. "You two planning on running off together?"

Joe glared at Tommy. "I would be so lucky if he would have me."

"Pay no attention to this jamoke," I said, for once getting to play good cop. "He wouldn't know romance if it bit him on the ass."

"But we need as much as you can give me so I can find out who sliced him," Tommy said, taking a long glug of his steaming hot coffee.

"Can you please be a little more delicate when discussing someone taken from this world so violently?" Joe asked. His manners were returning now that his plate was clean.

"I'm sorry," I said. "He really is that rough around the edges."

"You don't have to apologize for your man," Joe said. "He should do it for himself."

"I *am* sorry," Tommy said rotely. "I should have had more tact."

"Thank you," Joe responded. "Now. I really ought to have left those flowers at his hovel in Greenwich Village, but the landlords don't like me coming around."

"You know where he lived?"

"I'll give you the address, his full name, his roommate, everything," Joe said.

"Sounds like you knew a lot about this man," Tommy hinted.

"He was the most magnetic person I'd ever met," Joe said. "I struggle to think that he's no longer with us in this world."

"Joe, were you *together*?" I asked. "I don't care, but we need to know."

"Not in the way I would have wished," Joe said. "He knew me from the neighborhood. If I didn't have a place to stay, sometimes he'd let me in for the night. Buy me breakfast. He was kind. Kinder than anyone has been to me in my whole life."

"He had a roommate?" I asked, trying to put a plug in Joe's emotional tribute before the waterworks started.

"A girl, sweet but . . ."

"Troubled? Scandalous? Naïve?"

"That's the one, yes. Or the polite way to say it. Impolitely, as sharp as a rubber chicken. He had to send more than a few men away from the doorstep to whom she broadcast the wrong idea."

"Maybe she didn't broadcast it, but they wanted to hear it."

"Normally I would agree with you, but not Frankie. Pure as the driven snow, had no idea what she was doing. And look at the trouble it's caused."

"Are you sure that this attack involved Frankie?"

"Without a doubt in my mind," Joe said. "Henrik Fiskar was murdered because he stepped between a man and a woman."

"Can you give me Henrik Fiskar's address?"

"Corner of Bleecker and MacDougal," Joe said.

"And this fella you say got Henry," Tommy asked. "Do you know who he is?"

"Not by name," Joe said. "Tallish fella, but not strange tall. Just healthy. Broad shoulders, works at the port. Something like that. Only defining trait is a nice and puckery scar down his chin."

"Lotta ports in the city," Tommy said. "Can you be more specific?"

"I would have been if I could," Joe snapped. "Don't you think I want him caught?"

"Scootch out for a sec, Dollface, I have to use the facilities." Tommy shooed me out of the booth and disappeared down a hallway at the end of the counter. He was gone for a few minutes before Joe started looking around.

"I don't like this," Joe said, getting nervous.

"Tommy's just got to do what he's doing," I said. "Do you want anything else to eat?"

"Yeah," Joe said. "Get me a cake with a file baked into it."

"What do you mean?"

"Tell your man that I didn't run," Joe said. "He's going to hide in the back, isn't he?"

"I don't know what you're talking about."

"You will in about five minutes." Joe signaled Miklos and ordered another coffee and a corned beef sandwich, wrapped up in paper. "Lickety split, if you can, good sir."

He managed to get the sandwich into his pockets as the door to the diner jingled open and I felt a hand on my shoulder.

"Quite the early riser, aren't we, sweetheart," I heard Detective Jake Lawson croon. "Thanks for keeping this bum company."

Joe stood up and held up his hands. "You don't have to cuff me, I'm going quietly."

Tommy stood at the doorway next to the counter, close to the back hall, where there was a pay phone. Lawson spied him. "Thanks, Fortuna."

Joe left the diner and was tossed into the back of a waiting squad car. Despite the time of day, there was a little crowd of lookie-loos—a cabbie smoking a cigarette by the lamppost, Miklos's dishwasher, and a man in a dark overcoat and a muffler tied up around his whole noggin. Joe narrowed his eyes at everyone as the black-and-white pulled away.

"You called the cops on Joe?" I said. "What the hell for?"

"He knows everything there is to know about our vic," Tommy shrugged. "They need to question someone, keep 'em interested in the case. They can't keep him for more than a day. So tonight he gets to snooze in a real bed, not under a bench in Washington Square Park."

"They might hurt him," I said. "That's what cops do to men . . . *like Joe.*"

"He'll be fine," Tommy said. "So long as he had the presence of mind to drop that phony unemployment card. Oh, yup, here it is." He pulled a soggy piece of cardstock out of Joe's coffee.

"That was bad business, Tommy," I said, shaking my head. "He isn't guilty of anything other than vagrancy."

Tommy ignored me. "We'll go to that apartment in the morning."

"It *is* the morning," I said. "And I'm going home and going back to bed."

"See you soon, Dollface."

I stomped out of the diner, madder than a wet hen.

★ ★ ★

The sun was barely up before I heard the phone ringing again and I stomped back downstairs.

"Mrs. Kovalenko's Girls-Only Boarding House," I murmured. "Tommy, if that's you, I swear . . ."

"I'm sorry to be calling so early, Miss Valentine, but this is Mort Lobel," a cultured voice said over the line.

"I'm sorry to be short, Mr. Lobel," I said. "But I was out late last night on another case. How can I help you?"

"Tommy let me know this morning that the last round of work . . . with Rachel . . . didn't turn out and that you should be taking over that line," he said. "And I just wanted to let you know that she said she would be having an early lunch at Tavern on the Green today. Around eleven o'clock."

"Thank you, Mr. Lobel, I'll be there."

I took my time getting adjusted to being awake, and dressed myself for a day of sitting on a cold park bench in New York City in January—a white crew neck sweater with a man's burgundy cashmere cardigan over it, which I'd managed to accidentally keep from my time in Tarrytown from November. I found my longest wool skirt to layer over my regular stockings, plus knit knee socks, and my patent-leather boots. My black overcoat had lost its shape over the years and the wool sagged at the shoulders, but it was the only thing that would fit over so many layers. Topped with a beret to keep some of my heat in, a white muffler, and white leather gloves, I sauntered up to the restaurant in Central Park with my own thermos of coffee from Mrs. K and an ultra-small Minolta camera.

Settled on a bench just opposite the front windows, I paged through the newspaper and then a six-month-old issue of *Life* before Rachel showed her mug. She was in white fox, with a matching hat and muff, and looked absolutely outstanding with the gleaming silver fur next to her pale skin and dark, shining, curly hair. Two diamonds—or something that looked like diamonds—shimmered in her ears. She shifted uncomfortably under the awning of the restaurant before a man showed up and she gave him a hug around the neck. Five quick snaps and my morning errand was done and I could scurry away from this little scene feeling as though I had earned my hourly rate. But since I had no way of knowing if those five pictures would turn out, I knew I had to wait, my own squirming insides about spying on this chickadee be damned.

With what Tommy would call luck but I would call a curse, the restaurant must've been all but empty because Rachel and her companion were seated right before the tavern's biggest picture window. He was in somewhat shabby flannel, but her navy blue suit was cut specifically for her figure. The two watched as hansom cabs rolled by, each horse's breath billowing in the air like they were announcing a new pope. With every new addition to the table over the course of two hours—glasses of water, a glass of white wine, salmon filets, cups of coffee—I snapped a new photo of the twosome. If they were up to hanky-panky, it must've been below the tablecloth, because no hands met across the top. Rachel paid the whole bill with a stack of greenbacks, and they left the building, none the wiser to their tryst being caught on celluloid. A final hug, a pat on the lapel, and they were separated, Rachel back to Bensonhurst and her companion . . . who knows.

"If these don't turn out, I quit," I muttered to a pigeon. "This gives me the jeebies."

There was no place to go from here but to Thelma's apartment building. I tossed a nickel in a pay phone and jabbed in the number Tommy'd given me when we first started the case.

The phone was picked up with a grunt.

"Thelma Thompkins, please," I said as primly as I could.

"It's my private phone," she yawned.

"My apologies. This is Viviana Valentine. I was hoping I could stop by within the hour to drop off more film for Tommy."

"Sure." There was a click, and I supposed it was arranged.

By the time St. Paul's was bonging one, I was marching up the stairs to Telly's apartment, which now had a more pronounced lean than they had even a few days ago. She needed out of this building, and I was swallowing my reservations about having her at the boarding house. This wasn't a matter of my hurt feelings anymore—her life was at risk. My knock was greeted with another grunt, and I entered the apartment.

She was standing in the middle of the room, wrapped in a holey blanket and holding her cat. "Roll." She thrust out her hand with no patience to spare.

"I'm sorry, I haven't taken it out of the camera yet," I confessed. "I just got off the job."

"Jesus *Christ*." The cat hit the ground and she yanked the camera from my paws, turned the knobs that needed turning, and pulled the film from the back of the camera in a blink.

"Later today." She flipped her hand in the air and I left her place, lighting back to Mrs. K's as fast as my feet could take me. Tommy was on the stoop and waiting by the time I arrived.

"Lunch on the hoof," he said, tossing me a wrapped-up sandwich.

"Roast beef?"

"Of course," he said, whistling for a yellow cab. "We're going down to the Battery."

"Fine. Gives me time to chew."

Traffic from Chelsea to the southern tip of Manhattan was stop and go, with one hard brake by the driver so jolting half my sandwich slid to the floor of the cab.

"Son of a bitch."

"Don't worry, your landlady was already working on a whole turkey," Tommy said. "You'll be home for Sunday supper."

"Thank God. Sitting on a park bench watching people eat for two hours works up an appetite."

The cabbie swooped into a driveway and pulled the meter. "Don't worry about the horseradish in the floorboards," he said. "You're my last fare and it's getting hosed out at the depot."

"Thanks," I said, winging open the door and catching the wind off the bay.

"Now shut the damn door."

The cabbie was off with a squeal, ignoring a mother with two kids in tow waving her arms.

"Meet you back here in an hour," Tommy said, shivering. "My height. Dark. Big scar."

"You don't have to tell me, I was *there*."

Tommy hooked east and went toward Brooklyn and I wandered toward New Jersey and the squat and dirty wooden piers at the shoreline. The chopping waves of the bay smacked into the pylons and coated them in a gleaming sheen of ice. Some of the spray shot up and onto the walking paths, peppering me with icy shards of smelly, brackish water.

"This is miserable," I said, not even lowering my voice. There was no way anyone could hear me over the screaming wind, and I had to admit, one good thing about doing a manhunt on a pier in January is that there aren't too many faces to look at. The squat ferries and fishing boats in every slip were unmanned, and I scurried toward the large clock tower building to see if anyone was inside—no dice. Even the rats were taking the day off.

Tommy was walking my way after I finished peering into the building's windows like a creep. He cupped his hand to his mouth and shouted, but I knew I wasn't going to catch a lick of it. I ran full speed in my boots at him, and once I was within a few feet he tried again.

"Too many boats, too many people with Sunday off," he said.

"It doesn't feel right, either," I said. "This is tourist stuff. No one's hiring a man with a facial scar to greet lookie-loos to the Statue of Liberty."

"Not unless he's sweeping up the trash," Tommy said.

We walked through the park, sloppy with slush, to the corner of Battery and Washington.

"You head back," Tommy said, after magically hailing a cab and having one appear. I climbed into the back of the taxi and shivered.

"Crank the heat," I demanded.

"What were yous doing? It's freakin' freezing out there," the cabbie addressed me.

"Needed to find someone. Didn't." I was breathing into my hands and gave the cabbie the address of my boarding house.

"You're going to catch your death in this weather."

"Thanks, Mother," I said.

That shut him up.

★   ★   ★

In no time flat, I was tossing my coat on the rack in the vestibule of Mrs. K's.

"I'm nearly thirty years old," I said, unlacing my shoes. "Is there ever going to be a time that strange men don't lecture me?"

"When you are old and gray," Mrs. K said from just inside the door, setting the table. "Then they'll just act like you do not exist."

"From your lips to God's ears," I said, taking a deep sigh. "That turkey smells great."

"It's probably still got an hour to cook," Mrs. K said, bustling back toward the basement stairs.

"That's fine, I need some time to gather my thoughts." The last thing I wanted to do was tell anyone that Tommy and I were on the outs. "Let me see if Betty's in, and if I can steal her notebook." I was already out the door of the dining room and thundering up the stairs. A knock on the door revealed my housemate with shockingly white hair, and I didn't mention it.

"What's it doing, Boss?" She was in her jammies even though the sun was only just starting to set, and wrapped in a pink fuzzy robe.

"Can I snitch your notebook?" I said.

"I'll come help," she said.

"We don't pay you enough to work on a Sunday."

"You don't pay me enough to work Monday through Friday, neither," she said. "How did you make it work for so long, Viv?"

"I have my secrets," I said. "Better grab a sharp pencil, we have a lot to discuss."

We slipped into our usual seats at the empty dinner table, and Betty rapped her pencil against her steno pad. Oleks came up from the basement with a pot of coffee and five mugs.

"You two were in the paper today," he grunted.

"Oh, good grief," I rolled my eyes. "We're being harassed by some two-bit reporter who thinks the story is the engaged private detectives and not a murdered man."

"Is that the story?" Betty asked.

"It is until we find out why he was killed," I said. I turned to Oleks. "He bum-rushed us outside a girlie show in Times Square. Did your mother see?"

"Nah, I ripped it to shreds and it's already in the can in the alley."

"Thanks."

"So, what's new?" Betty asked, while he poured.

"Well, Mr. Floristan's theft case is waiting to see if Rocío can decipher that latest puzzle, I said. "Lord knows how long that will take."

"A dollar says she has it tonight," Oleks said.

"You're on."

"And then the missing banker . . . all we have is that post-card," I said.

"Any ideas what it's a picture of yet?" Betty asked.

"Haven't even had time to think about it," I admitted. "What would you do if you had to find a missing person?"

"Call the cops." Betty shrugged.

"I wonder why Mr. Bowen didn't . . ."

Oleks grunted. "The missing fella knows why."

"True, true. And Ms. Thompkins has the latest roll of film from Morty's case."

"She'll have it in a day," Betty said.

"And the murder?" Oleks asked.

"We have an apartment to case, a roommate to question, and a suspect to track down," I ticked off on my fingers.

"So, actually not that bad," Betty said chirpily.

"We'll have more once Joe gets out of hock," I added.

"Who's Joe?"

"Someone who knows the victim. Joe let on that he was sweet on Henry, the dead fella. Tommy got Joe locked up for the night, which was some lousy business," I said. "He was trying to help."

"Why'd he do it?" Betty asked. "Did he kill Henry?"

"I don't think he did. Said he really cared for him. Tommy said Joe needed a bed to sleep in," I said. "Said Lawson didn't suspect him either, but I still don't like it."

"If there's a next time, you can call Saint Volodomyr's," Oleks suggested.

"Church shelters would try to make him repent his sinning ways," I said. "Best I can hope for is that Lawson just gave him a night's rest and didn't even take the sandwich."

"*Lawson* likely wasn't guarding him," Betty shuddered. "And you know how cops are to men like Joe."

"Ya know, I said the same thing about Tally—cops shouldn't care about a damn thing, unless someone is hurting another person, and Joe sure isn't. Not by leaving flowers for a fella in his memory." I took a long, deep sip of my coffee. "I hate this damned city sometimes."

"Me too."

I stared at the oil creating a sheet on the top of my cooling brew. "I'm going to need to ask Tommy for a favor."

"What kind of favor?" Oleks asked.

"When those pics come back from Thelma, sooner or later, I have to have a sit down with Rachel," I said.

"I don't think Mr. Lobel will like that," Betty scowled.

"I don't really give a flying fig what Mort likes," I said. "That wasn't a romantic meet and greet today, and I know it in my guts. I just want her to let me know what's happening before we tell Mort."

"We'll have to reach out to him to ask when she's heading out next, and you can cut her off at the pass."

"That would be the only way, yeah."

"What do you think it is, Viv?" Betty asked.

"Something sad," I said. "But I don't know what."

"What isn't sad lately?" Oleks asked.

"It sure does feel like the shine wore off," I said. "After the war, we were all excited. And now it just feels like nothing got fixed."

"Plenty got fixed," Betty said. "But not everything."

I looked at her. "You don't care that Thelma isn't a white girl, do you?"

"News to me, but no, I do *not*," Betty pounded her first on the table. "The way other nurses at the hospital would treat folks always had me steaming."

"Because her walls had a mighty fine lean to them," I said. "That building might collapse with her still in it."

"What is Moses *doing*?" Oleks asked. "These are neighbor-hoods with families in 'em."

"They're wrecking the city, is what they're doing," I said.

"Making it so no one wants to live here," Oleks said, polish-ing off his coffee. "I'm going to go check on dinner."

"Tommy will probably suggest we move up to Bronxville," I said. "Near his family. But the thought of leaving Manhattan makes me want to spit."

"His mother lives in Westchester?" Betty asked.

"That was a whole conversation," I told her. "I feel strange, but what are you going to do."

"Pay your staff more," Betty said. "I'll bring it up with the boss."

Oleks ambled up the stairs like a cheetah, his arms holding a tray filled with at least ten pounds of dishes. "Work off the table, Mom says I have to set it for dinner."

NIGHT 8

Dottie was conspicuously absent from the dinner table, and Oleks, Mrs. K, and Betty tried to play off like this was a normal occurrence.

"How are our two private investigators?" Mrs. K asked, plopping a golden-roasted bird in front of us.

"I've been freezing *mio culo* off all day," I told her, eyeing a drumstick as she slid in the knife and carved it right off. The leg didn't even hit the platter before she gave it to me. "I can't wait for springtime."

"You left the house in the dead of night," Mrs. K said. It wasn't a question. And she wasn't looking at me when she said it. She stuck the breast of the turkey with the pointy end of the knife for emphasis.

I got the message good and proper and gulped. "Tommy had a suspect and he needed help with questioning. It's all right, though, Mrs. K. I knew what I was getting into when we became partners. I'm just sorry about the late-night call. It must've woken everyone up."

"It happens," Oleks shrugged. "Did you find out everything you needed?"

"No."

The front door clanged open and Dottie came stumbling inside, followed by Rocío. "Sorry we're late!" Dottie laughed. She was behaving like a teenager, and it was beyond endearing.

"How was the zoo?" Oleks called out.

"Great! Freezing!" Rocío responded. Both her and Dottie's shoes were off and they padded to the table in stockinged feet. "I was planning on going home, but I had to tell you in person."

"It took you a *day*?" Betty gasped.

"I had to call a former colleague," Rocío said. "But we went through it and managed a cogent message." She pulled a piece of paper out of her cardigan pocket and handed it over.

"I don't know if I want to read this," I said. "*More* spies?"

"Well, festive spies," Rocío said. "Read it. I swear."

I unfurled the paper before Oleks snatched it from my hands.

"*And surely ye'll be your pint-stowp, And surely I'll be mine, And we'll tak a cup o' kindness yet. For auld lang syne.*"

He gave me back the paper and I groaned. "Whoever is giving Floristan the run-around is an absolute ass."

"And an ass who is familiar with German double-transposition ciphers from World War I," Dottie said. "Or that's what she said."

"They require a code to break them, and whoever it was made that easy by putting a good one in all caps at the top of the top of the note. The key was the word SECRET," Rocío said. "He could've made it much, much harder."

"It was Reds over the summer and now it's Nazis?" I asked. "You guys, I want out."

"No, no, no," Dottie said. "Roci says that the code has been pretty common knowledge since the teens. No Nazis, just someone who is obsessed with puzzles. Difficult ones."

"Does anyone know what the hell a pint-stowp is?" I asked. "This doesn't feel like English."

"It isn't . . . sort of," Betty said. "It's Scots. Sort of."

"How can something be sort of English and sort of Scots?" I asked.

"Well, that's just what Rabbie Burns wrote," Betty continued. "The puzzle is a bit of his poem, 'Auld Lange Syne.'"

"Do you memorize a lot of Romantic poetry?" Rocío asked.

"Just the greatest hits," Betty said back. "Besides, I worked a few New Year's Eves in the hospital, and I called the library once to ask about the tune everyone was humming."

"The info line must have really loved you," I teased, elbowing her in the side. "We can't let you be idle, you're the death of librarians."

"But what was the last clue?" Dottie asked. "It sent you to a statue, didn't it?"

"First, we thought Joan of Arc, but then it was that big angel in Central Park," I said.

"Is there a statue of this Burns fella somewhere?" Oleks asked, scooping up some green beans.

"Couldn't tell ya," I said.

"Library can," Betty said with her mouth full.

"What's the number?" I was halfway out of my chair.

"After dinner, pretty girl," Mrs. K scolded.

"Yes, ma'am."

Almost like it was bewitched, the phone upstairs starting ringing, and Betty raced up to answer it. It was a handful of pleasantries before she descended back to the table.

"Thelma's got the pictures," she said. "I'll go and pick them up and bring them to the office in the morning."

"Thanks, Betts," I said.

"Gotta earn a new salary," she said.

"Mrs. K—you still have any of that brandy from the other evening?"

"Of course I do," she said. "Oleks—help me downstairs."

The turkey carcass and all the half-eaten trimmings disappeared in minutes. The doorbell rang and I got up to answer it.

Tommy was on the stoop, looking dejected.

"Come on in," I said, leaving the door open for him to follow. "You missed dinner."

Tommy followed me into the dining room and put on a cheery smile when he saw the assembled housemates. He sat down at the table next to Betty and didn't even turn to me to say hello. Dottie and Rocío were having their own whispered conversation.

It felt nice to not have to say a word to anyone for a while—ever since the summer, it felt like I was in charge of providing dinnertime conversation. But for a solitary half hour, I listened to laughs and questions that had nothing to do with me, and I could switch off my own brain. Tuning in and out, I heard Dottie discussing blackboard chalk while Betty was ribbing Tommy over all the men he was pulling out of his mental file for her to date.

"Marlon did a few years in minimum security," Tommy said, and Betty shrieked with giggles.

"Oh, could you imagine," she said, whipping tears from her eyes. "My mother would have an actual conniption."

"There's always Terrence, who hasn't been caught yet, but the clock's ticking on that one."

"Anything violent?"

"No, but you might find your basement or spare room filled with objects that fell off the back of a truck every now and then," he said.

"That doesn't sound so bad," Betty mused. "I know I have to take a man's name, but I don't want to also take his rap sheet."

"I don't want to take your last name!"

The dining room conversation screeched to a halt and every head turned to stare at me.

"Say that again?" Tommy asked.

"I don't know why I said that," I stammered. "I'm sorry, I just . . ."

"You don't want to be Viviana Viola Fortuna? Or even Viviana Viola Valentine-Fortuna?" Tommy asked. He smoothed the linen napkin that had been left stranded on the table when Oleks had picked up all the dirty plates.

"I don't . . . think so. I've been Viviana Valentine for almost thirty years, and I like it. I just like my name. It's mine. It's me. I just . . ." I had tears coming to my eyes, and Dottie and Betty shifted uncomfortably while Rocío stared at the floor.

"I like your name too," Tommy said. "I suppose it's your choice if you want to take my name or not."

"You won't hold it against me?" I let out a breath I didn't know I'd been holding in since Thanksgiving.

"*I* won't," he said. "But that's going to be an interesting conversation you have with my mother."

"What business is it of hers?"

"I'm her son," Tommy shrugged. "But what's on your driver's license is your business, I guess."

"You still haven't taught me how to drive!" I said. "That Cadillac is sitting in a garage by the Garden!"

Dottie looked at her friend. "It was a gift from the heiress, Tallulah Blackstone; none of us can afford a Cadillac."

"You all are something *else*." Rocío leaned over and pecked Dottie on the cheek. "But I should head home. I have to prepare lesson plans."

Oleks and Mrs. K emerged from the basement with a tray of glasses and the brandy just as Rocío was putting on her shoes. She raced back into the dining room to clasp our landlady's hands and thank her for dinner, then raced back out the front door chasing down a taxi.

"She's a blast," Oleks said. "A real live op! In our house!"

"You live with a private detective and soon there may be two." His mother raised an eyebrow at him, and Oleks ignored her.

"Do you think she might take the time to explain all the codes she knows?" he asked Dottie.

"Of course, we'll have her around later this week," Dottie said, clearly thankful for a reason to have the math teacher in her home as much as she could. "If she's free."

"I wish *she* was moving in," he said devilishly. Tommy ignored the rebuke, but Mrs. K did not.

"Oleksandr Grigoriy Kovalenko, if I hear one more statement like that out of you I will . . ." She held her tongue but also held her napkin like she was ready to wring its neck like a chicken.

"How do you want me to feel about it?" he shouted, standing from his seat at the table and launching himself toward the front door. Suddenly I saw him for what he was—a sizable young adult, stubble on his chin, and the man of his house since before he even hit junior high. "I'll move out as soon as I graduate. Somewhere *I* want to go." He was in his overcoat and galoshes and out the door before Mrs. K could even let out a sob.

"No one say a word." She stood from the table and slipped downstairs before even an ounce of comfort could escape our lips. I tidied the table and we all returned to where we came from—Dottie, Betty, and me to our rooms and Tommy to his apartment a twenty-minute walk away—before we uttered another sound.

DAY 9

Dottie was up, bathed, breakfasted, and out of the house first. Not that this was unusual, but I think she had a greater drive to get to school lately than normal. Second was Betty, who offered to go and pick up the photographs from Thelma. That meant I was still in bed and enjoying my slumber when the phone began ringing on the floor below me, and I nearly slid down the stairs in my socks to pick it up in time.

Tommy cut me off before I could finish the full, standard greeting. "Viv—let's go to Brooklyn," he said, yelling into the phone.

"No."

"We have to do recon at more ports," he said. "I'm coming to get you, then we're getting the Caddy."

"Oh, please, dear God, *no*," I whined. "I hate that car and the last time we left Manhattan we were almost sent to the chair for espionage."

"We were not," Tommy said. "I'll get the Caddy and *then* pick you up. *Bene?*"

"Fine. But I'm not driving."

"Of course you're not, you're not licensed. I don't want to end up in the river."

I took my time showering and getting properly coiffed and met Tommy at the breakfast table, where we munched some cold toast with even colder coffee and slipped back out the front door. The enormous, luxurious car sat like a tank on the otherwise vacant curb. "Lord, I hate this car."

"It's fine. We want to catch a murderer, right?"

"We do."

"The main clue we got was that he works at one of the ports, correct?"

"Correct."

"Can you think of a more expedient way to get from Chelsea to the Port of New York and New Jersey?"

"I cannot."

"Then, the car it is."

"We're never going to find a random man with a facial scar at the port, Tommy," I said. "It must employ thousands."

"So, we'll just ask around. Never hurts to ask."

"This is a waste of time," I said. "We'd have better luck with the apartment." I slammed the heavy metal door after me, and the shock wave reverberated through every inch of frozen steel in the car. The leather seats were ice against my thighs. All I wanted to do was head into the office and take a gander at the snaps I'd caught at the tavern the other day and figure out what Morty's fiancée was up to.

"The apartment is just one person who knew the victim, not the murderer," Tommy said. "Humor me. Maybe we'll find the needle in the haystack. Maybe we won't."

"We definitely won't," I said as Tommy checked his mirrors. "We don't even know what shift he's on. Midmorning on a Monday! We'll sure find a felon at his day job, responsibly clocked in and rarin' to work. Saying *yes, sir* and *no, sir* to the foreman, maybe he even brought everyone donuts."

Tommy was silent for a minute.

"Take a snooze," Tommy told me as he turned the key. "It's gonna be a while."

"Come to think of it, do *you* have a driver's license?" I asked. Tommy turned on the radio.

It was nearly an hour of driving in nauseating traffic to Red Hook over the Manhattan Bridge and twenty minutes of circling the through lines of cars before Tommy found a slice of pavement to park the Caddy. We jumped out into a damp lot that smelled of motor oil and fish guts. The sound of the docks was deafening. Trucks beeped, horns honked, men yelled, and metal clanked.

"You stay here," Tommy instructed. "I'm gonna go talk to a man with a clipboard. You look at faces."

I sure as hell tried, but every face had a beard, a scarf, or a hat pulled down over its eyes. Every man looked the same—dirty and mad, and I would have been too if I had to do this much physical labor in the freezing cold just so someone could buy a stupid French tchotchke or a manufacturer's piece for an imported car.

Besides, nearly every man on the docks was sporting some kind of noticeable injury. Gashes and bruises, sores and scars—if they weren't from getting whacked in the kisser by a crane hook, the wound was from the Navy, Army, Marines, Air Force, or hell, even the Coast Guard sometime during the war. There were few men between the ages of twenty-five and fifty who didn't have some kind of mark on 'em. And I wasn't going to find the right man in this parade of mugs, no matter how many questions Tommy asked.

"Nice ride, sugar," a man whistled at me as he walked by with his lunch pail. Wasn't yet ten AM, but I supposed breaks depended on what time your shift started and ended, and like the city itself, the port didn't sleep. "Why don't we make use of that big back seat?"

"Buzz off!" I shouted, taking a good look at his face. It was ugly, but it didn't have a puckered scar.

The man walked a little bit closer. "What's a dame like you doing around here?"

I eyed him up carefully, but he certainly wasn't our man—he was missing his left ring finger down to the second knuckle and the little finger didn't look healthy, either. I decided honesty was the best policy. "Looking for a murderer, actually," I said, casually pulling my investigator's license from my purse. "Anyone do a scamper after New Year's Eve? Someone with a nice gash on his mug?"

The man didn't miss a beat. "There's always a few that go missing after the first," he said. "Usually they're fished out of the drink. Showing off to some little chickadee or checking out permanently, it's never an accident, you know what I mean? But sorry, ma'am, wish I could help you." He tipped his hat to me and scurried off.

"Making friends?" Tommy came up on the driver's side and opened the door.

"Yeah, but they're no use to me," I said. "Every man I see has a scar, Tommy. We need to go to that apartment."

"You're right," he said. "The foreman said that the description I gave him matched a hundred guys. We're not finding our fella here."

"Let's go drop this hunk of junk at the garage and meet up with Betty," I said. "See what she's seen in those pictures for Morty and wash our hands of that mess as soon as possible."

"You know you can sell it, right?"

His words hung in the air for a minute before I processed what he said. "I . . . I hadn't thought of that."

"I'm going to drop you off at the office and then bring the car around to a friend of mine, he can tell us how much you'd get for it."

"Do you think Tally would mind?" I asked. "It was a gift."

"If you regretted selling it, she'd just buy you another one," Tommy said. "Take a snooze. Or at least do what you have to do so you don't get carsick."

"Thanks." I nestled into a cocoon of coat and scarf against the door, but kept my eyes stuck on one corner of the windshield so I wouldn't feel the need to upchuck all over the floorboards. Within no time we were back in Hell's Kitchen and Tommy poked me in the side to get me out of the car, which had finally become all nice, toasty warm.

"Be back soon," he said as I ran upstairs to Betty to see what was cooking.

"Viv!" she shouted at me as she startled from the desk. "You got something, all right." The three-by-five photos were splayed out on the desk and clear as day. She was a beautiful girl, in person and in pictures, smiling her way through lunch with a man who wasn't her intended.

"I took snaps of as much as I could without drawing suspicion," I panted to Betty. My run up flights of stairs in full winter gear was making me dizzy, and I stripped down to my shirt while I sweated and stared at the photos. "What do you see here?"

"Well, that ain't Morty," Betty said, stating the obvious. "He's pleasant to look at, she could do worse."

"Dark hair, dark eyes," I said. "The coat used to be nice."

"The shoes are new," Betty said. "They even still have a slight shine in this weather."

"You know, she never smooched him on the lips," I pointed out. "There was a cheek kiss, but if you were having a steamy, hidden affair at a nice restaurant, wouldn't you go in for a real kiss?"

"People have all sorts of different manners," Betty shrugged. "But yes. *I* would."

"Well, now I really have to get her by herself," I said. "I'll call Morty and tell him that this round also turned up nothing and I need another stab at it."

"And then ask her what's up?" Betty said.

"That's the gist."

"Speaking of . . ." My secretary petered off, and I already knew where our conversation was heading.

"So what'd you think of Thelma?" I asked.

"Well, as your friend I want to tell you that she's a drop-dead beaut and you weren't wrong for feeling a bit of a twinge of jealousy, honey," Betty said. "What a *knockout*."

"I told you it wasn't for nothing!" I poured myself a hot cup of joe now that we were at the gossip portion of our day.

"And I caught her before she was even dolled up," Betty said. "And she looked like she'd been crying on and off."

"I'm sure it can't be easy to watch your neighborhood get torn down around your ears," I said.

"That's what I said, but she said that she finally got a place in Harlem all lined up, she just needed to get the utilities turned on before she moved," Betty explained. "So she's not coming to Mrs. K's."

"Then what's the rub?" I asked.

"Gol*ly*, Viviana, for a girl who reads the paper back to front daily," Betty said. She snatched a front page from a pile of days old *Times*. "In between stories about CiCi's legs and the weather, you may have noticed there's a war on. Her brother's in Korea. He's stationed in gee-dee *Seoul*."

The headline from the paper announced a battle in the city, and a significant number of casualties.

"Oh God, Betts, I've been an ass."

"Well, I'll say you've had your head up yours for a while," she said. "I say it as a friend."

"You're right. I need to apologize." I thought back to Norma and how badly I needed to make amends to so many different women I'd met in the last week.

"You'll send her a housewarming present when she's settled in a few weeks," Betty said. "Until then, if there's more pictures, I'll do the running."

"You two hit it off?"

"She's bringing me uptown to go dancing on Friday."

"How do you do it?" I asked. "Put everyone so at ease?"

"I'm a nurse," Betty shrugged. "And a damn good one. If someone isn't screaming in pain when I meet them, I'm already at an advantage."

I slugged back the rest of my coffee and winced as it went down hot. "This whole time I've been missing the obvious," I said to her, shuffling back into my layers so I could hit the streets again. "I have to run an errand. Tell Tommy to cool his heels if he gets back before me."

I slammed down the stairs and out to the sidewalk, flailing for a taxi cab.

"Calm down, kitten, nothing's on fire," the first driver said as I slipped into his back seat.

"I need to get to the Diamond District, as fast as you can," I said.

"No one needs to buy rocks that fast," he said, eyeing me as he started the meter.

"I can't afford them anyhow," I said. "But I need to ask a man a question."

The cabbie zipped five blocks east in no time flat and gave a thank-a-you when I tipped him. I found Mr. Doroshenko's building no problem, ran inside to the elevator, and hit the button for his floor with gusto. The clunking lift moved slowly, but I took the time to take ten deep breaths to calm myself before I went rapping on his door. He wasn't expecting me, and I didn't want him to think there was something wrong with his sister and nephew.

I slipped out of the elevator and made my way to his suite. A soft tap at the door was met with a booming, "Enter!" and I stumbled into the pitch-black office. He sat where I had found him this past summer, behind a massive desk covered in black leather satchels, each one containing handfuls of diamonds—same black suit with a crisp white shirt, black jet shirt studs, black jet stone cufflinks. His jeweler's glasses made his eyes appear to be the size of baseballs, and he craned to make out my face from underneath his lamp.

"You're one of Lana's girls?" he asked.

"The troublemaker, Viviana Valentine," I said. "I was wondering if I could ask you a few questions. About the construction?"

"Yes, yes." He motioned for a nearby chair.

"I'll only take a minute," I assured him. "I'm just nervous about Oleks. He's not acting like himself."

"Of course he is not," Mr. Doroshenko said with a shrug. "His entire home is being ripped apart."

"I feel awful."

"Do not. This was a long time arriving."

"The construction?"

"No!" he laughed. "My sister taking that boy out of the city!"

"You're joking!" I gasped. "They can't move!"

"Of course they can," Mr. Doroshenko said. "We are turning the whole building into apartments. We just needed people to say they would rent them."

"Well, that's just awful," I said. "Just awful. What will happen to Betty and Dottie? And what about breakfast?"

Mr. Doroshenko raised his eyebrows at me. "Breakfast? That is your question?"

"Well, no, but Betty and Dottie are my concern," I said.

"They are more than welcome to rent their floor. Perhaps together as roommates."

"Oh, I'm not sure they would like that . . ."

"Boarding houses are very old fashioned, Miss Valentine," Mr. Doroshenko said. "Modern people want their privacy more than they want bacon and eggs. But it will be some time yet before the conversion is made."

"Thank goodness for that," I said. "And Oleks—where are they moving to, sir?"

"The suburbs!" Even in his strong Ukrainian accent, the joy was palpable. "On the Long Island."

"Oleks is eighteen pretty soon," I said, getting up from my chair. "He may not go."

"He may not," Mr. Doroshenko agreed. "But boys . . . they will be kind to their mothers."

I shook his hand and started the mile back to the office, sorry I'd even talked to Tommy about moving in.

I knew marriage was a big change in a relationship, but it shouldn't be this disruptive to *so* many people. Should it just have to do with the two people who say "I do"? I thought back to the summer, to Tally Blackstone, whose daddy ruined so many lives because he wanted her to walk down the aisle to marry someone she would never love in the way everyone wanted her to. At least I didn't have that issue with Tommy— when I said he was the one and only, I damn well meant it. The hiccups we were having were normal bumps that happen when two roads merge.

It was only afternoon, but the sun was already dipping behind the taller office buildings on the west side of Manhattan. I slipped into a pay phone on the corner and dialed the office.

"Hey, Betts, let me speak to Tommy," I said.

"No prob." The phone hit the desk for a second before he picked up.

"Tommy."

"It's me," I said, even though I was sure Betty had already told him so. "I'm going to take a breather. I need some time to focus on something that isn't a case or my landlady's ornery son."

"Sure. Do what you gotta do."

"I'll come by your place later?"

"Sure."

"Thanks. Patch me back to Betty, would you?"

He grunted again and Betty picked up her extension. "What's doing, Viv?"

"Could you maybe grab me the number for Mr. Bowen's office?" I asked. "The banker."

"You bet." It took a few seconds of flipping and flapping through her files but she had it. "Pennsylvania 5-0113."

"Thanks, Betts." I depressed the plunger and slipped a nickel into the coin slot, dialing the number my secretary gave me.

"Keller Bachmann, Mr. Bowen's office, how may I help you?" A pleasant voice came down through the wire.

"Hi, yeah, this is Viviana Valentine, one of the, um, helpers Mr. Bowen came to see last week?" I said. I couldn't think of a harmless euphemism for *private eye* and I wanted to keep it vague just in case someone was listening in at the bank's office.

"Do you have a report ready for Mr. Bowen?" the voice asked.

"No, not yet, but we are chasing down a few leads," I fibbed. "I was just wondering—am I speaking to Peggy, the secretary girl?"

"This is she."

"So, I was just wondering—would you be open to meeting for a drink tonight? I'd like to ask you a few questions about the missing man, Trevor."

"Of course." Her voice was suddenly a whisper. "I live in Alphabet City—Avenue A and 13th Street, there's a little hole-in-the-wall. George's. I can be there at eight."

"Thanks, Peggy."

"Don't mention it. *Really.*" She hung up and my coin rattled into its new home in the collection container.

Well worth five cents, I'd say.

It was a long walk from the Diamond District to anywhere I wanted to go, especially for a cold day that was rapidly becoming colder as the shadows loomed. But I needed a clear head, and focusing on my footsteps—and not murder—was just doing the job.

There was a man roasting nuts by Radio City, and I pulled a few coins out of my pocket to nab a small bag. The heat of the oils seeped through the paper and into my gloves as I popped the candied, sweet confections into my maw. I spun around on my heel.

"How do you do that?" I asked the gent without thinking.

"Do what?"

"Make 'em smell like heaven but taste like gee-dee cardboard?"

"Why do you think they only cost a dime, sweetheart?" He roared with laughter and set about tossing the caramelized and burning nuggets at the bottom of the roasting pan. I tossed the nuts into the trash can in front of a waiting customer, and she slid her two nickels back into her purse and moved on.

Night 9

Across the street was a discount cinema, still playing the latest Jimmy Stewart movie from November. It was the kind of movie I just can't stand—something happens and hijinks ensue; not to mention, Jimmy Stewart cast as an everyman always makes me hoot. You can't fool me with that jaw and accent, he came from bucks—but you can't expect a lot from Hollywood this day and age. If you wanted to cast a college professor or a fella with a million dollars, I'd cast Jimmy Stewart. But a fella who works at a shoe store? Well, sorry, my friends, but you need Donald O'Connor. I'd have to write Tally out in Los Angeles and ask her a few questions about what all these picture executives were thinking.

On top of that, it's a hard sell to have a bunch of stars act like they can't afford the tax bill after winning a diamond ring in a puzzle. Seven thousand dollars would be a drop in the hat for Jimmy, that's for sure. Maybe he was better in the movie with the invisible rabbit, but that wasn't in the second-run theaters yet.

A mindless ninety minutes plus newsreel was just what I needed, and I beat feet back to Tommy's apartment once the house lights came on and my fingertips were scraping the bottom of the popcorn box. No one accosted me on the sidewalk this time, and I made it up the stoop unmolested and lost in my thoughts. Concentrating as I pulled the janitor ring out of my purse and unlocked the front door, I ran up the stairs to Tommy's, bursting open his apartment and shouting the only word I had on the tip of my tongue.

"Taxes!" I said, throwing my purse to the ground. "It has to be about taxes!"

"What does?" Tommy was in an apron and frying up chicken cutlets. It smelled like hot oil and oregano in his apartment.

"The banker," I said. "The guy with the long name who's done a scarper."

"Running away from things is a bad idea if you owe the government."

"*He* doesn't owe anything. Dollars to doughnuts it's the bank."

"Then why does the bank want us to find him?" Tommy asked.

"Proof! I bet the missing banker has proof!" I was salivating at the scent of dinner, and the memory of two disappointing bites of my sidewalk snack that had cost me a hard-earned ten cents. "Man, that smells good."

"Thank you," Tommy said, placing our dishes of food down on his tiny little dining table. "I always thought if the PI business went belly-up, I could start a little restaurant."

"There's no danger of it dying, is there?" I swirled some spaghetti around my fork and slipped it into my mouth. Perfect, really, and the sauce was just divine.

"Only if I do," Tommy said.

"You're not planning on *that* either, are you?"

"Only two things in this life you don't escape, Dollface, are death and taxes."

"But the *far* future, you mean. After we retire."

"Retirement comes at some young ages for private investigators. If I turn up my toes, you have my permission to sell the joint." He was giggling, but I wasn't quite as amused.

"And do what, exactly? Retire to my knitting?"

"You knit?"

"I don't know what else widows do," I shrugged. "Anyway, let's not talk about all this morbid stuff right now. One death a month, if we can manage it, please."

"No problem," Tommy agreed. "Though technically that death happened in December."

"I don't know what came over me the other night," I said. "Money is such a sore spot for me, I don't behave quite right when I talk about it."

"I should've read the room better, Dollface. I can tell when a fella's about to pop me in the jaw, but I couldn't tell that you were getting upset," Tommy said, picking up my hand and kissing my fingers. "That's on me."

"People from money—and I know you're not like *Vanderbilt* loaded, Dottie just called you *comfortable*, but people from money expect the people in their lives to be a certain way, and I don't think I can ever be that."

"I don't think my mother . . ."

"Even if you don't expect it, you may not be able to see it, but it'll *happen*. They'll ask if I read a certain book or if I ever been to someplace on a plane, and I gotta say no."

"You've been on an airplane, right?"

"Nope, never once." I kicked the toe of my shoe into Tommy's floor. "See, that's what I mean. It ain't normal to have been on an airplane, Tommy."

"I really gotta think before I open my trap, Viv."

"I think assuming I've done things is better than treating me like I'm some dummy for never having done them," I said. "It makes me feel so small. I know Paris exists, I've seen the film reels, Phyllis writes me letters telling me about her modeling jobs she's had in the last few months. I just never thought I would see it in a million years, and there's no reason to think I will."

"We'll try to go one day."

"Thanks, I guess. But I don't *need* to, you know that, right? I just hate feeling like there's something wrong with me because I grew up in a two-room shack with no running water."

"You just described most people who grew up in the Depression, Viv. I know I'm not usual."

"No, you're one of the most unusual men I've ever met," I laughed.

Tommy smiled. "Is your chicken cooked through?"

"It better be, I ate most of it already."

"Atta girl. What'd you do all afternoon?"

I recounted the ridiculous flick to him, and his eyes started to glaze over. Tommy wasn't one for movies and usually fell asleep in the theater. We ate in silence for the last little while, washed the dishes, took in a program while snoozing on the couch. It felt almost like normal people, not fiancés who were in the mutual business of apprehending crooks and liars. It'd been a while since the nearby church bonged seven PM, and I had places to be by eight.

"I gotta go," I said, pulling myself from underneath Tommy's half-asleep body and all the warmth that came with it. "I called Mr. Bowen's secretary today, and we're having drinks. I need to cultivate some girl talk. Will you call me up a cab while I get my coat on?" Tommy reached behind him to grab the black Bakelite phone and spun the dial, murmuring to the operator while I slipped into the bathroom to comb my hair and touch up before I had to see a girl about a boy.

It was only a few minutes before there was an impatient *beep-beep* from the curb.

"How do they make even the horns sound surly?" I asked, kissing Tommy's cheek.

"A skill of the profession," Tommy said, taking a fiver out of his wallet.

"No need," I said, pushing it away. "I'll just bill it back to you." He swatted me on the rump as I ran down the stairs giggling and into the smelly, warm interior of the cab.

I was heading toward a part of the island I didn't know one bit, but the cabbie got me right in front of a seedy little joint with a flashing neon sign reading "G org 's" no problem.

"I assume this is the joint," I said.

"Order a bottle of beer," he sneered. "No glass. Trust me."

One quick hop across the sidewalk and I was inside, looking for a girl who looked like a banker's secretary among pool sharks and bikers. There was an older woman in the corner in blue jeans and a leather jacket, and I took my chances.

"Are you Peggy?" I strode up to her and asked.

"You're Viv." She motioned to the bench across from her, stuck two fingers in her mouth, and whistled so loud my hands clapped over my ears without a second thought. "Two Genesees! And step on it!" She had a voice like a smoker but her teeth were pearly white.

A man in a flannel shirt with the sleeves ripped off came by with two bottles of beer and two filthy glasses that looked like they'd never seen a scrub in their lives. He popped off the caps with his unwashed thumbs. Peggy waited until he left before she rubbed the mouth of the bottle on her cuff. "Cheers."

I did the same.

"You are not the Peggy I was expecting," I said.

"I get that all the time."

"You work for a bank?"

"I have to pay the bills somehow," she said. "We're not here about me. How can I help with Trevor?"

"Can I tell you in confidence?" I asked.

Peggy held up her finger while she drained her beer. "I hate that bastard Bowen with the passion of a burning star, little girl. I keep secrets."

"We have one small lead, but if it doesn't pan out, then we're up shit creek."

"Well, maybe Trevor wants to stay hidden, little girl."

"Does he have any family aside from his parents?"

"Not that I know of," Peggy said. "But Trevor doesn't treat work like a bar. He doesn't chitchat. Doesn't try to make friends. He does his job. And damn well, little girl."

"Stop it with the 'little girl' bullshit," I finally snarled. "I'm nearly thirty, Peggy. If I can't get some fucking respect at my age, when am I gonna get it?"

"I'm fifty-two," Peggy said, sighing. "The answer is never. But you'll get it from me, Viviana."

"Thank you. So, no family that you know of outside of his parents, no emergency contacts in his personnel file?"

"Thinnest file I've ever seen," Peggy said. "Nothing to even send, really."

"What do you know about him personally?"

"He liked a few things that he'd talk about. He liked going to Grand Central and watching the trains come in. He liked building watches."

"He *built* watches?"

"From the cogs on up," Peggy smiled.

"God, that must give anyone a headache," I said. "If I need a watch, I just steal one."

Peggy nodded toward a particularly sweaty fellow standing by the jukebox. "Bet you can't get Gil's."

"Time me."

I sidled up to Gil and peered over his shoulder at the pages of the jukebox. "'The Cry of the Wild Goose'? Here?" Gil whipped around to look at me and as his arm fell, it hit my right hand. I grabbed his wrist. "Hey! Don't get handsy with me!" I reached up to smack his face, without letting go of his wrist.

"What's the big idea!" His other hand reached up to stop my slap, and I was in like Flynn. Two quick squeezes and the strap on his wrist was unbuckled. "You came over to lean up on me!" He shoved slightly to move me away from him, and I stumbled back, falling harder than he pushed, to slip the watch up my sleeve.

"You big lug, I was just looking at the songs."

"Peggy, come get your girl!" He hollered. "She done lost her mind."

Peggy came up next to me and fished the watch out of my sleeve. "I bet her she couldn't snitch this and she proved me wrong." She tossed the timepiece at her friend, and he reddened.

"Sorry," I shrugged. "I swear I didn't get your wallet, but he might." I nodded at another gent hovering around the music box, looking like a menace and holding a pool cue.

"That's Larry," Gil shrugged. "He tries to get my wallet every week."

"You still owe me fifty dollars," Larry grunted, chalking up his stick.

"What did I tell you?" Gil said through his teeth. "You gonna teach me how you did that, girlie?"

"Not on your life." I curtsied and headed back to the dark corner I shared with Peggy.

She settled down across from me again and whistled for two more beers. "I like you."

"I like you, too," I agreed, rubbing my beer without being instructed.

"I wish I could be more helpful."

"It's fine," I lied. "Did he ever go on vacation? Did he and his parents go away at any time?"

"They wouldn't've had the money," Peggy said. "Never took a dime from Trevor, but they did live with him. They—the parents, that is—were coal workers in Wales before they came here. Lungs completely shot."

"Don't lungers usually move where it's hot and dry?"

"Why do you think Trev was workin' so hard?" Peggy asked. "So if they're anywhere, they mighta caught a train to Phoenix."

"Thanks. I'll check the train ticket sales," I said. "Listen, I need to know . . ."

"I'll tell you anything you want, so long as I have a new job before you testify."

"There's a scam going on, yeah?"

"Quick fingers, quick mind," Peggy said approvingly.

"Bowen's been hiding his trail with fake incompetence, I'm guessing," I said.

"Bad records and a high staff turnover," Peggy said. "He thinks I can't tell."

"You never planned on blowing the whistle?"

"Who's going to listen to an old blue-hair who they think just answers the phone?" Peggy asked. "It has something to do with the stocks they're selling, for how much, and when they're doing it."

"But Trevor has something." It was not a question.

"That's the only thing that explains this whole charade," Peggy said, lighting up a menthol and blowing a smoke ring into the light hanging over the table. "He's a smart cookie. He doesn't need the job, not anymore."

"I spoke to Steve and Bill and—"

"Those clowns?"

"They were nice enough," I said. "Dim. But nice enough. They say they want Trev found just for his sake. And that he's built up a nice nest egg."

"On the level, he did, too," Peggy said. "Unlike some of the other fellas."

"But the kid may not ever show his face again."

"He will when the time is right for him," Peggy said. She took a long drink at her beer and pretended not to be eyeing me up and down. She killed the whole bottle with a gasp and smacked the empty down on the table, letting out a hollow *thunk*. She nodded at my hand. "Next time you come to Alphabet City, leave the ring at home, little girl."

I threw a fiver down on the table for the beers. "I'm leaving with it now, though, you old besom."

Peggy laughed. "Nice show."

Gil and Larry eyed me as I left the bar, and I whistled for a taxi on Avenue A. This wasn't my neck of the woods, but it was worth the trip.

DAY 10

Tuesday, January 9th, 1951

There was a light knocking on my door first thing in the morning. The noise I made upon waking was particularly unladylike, but there was no one in the house who hadn't witnessed worse from me, so I flopped out of my warm sheets to open the door.

"Viviana, I'm sorry to wake you," Dottie said. Her eyes were a little wild. "Do you have any stamps?"

"At the office," I said.

"That's what Betty said as well." Dottie was down in the dumps.

"I can take whatever you want to mail and mail it myself after I hit it with postage," I assured her. "It's no big deal."

"Oh, thank you, that would be so kind. I just don't have time to stop off at the post office before school. I bought my sister a series of postcards at the zoo, and I'm sure her children will just love them." She folded the cardboard into my hands and checked her dinky, scratched-up watch. "I'm off. Thank you again!" She skipped down the stairs and I slipped the cards into my bag for later.

The one good thing about the third floor was that I did have my own bathroom, but after Dottie, Betty, Mrs. K, *and* Oleks finished their ablutions, there was really only enough left in the boiler for a five-minute shower, which I tried to make as luxuriant and relaxing as I could. I still had a sliver of lavender soap left over from summer, and the scent filled the whole upstairs and made it smell like heaven. I'd made a mental note to write my own letter to Paris and the girl who gave me the soap, to catch up with Phyllis to see how everything was going.

I didn't feel like another breakfast of cold toast, so I ran out and picked up three *sfogliatelle* from the nearby Italian bakery en route to Tommy's. Betty was already there with the door unlocked and the percolator percolating.

"Catch," I said, and tossed the bag of pastries at my secretary. "Dottie left me her mail. Could you stamp it and give it to the mailman when he comes up?"

"Of course!" Betty grabbed the cards and set to licking the one cent stamps. "This one with the penguins is adorable." She handed me the card.

"Too bad they stink something awful," I said. "They are plenty cute."

"So charming in their formal wear," Betty giggled.

I picked up each photograph as Betty stamped them. "They've got lions . . ."

"You can hear 'em sometimes," Betty admitted.

"Tigers?"

"Maybe it's the tigers."

"And . . . oh my God!"

"What?" Betty shrieked.

"Get me the file on the missing banker!"

Betty tripped over the wastepaper basket and almost ate the floor on her way to the filing cabinet. "Viviana, you can't yell like that!"

"You will too when I show you!"

Betty emerged with the manila folder and I flipped it open, yanking out the clue we'd pulled from the overstuffed mailbox. "Put that in your pipe and smoke it, Betts."

Side by side were two identical photographs of a stone eagle. And since I knew Dottie got hers when she was at the Central Park Zoo with Rocío, I knew exactly where to meet Trevor Penhaligon at one o'clock, as soon as I could fit him into my schedule.

"Dottie's going to flip her wig when you tell her," Betty said, admiring the card I snitched from Trevor's mailbox. "The back says the sender will be there every day at one o'clock."

"I've got a few hours until the meeting time," I said, checking my watch. "I gotta go make some calls. Just check off a few boxes."

I flopped down at my desk in the back office and yanked up the receiver. A quick spin of the dial got me the operator. Even though I knew better, in my mind I was always connected to the same girl, whose job it was to help me to the bottom of the case. Today, my girl was trying on a Queens accent instead of her usual Brooklyn.

"Operator," she started. "How may I connect your call?"

"Grand Central ticketing office, please."

"Hold on."

She rang for a few seconds before connecting back in. "This always takes a while. Give me a minute."

"Thanks for your patience." My regard got a grunt and she went back to ringing until a voice picked up.

"Terminal."

"Hi, I'm trying to find out if my cousin managed to catch his train to Phoenix last week," I fibbed. "I haven't heard from him in ages, and I'm starting to get nervous."

"We're not allowed to give out that kind of information, ma'am."

I hiccupped a fake sob. "Oh, but he's in such terrible health! My mother's going to lose her absolute *marbles* if I can't find him!"

The man on the other end of the line sighed. "Hold on. What's the name?"

"Trevor Penhaligon."

"You're gonna have to spell that."

"Papa-Echo-November-Hotel-Alpha-Lima-India-Golf-Oscar-November."

"*Jesus.*"

"It's Welsh."

"I don't care. Gimme a minute." The line went quiet, and I started to hum "Here Comes Santa Claus" to fill the space. It'd been two weeks since Christmas but it was the only song playing in my head. It was the world's most ridiculous song—sure, *Santa* knows we're all God's children, but it didn't make everything right. I had a murderer on the loose and a whole bunch of blackmail on my plate to solve. Santa could stand to bring everyone just a little bit more kindness, this day and age.

I had to stop my singing when I heard heavy breathing come back on the other end of the line. "I checked back as far as I wanted to, until I lost patience," the man grunted. "Nothing under that name or even close to it. But he could've bought tickets in cash on the train."

"Thanks again." I hung up and spun my operator again.

"How may I direct your call?"

"Penn Station ticketing office please."

The whole charade was repeating, down to the results.

"Well, *damnit*," I spat into the office. Betty came in to check on me.

"Whatsit doing?"

"Jack nothing," I said. "One of the missing banker's coworkers said to me that if he and the family had skittered off anywhere, they would've gone to Arizona. Neither train station ticket office has a record of them moving out. But that's not saying a whole lot."

"You know what Dottie says . . . ," Betty started.

"Yeah, yeah. Even closing a line of inquiry helps with a mystery, but I'd like one to stay the hell open for once." I was pouting. "By the state of their mailbox, they didn't leave a forwarding address with the Post Office. No record of train tickets to their most likely destination, and I can't exactly ask Grand Central or Penn Station to check ticket sales for every possible train stop in America."

"Or Canada or Mexico," Betty added helpfully.

"The fellas at the office weren't keen on being helpful, either."

"You're just narrowing down to the solution," Betty said. "Like a doctor making a diagnosis. You start with the most obvious and rule things out."

"We're ruling ourselves to a Hail Mary of meeting someone at a random place in the city we just narrowed down to ten minutes ago."

"But it's still something!" Betty was full of fightin' spirit.

"Well, fine. On to the next one. What's that library info number again?"

Betty spun it on the rotary and handed me the receiver.

"New York Public Library," a soft voice said over the line.

"Hi, I was just wondering—does New York City have a statue or monument to the Scottish poet, Robert Burns, anywhere?"

"Of course!" The woman got chipper without even taking a pause to look up the information.

"Could you . . . tell me where it is?"

"Oh yes. Naturally. The east side of Central Park, about on parallel with 67th Street. It's called the Literary Walk. Did you know that Robert Burns is the national poet of Scotland and—"

"Wonderful, thank you so much." I hung up on the librarian but felt a little bad about it. I wasn't really in the state of mind for a history lesson, but she seemed very excited.

"Looks like I'm going back to the park for most of today, Betts." I put my warm clothes back on and opened the kitty at the office for cab fare, but there were only a few loose quarters sliding around in the tin.

I should've taken that fiver from Tommy after all.

"Rats. Looks like I'm hoofing it. Hopefully we'll catch this fool who's harassing Mr. Floristan soon. And if Tommy shows his ugly mug by noon, tell him I'll meet him at the zoo. If he's not here by noon, call his house, and if that doesn't work . . . well, I'll try to do it all by my lonesome."

"Got it, Boss." Betty sat down with her pastry and began munching. "This isn't bad."

"Glad you like it! I'll report back, with or without ol' Tommy boy, after lunch."

I swear up and down, I must've walked the equivalent of the equator this week, with all the trekking I was doing for these damn cases. I rewarded myself with a pretzel and kept my sights on the far side of the park. Again.

I approached the park by its southern border along 59th Street and once again spied the awning of the Plaza taunting me from down the sidewalk. I could only daydream about what it would feel like to wake up in a hot hotel room, in an enormous king-sized bed. You'd have to be rich as a banker to get that experience, and I felt a little zip of electricity burn through my toes as I tried to convince myself I was wrong.

But curiosity got the better of me.

I slipped into the marble foyer of the hotel and approached a desk clerk.

"Excuse me, sir," I whispered, like I was in a church and not a bustling, big city hotel. "Could you tell me if you happen to have guests here by the last name Penhaligon? Might've come by around New Year's, or a few days after."

The man didn't say anything but went to his ledger book and flipped through the handwritten pages. He looked up and shook his head.

"Thanks anyway."

I was getting real tired of the winter wonderland splendor, wet socks, and stiff wind by the time I made my way north through the park and spotted a little red package tucked *just so* at the base of the monument, underneath Burns's cloak and what I think was meant to be a scroll of parchment, even though I think they were just using regular paper in the 1800s.

"How is no one *stealing* these godforsaken things?" I asked the wind. I reconned my surroundings, saw no cops, and clambered up a marble pedestal for what I hoped would be the last time this week. The leather soles of my snow boots slid on the slick and frozen stone and I whacked my cheek into the edge of the monument, right by Rabbie Burns's tootsies.

"I'm really starting to hate you all," I said to the statue. He remained stoic. "Never gonna buy one of your books now, I tell you what."

My cheek smarting, this time I decided just to hop and make a snatch at the small red box. I'm above average in the height department—no one would dare call me petite, I'd say—but it took more than a few squatting high-jumps before I worked up the technique and altitude I needed to lay my hands on that loud and garish paper. Everything on me, from the toes on up, was now frozen and hurting from the wind or burning and hurting from my athletic pursuits or thudding and hurting from my smacking it into a two-ton piece of ice-cold, solid rock. I shoved the stupid little box into my purse and hightailed it out of Central Park, my feet leading me away from the soggy asphalt and right into a diner just outside the boundaries. It was a fancy joint that smelled less like frying onions and more like coffee and vanilla, but I didn't care. I needed to thaw and collect my thoughts before I scurried back to the zoo to see if someone—anyone—was still spending his lunch hour there.

I fell onto the swivel stool at the counter and it felt like it was the first time I'd been *really* alone—and not too distracted by the rocky road of my relationship—to collect my thoughts on all the cases since New Year's. Not that I don't appreciate all the time I spend with Tommy and Betty, but sometimes a girl just has to sit with her own brain and see what comes from her own thoughts.

Something was still fishy with every single one of our cases, that was for sure. I didn't have the solution for any of 'em, but I felt like Trevor Penhaligon was going to wrap up the soonest. Whoever drove him out of town had invited him to a meeting down at the zoo, and something was as rotten as elephant shit with what was happening to that poor boy. I had a feeling that whatever was in that little red box I had just nabbed from Rabbie Burns was going to need a woman smarter than me to figure it out, and I sent a silent prayer to whoever or whatever was listening to thank them for delivering Rocío to me and Dottie. I knew I was going to have to stalk poor Rachel one more time to figure out what Morty's whole deal was, and I wanted to spit on the ground about it, but one quick glance at the floor of my diner showed it was marble tiles and they wouldn't take too kindly to me befouling 'em with my feelings.

And then there was poor old Henrik Fiskar.

This new year of 1951 was shaping up to be the real pits. I don't think Tommy and I had ever been that mad at each other before, but I had to remind myself over and over—just like Dottie and Betty had been reminding me for the past week—that Tommy and my relationship had changed, and there was no going back to the way it was, with us being easy-breezy friends and me solving as many of his problems as I could between the hours of nine and five. Not that that was the relationship Tommy had wanted for us, unbeknownst to me, for the last half a decade, but it was hard for me to really get my bearings in this new normal. Not that this was a bad normal.

Everything felt like bumper cars lately, and I needed a break.

But after three cups of steaming hot brew, I could feel all my extremities again and my nose had stopped leaking, so it was time to carry on.

I threw a few nickels down on the counter for my coffee and tip and exited the way I had come in—back onto the sidewalk, where I was hit with a blast of wind so cold and so forceful my curses were lost to the ether.

The light changed and I stayed in the pack crossing 5th Avenue, fixing my eyes on the fencing to the zoo. The stench was already hitting me, and I slowed down, observing the herd of people now making their way to the park. One of these fellas could be our mysterious person, out to get Trevor Penhaligon, and I fell to the rear to make sure I could keep everyone in my line of sight. Out of the corner of my right eye, I saw what I knew to be a yellow cab, careening southward down the long street, not even tapping the brakes, running and gunning to make it through the intersection as soon as the light turned green, even though I knew if I kept my current pace, I'd still be in the street when he got here.

This cabbie had no intention of stopping for pedestrians.

I put on the jets and sprinted to get out of the giant car's way, splashing my boot square into a sloshing puddle, and felt my ankle wrench. Knees, elbows, hands, and face hit sidewalk, but my body was fully out of the way of the chromed bumpers of the yellow cab. All he could do was splash me with the filthy muck from the puddle that still trapped the toe of my snow boots. Insult to injury—I was now covered with God knows what from the runoff of a Manhattan gutter, bleeding from at least three surfaces, and in what I could only describe as a God damn ton of pain.

I was not getting off the sidewalk under my own power, and thankfully, a couple of meaty hands got under my armpits and wrenched me upwards.

"Betty told me to meet you," Tommy said. "We're going home."

"But the one o'clock!"

"He's been doin' it every day for a week, Dollface, one more day won't kill him."

"I'm going to write a mean letter to Impellitteri about this," I said through a fat lip. I had snot running down my face and I wanted to wipe it with my mitten, but that mitten was covered with filth. I was fresh out of dignity and frozen to the bone.

"The mayor doesn't give two shits about the sidewalk, Viv." Tommy leaned me against a mailbox and left to go stand at the curb. I closed my eyes to concentrate on staying vertical while I heard his signature whistle. A few more minutes of, well, not *silence*, but nothing that sounded like a cab pulling to the curb and asking "Where to?", Tommy let out another whistle and a robust "Tax-EEEEEEEE!" And still nothing doing.

"We might have to hoof it, Viv," he said, taking my arm and throwing it over his shoulder to leverage me into a stand. "The cops are gonna think I gave you a five-finger explanation in a dust-up, I swear it."

"And then what? Shoved me into a damn latrine? No, if anyone stops us out of civic concern, they'll believe I took a spill, it's fine."

"What happened?"

"Cabbie. Had to sprint to not get hit."

"Think it was one of last summer's goons?"

"Nah, we're too far afield for that, and I think Lawson got all of them last year, anyhow."

"I spoke to him last night."

"My former beau?"

"No, Lawson," Tommy explained, hitching me up and leading me down the asphalt pathway in the park to the west side. "Joe's at the YMCA, and the police know he has nothing to do with our stiff from New Year's."

"Henry."

"Henry. Sure."

"We need to go check out that apartment."

"*We* aren't doing anything. I'm depositing you at the landlady's and then *I'll* go stake out the apartment."

"You can't leave me and do it by yourself!"

"I did it by myself for a full decade, Dollface. I'll be fine."

"I don't mean physically, I mean it's my case too, you bozo."

"You can take a breather. You can't even walk."

"Damn. Damn, damn, damn, damn, *damn*."

"Sorry, Dollface, you're human and sometimes humans get hurt."

"But it's not real hurt, like when you get punched or knifed. It's just a stupid mistake."

"Do you know how many of my shiners over the years have been from me just walking into something in the dark?" Tommy laughed. "Forgive yourself, it's just basic human frailty."

We thumped and grunted as far as we could and made it to Columbus Circle, where there was usually a line of cabs waiting to take the crowd of sightseers back to their Times Square hotels. Today, there was just one, sitting alone like a sad little duck on a pond of dirty snow. Tommy opened the back door and dumped me unceremoniously inside, handing the cabbie a bill and giving him Mrs. K's address.

"I'm just gonna go check on that apartment," Tommy said. "Tell Lana to call a doctor, on me."

"But . . ." The car door slammed before I could make another case to go with him to the apartment at Bleecker and MacDougal.

"How far *is* it to Bleecker Street, anyhow?" I asked the driver.

"Over three miles, sweet cheeks."

"Oh."

The cabbie pulled up in front of Mrs. K's brownstone and pulled the meter. "You can keep whatever's left as a tip if you help me out of the car and up the stairs," I said.

"Sure, sweet cheeks." He threw it in park and lumbered out of his seat with a heavy amount of groaning.

"You okay?"

"Do you know how hard it is on your back to sit for twelve hours a day in the same busted-up chair?" he growled. "What I wouldn't give for a job that had me upright."

"I don't, but the way you're stooping, it must be awful. Sorry to ask for your help."

"I appreciate the opportunity to walk more than a few feet." He was about my height or a little shorter, a little Mediterranean meatball of a man with a big push broom mustache. We got up the first step to the stoop and I stopped to get out my keys and take a breather. "Your luck you live on the third floor, huh."

"I do, actually."

"I ain't helping you up there."

"No, you won't." Oleks had heard the commotion on the front porch and opened the door. "I will."

"He's a little young for you, sweet cheeks." The cabbie tipped his hat and beat feet back to his car, pulling away from the curb with a crunch of ice and hightailing it back to a major avenue in order to scare up another fare.

"What happened this time?" Oleks said, bending down, throwing his arm behind my knees, and swooping me off my feet. He carried me up the last few steps and into the house. He didn't seem to mind or notice that his sweater was siphoning up all the damp filth I was soaked with.

"I almost got hit by a cab, twisted my ankle, then fell into the gutter."

"Well, you did a great job of it. You're caked in blood. I'm gonna go get her." He put me down in my favorite spot at the dining table, and I hoisted my bum foot onto Betty's chair.

I hollered after him as he started going down to the basement. "Tommy says to call a doctor and he'll foot the bill."

"Okay, but I'm still *getting* her." Oleks's voice cracked ever so slightly, and I knew that in his mind, no one was going to solve the problem better than his mom.

Within no time flat, Mrs. K was bustling up the stairs with an old, red sewing kit.

"I don't need stitches."

"That's bandages and iodine and stuff," Oleks said. "The blue one is for sewing."

"Oh."

"Go upstairs and get her robe," Mrs. K commanded her son.

"Is it okay if I go in your room?" he asked.

"Of course," I told him. He bounded up the two flights.

"While he is gone, take off that filth."

I did as I was instructed, down to my stockings and slip. Oleks thumped back downstairs, just to stand in the hallway and thrust his arm through the doorway with my robe in his hand. "Here, Ma!"

She stood up and grabbed it, and Oleks came back in once I was decent. "I'll take all this down to the laundry." It wasn't until my clothing was out of the room that I realized how bad it stank.

"I should just *bathe* in iodine, huh?" My hands and knees looked like chopped meat.

"It could not hurt." Mrs. K dabbed at all my cuts and bruises. Oleks was back upstairs and she sent him right back down. "Get her ice for the eye."

"That was from a statue," I said. "The case that comes with puzzles, the thief hides things on statues around the city, but what he leaves is hard to reach."

Mrs. Kovalenko raised an eyebrow at me. "What is today's puzzle for Dottie's friend?"

"It's in my purse. Toss it to me?" She put down wads of bloody gauze and heaved my purse in my direction. I pulled out the red box and tore off the wrapping. Inside was another wooden chest with not a single clasp or hinge.

"Another one of those physical puzzles," I said. I shook the box and something inside made a clacking noise. "The last one just had paper inside, but this sounds more solid."

"Give it to my boy, he will get it."

"Without taking a hammer to it?" I asked.

"I did not say that." Mrs. Kovalenko laughed.

"Let me have a go at it for a day, then he can do whatever he wants." I slipped the object back into my purse

"Of course." Most of my extremities were swathed in bandages at this point. "I will go get you some tea. And call Betty at your office to tell her you are all fine."

"Thanks, Mrs. K."

I was alone for a few minutes before the phone rang, and there was no way my busted butt was getting up *or* down a flight of stairs to answer it. I would have to wait for a report from either Kovalenko, and the seconds ticked by too slowly for me to stay calm.

It was Oleks who made it upstairs first.

"Here. I know it's cold, but it'll help." The bag of ice stung my cheekbone more than the marble had in the first place.

"Tommy usually puts a steak on it." Oleks made a puss when I said his name. "You know what? Just tell me what's eating you already."

"Do you know where he wants us to move?"

"Tommy doesn't want you to move anywhere."

"Not him, *miy dyad'ko.* Sorry. Wrong language. Uncle Sergiy. He's been scouting for a little place for mom in Oyster Bay Cove."

"That's some pretty pricey real estate there, hon."

"Don't I know it! I'm not meant to be in places like that. I'll be arrested as soon as I step foot on someone's perfect, green lawn."

"I take it you've said something to your mother?"

"Yeah, *and* to Uncle. Even though I've lived in this house since Dad died, they seem to think it's this pigsty I should be happy to leave. But *look* at it." Oleks threw open his hands as if he'd just walked into Buckingham Palace.

Mrs. K's had just been Mrs. K's for as long as I had lived here, but I squinted to take in the details. I had no idea when it was built, but when it was, someone had paid attention to the details. The newel post of the banister was carved and ornate, kept to a spotless polish by countless hands and Mrs. K's swiftness with a dust rag. The cornice above the door to the dining room was just as fancy, two little peaks of wood meeting at what I realized now was a hand-carved pineapple. The tiles around the edge of the foyer might've been missing in a few places, but the pattern was complex and colorful. The plaster on the ceiling was chipping a bit in the middle of every room, but there was crown molding underneath forty layers of paint that might've been grand at some point in the not-too-distant past.

"And all they're going to do is turn this into four identical, dinky little apartments," Oleks said.

"Have you been out to Oyster Bay?" I asked. "How do you know you won't like it?"

"I'm sure it's fine," Oleks shrugged. "But it isn't here."

The boy shut his trap as we heard his mom come up through the basement door.

"Pretty girl, we will wrap your ankle," she said, coming at me with a long Ace bandage and some safety pins. "I could not get the doctor to come and visit, but this is on his advice."

"Thanks, Mrs. K. It's already all starting to feel better," I fibbed. "I don't suppose you got any aspirin?"

"We do," Oleks said, poking through the first-aid kit and coming up short. "I think it's in my room. I'll get it." He went back downstairs for the umpteenth time, and I turned to address Mrs. K.

"Can't he just stay here?" I asked.

"If he can come up with seventy-five dollars a month in rent," Mrs. K shrugged.

"That's not that much," I said. "I paid twenty a week for that windowless room."

"And I also cooked your meals, did your laundry, and you do not pay extra for electricity, water, or gas."

"When you put it like that, why aren't you charging us more?"

"I ask Sergiy this question often."

"Would you like me and Betty to take him out there one day?" I asked. "Look at the town with a younger set of eyes?"

"If you think it will help." Mrs. K was ambivalent. "If he works and pays rent, he may stay in his home. If he does not, he comes with me. Those are his choices."

"Poor kid."

"How old were you when you arrived here, pretty girl?"

"Two years younger than Oleks."

"The case. It is rested." She yanked on the bandage to put pressure on my swollen ankle. "Stay here. Do not try to go upstairs."

"Could you call the office and tell Betty to come home?" I asked.

"It is already five o'clock," Mrs. K said, looking at her watch. "She will be home soon."

"This really is a beautiful building, though."

"It has a lot of memories," she said, standing up. "Though you will understand not all of them are pleasant. I must go start dinner."

NIGHT 10

Tommy, Betty, Dottie, and Rocío all showed up within the hour and congregated around the large dining table, waiting for the surprise of house dinner. There was some immediate oohing and aahing over my injuries, but by and large, they left me to throb and seethe in the chair before doing what they always do when they get home from work.

Tommy ran up two flights of stairs to use our facilities and was back at the table in no time flat in his favorite flannel slacks and his cardigan with leather patches on his elbows, looking like a college professor who could talk at length about Shakespeare.

Betty was up the stairs and back down in a flash, ditching her work clothes for her favorite winter housecoat and slippers. A new pulp novel was half sticking out of her pocket, like she intended to read at the table. From the looks of the cover it was new, but same ol' same ol'. There was a girl wearing a nightie and a man behind her wrapped his long fingers around her collar bone. I said a little prayer that Betty got out of the private investigator business before murder lost its entertainment value, or else I had no idea what she was going to read at night.

Dottie stayed in her tweedy uniform from school—everything short of her oxfords, which she'd replaced with her house shoes—but Rocío had managed to find time to change in between lessons and dinner plans, and was seated at our table in dark blue jeans, a red and white flannel shirt tied at her narrow waist, and a red kerchief tied up in her hair. She looked like a glamorous, Puerto Rican Rosie the Riveter.

"Gotta be a ham," Tommy said, taking a deep sniff.

"Steak," Rocío challenged him. "And potatoes. There's definitely potatoes."

"Bet a dollar?" Tommy goaded.

"You're on." They both reached into their back pockets, took out a billfold, and threw their bucks into the middle of the polished wood and grinned.

"Tommy, go grab my bag for me?" I asked.

"You have to say what you think dinner is first," he said, getting up. "That's the rules of the wager."

"I'm not betting, I know it's meat loaf, mashed potatoes, gravy, and green beans," I said. "But I still need my purse. I want to show you the latest clue from the cipher case."

"Oh, you found it?" Betty squealed.

"It's how I got this," I said, pointing at my bruised face. As soon as my purse was in my lap, I broke out my compact to assess the damage for the first time since coming home. I was puffy but not deeply bruised, thank the Lord. "Those monuments are tall, and I had to take a flying leap at it to reach the thing."

"You're supposed to land on your feet, not your face," Oleks said, emerging upstairs with a huge tray of tableware, glasses, and silverware, as usual. He left the tray, and Betty and Dottie stood to divvy up the utensils to each place at the table.

"Or your ass," Tommy said. "Like you did over the summer."

"Thanks for the advice, boys. The rest of this is from taking that spill on the sidewalk. But here," I tossed the clue at Tommy who nearly fumbled it into the window. "Take a peek."

"There's no opening." He tossed it to Rocío, who plucked it neatly out of the air.

"My uncle used to make these," Dottie said, admiring the shining wood of the box. "They're their own kind of puzzle. Not ciphers, but there are ways to pull and put pressure on the pieces to make the whole thing spring open."

"Betty opened the last one," I said. "Said the hospital gave puzzles like this to people with head injuries."

"They're hard enough to master if you haven't been clocked in the melon," she told everyone. "Making hurt people do this stuff can be really mean, even if I do know what the doctors are getting at."

"You want to take this one?" Rocío said, handing over the clue to Dottie. "I'm much better with linguistic ciphers."

"I shall do my best. But later." Dottie turned around and placed the clue on the buffet behind her. "How are the other cases?"

"I think we cracked the code on the missing banker, thanks to you," I said. "Your postcards from the zoo. One matched the one we found in the missing banker's mailbox. It's one of the giant eagle statues."

Dottie nodded. "By the sea lion pool. They're really quite imposing."

"Why would you put enormous concrete birds next to the seals?" Tommy asked.

"Sea lions," Dottie corrected and slapped her hands over her mouth.

"They're different animals," Rocío said. "And so are teachers. We can't not tell you if you're wrong about things. Bad habit."

"I don't mind," Tommy said. "I have three sisters, I'm used to being corrected. What's the difference?"

"There are a few," Dottie lectured. "Size, initially. Sea lions are rather large, though some seal species can also weigh more than a ton, but those are rarely kept in captivity. Sea lions also have external ear flaps on the side of their heads."

"Seals don't have ears?" Betty asked.

"They do, but seals don't have anything on their heads to tell you where their ears are. Sea lions have ear flaps, like we do," Rocío said, pushing her own ears forward in demonstration.

"What else?" I asked.

"Seals have more of an undulating locomotion on land," Dottie said.

"They scoot like slugs," Rocío translated, stretching her body out as long as she could before contracting back on herself.

"And sea lions can bend their back flippers and do more of a shuffling walk on land," Dottie explained, wobbling back and forth in her chair in an excellent imitation of a beast.

"How do you know all this stuff?" Betty asked.

"Usually, a student is the one who tells you," Dottie said. "Children become . . . somewhat obsessive over topics at times, and it's difficult to keep them on task."

"You mean it's hard to make a kid shut up," Tommy said.

". . . Yes." Rocío laughed.

"So what are walruses?" Betty asked, miming tusks with her two index fingers.

"Walruses," Dottie shrugged.

"So, anyway, we'll be hanging out with the sea lions tomorrow afternoon," I said. "To see whoever we can see who might've sent the missing Penhaligons a cryptic postcard."

"What did it say?" Rocío asked.

"Not much," Betty responded.

"That someone would be at a location—presumably the sea lion pool—every day at one PM," I explained.

"How do you know whoever sent it isn't waiting to whack you?" Rocío asked.

"Eh, now that we know where it is, it's too public and there's too many kids," Tommy said. "If they'd said, 'Meet us down under the Manhattan Bridge,' then we'd know they were up to something violent."

"And if they want to take you to a place more private?" Dottie asked.

"Scream bloody murder," I said. "They're still not going to shoot you in front of kindergartners looking at the seals."

"Sea lions," everyone corrected.

Oleks came back upstairs, followed by his mother, carrying the exact array of dishes I had predicted.

"Did she tell you?" Tommy asked, picking back up his dollar, and handing Rocío hers. "While she was fixing up your ankle?"

"No, but it's the second Tuesday of the month," I explained. "Barring special occasions, the second Tuesday of every month is meat loaf night. So is the fourth Thursday."

Mrs. K beamed at me. "Pretty girl *and* brilliant."

"Even I didn't realize that," said Oleks, chopping off a quarter of the meat loaf just for himself.

"We all have our patterns," I said. "Dottie sharpens her pencils after she washes her face but before she brushes her teeth. Betty buys new nail files once a month, sometime between the seventeenth and twenty-first, and Oleks does too many loads of laundry when he's got a science test coming up."

"It's very calming," he said with a shrug.

"You're gonna make a hell of a husband one day, kid," Rocío winked. "If you clean when you're nervous."

"People are just interesting," I reasoned. "It's why I know that Rachel—Morty's Rachel, who we're following—isn't up to no good."

"She'll be back out again on Thursday," Tommy said. "She has lunch at the Rainbow Room."

"Fancy!" Betty squealed.

"You'll come with me to shadow her," I said. "I'm not going to that place alone."

"Not that I'm complaining about the ritzy lunch, but would it kill someone to go to an automat?" Betty asked. "You're not the only one who gets self-conscious at the nice joints, Viv."

"So that's where we stand on the paying cases, at least," I said, ticking them off on my fingers. "Mr. Floristan's next step is in that infernal puzzle box, Morty's Rachel gets trailed again the day after tomorrow, tomorrow we hopefully get a lead on Trevor Penhaligon."

"And then there's the murder from New Year's," Tommy said. "I went to that apartment today."

"Did you see this Frankie character?" I asked.

"I did."

"Anything doing?"

"She was in a rush, so I figured we'd swing by in the morning," Tommy said.

"And catch her off guard?"

"No one expects a breakfast meeting," Tommy said, taking a bite of green beans.

"Do you think we're going to get the bastard that did this?" I asked.

"God, I hope you do," Betty said. "I don't love the idea of a murderer roaming the streets."

"This seemed like a pretty deliberate hit job," Tommy said.

"That's not as soothing as you think it is, ol' Tommy boy," I said.

"Do we want to let Detective Lawson know about any of this?" Betty asked.

"Nah," Tommy said, throwing down his napkin. "They'll only get in our way. Thank you for another lovely evening, everyone. I'm going home to catch some shut-eye."

I followed Tommy to get his coat, hobbling the whole way, just to prove I could get up and get around. I could tell everyone wanted to stop me, but no one said a word.

"If this case goes on any longer, I'm going to lose steam. We can't check out every dock worker in the tri-state area."

"I don't like this bird we're seeing tomorrow," Tommy growled. "And you won't either. I didn't want to say it in front

202 of everyone, but she's some rotten business. Careless, mean. You

of everyone, but she's some rotten business. Careless, mean. You know the type. You remember the address?"

I nodded and Tommy put on his hat. "Bright and early, Doll-face. See you there at five sharp."

He kissed me on the cheek and disappeared into the night, whistling "The Tennessee Waltz" into the cold air.

DAY 11

Wednesday, January 10th, 1951

My tinny little alarm clock was screaming its bells off long before the sun even threatened to rise, my hand instinctively knocking it to the floor to kill it and to keep the racket from waking my downstairs neighbors. There was no way that Dottie or Mrs. K were up and shuffling around this early, and my only solace when peeling back my covers was that I'd have first crack at the contents of the water heater. The shower head was working overtime to steam up my third-floor apartment, but the hot water was having a healing effect on all my bruises from yesterday. I shuffled into two sweaters and a cardigan before putting on my overcoat and shoving my chignon into the wooliest hat I could find.

I knew that the streets would be dead as a doornail, so I didn't even bother glancing around for a cab before immediately hooking a right and heading south toward the Village. I was reminded of one of my last jaunts this a-ways, in the heat of the summer, which was a hell of a sweaty endeavor, and I had to admit, I didn't know which extreme I preferred. I think I just preferred the month of May.

But the city isn't ever *really* dead, and a quarter to five in the morning just entertains a whole different type of people than I'm used to seeing closer to nine o'clock. The rats are bigger in the dawn, I tell you, and the garbage men in their open-backed, white trucks moved faster than the vermin as they picked up clanging, stinking, sticky, tin dustbin after dustbin.

The closer I got to the Village, the more people I saw up who clearly hadn't yet been down. I knew it was the neighborhood of poets and playwrights, but it also looked to be the neighborhood of folks who had something to prove to their own livers. A man was dangling off his fire escape at the waist, dressed in a white terrycloth bathrobe and nothing else.

"Behold!" he shouted, raising a wine bottle to the sky. "Behold the grandeur of dawn and the endless glory of creation! I am your king and conqueror! Let me drink your life's very blood!"

"Is that . . . Tennyson?" I asked, name checking the only poet I could recall from ninth grade English, even though it felt very wrong.

"Thelonious!"

"His stuff don't got words!" I shouted back.

"You aren't"—he paused, to expel a cascading stream of vomit onto the windowsill of his downstairs neighbor—"listening *sufficiently*."

This interrogation couldn't be over soon enough.

It was only another few minutes of schlepping til I found the corner of Bleecker and MacDougal and spotted Tommy in his blackest overcoat and darkest hat lurking outside the building.

"Do we buzz?" I asked, and he jumped like I'd stuck him with a hot poker.

"Nah." He pulled out a thin, flat piece of metal the size of Dottie's library card. "They don't have a deadbolt. I can slip it." In no time flat, he managed to push back the latch of the door, and we were inside.

"Isn't any warmer in here," I said, my voice echoing around the tiled vestibule next to the mailboxes. It stank like a public restroom. There was a pile of rags at the far end of the hallway, between two apartment doors. It shifted slightly and revealed itself to be a person as it scratched itself and settled back down into sleep. Whoever it was looked warm enough and was definitely better off than the poet on the fire escape. Though it was long before the sun would think about rising, the building bustled with the sound of clanging pipes, alarm clocks, and voices. Extremely loud voices, none of them discernible as they echoed through the derelict building.

"That's the Village for you," Tommy said, scrutinizing the names on the boxes, squinting to concentrate and tune out the din. "Landlords probably sold the pipes for scrap during the war and never remembered to fix it. Here we go—apartment 2A." He led the way to the stairs.

"Tommy, is Mrs. K right? Is the city getting worse?"

"Nah," Tommy said. "Same people everywhere, just like always. The Depression just never ended for a *lot* more people than they'd like us to think. Now shush. We're *sleuthing*."

We approached the front apartment on the second floor and the door was wide open. A crystal-clear soprano was coming from inside the room and I could finally tell what one of the voices in the vestibule was saying.

"Something-something-something-something *reveille! He's the Boogie-Woogie Bugle Boy of Company B!*" A pile of heavy things of unknown type tumbled to the floor. "Oh, whoops!"

The girl was *probably* stoned, and you could *probably* hear her shouting on Mars.

Tommy turned to me with his eyes wide. It was clear to me that he'd expected to catch this girl off guard and question her right out of slumber. I took the front position and toed open the door farther. Tommy pulled at my coat to hold me back, but I advanced. With a limp, but it was advancement all the same.

"Frankie?" I asked. "It's Viv and Tommy. We came to ask you some questions about Henry?" I walked in through the door, craning my neck to find our screwball chanteuse. And to see if she had any company.

"Hiiiiiii!" A familiar-looking broad threw herself at me and gave me a big hug. She was wearing a silk nightgown, one heeled evening shoe, and a knee-length chinchilla. The studio apartment was empty of other human beings, but chock full of garbage. A sofa was set up under the window, and a full-size mattress was on the floor next to the tiny gas stove with only two burners. The door of it was held on with wire. A giant, claw-foot tub was surrounded by a ragged shower curtain and stank like mold. There were red scarves over every lamp. The entire apartment looked like it held a depressed and slovenly genie who had never thought to conjure up a bottle of Lysol.

"Hi, Frankie." I pried her off of me. "Glad to see you're up."

"This lug said you were coming to see me today," she said, flirtatiously punching Tommy in the shoulder. "But he never said when, so I stayed up all night!"

"That's . . . commitment," I said.

"Boy, am I glad you didn't want a lunch meeting. Hoo-weee!"

"We'd never do that to you, honey." I scanned the apartment real fast, looking for a distraction, and my eyes settled on a stovetop percolator. "Hon, can I make you a cup of coffee? Why don't you sit down on that davenport right there and I'll take care of it all."

"Smart move, sweetie!" Frankie flung herself at the sofa and rested her one shod foot on the back of the couch, all but flashing us her full nether region. She snuggled down into her fur, pulled a pack of Old Gold cigarettes from the pocket, grasped one with long, dainty, shell-pink nails, and lit it with a gold lighter. "God, I just haven't been myself since Henry. I miss that boy!"

Tommy leaned against the window case, closer to Frankie's top half, and peered out over the front entrance. "No new roommates lined up?"

"Couldn't possibly," the girl said, her matching pink lipstick leaving faint stains on the tip of the cig. "I loved him just *that* much."

I flipped over the percolator to find what looked like two weeks' worth of grounds stuck to the filter. It took all my strength not to gag. But I had promised coffee and coffee I would deliver, so I dumped the moldy brown crust into a bowl and set to scrubbing, all while peppering our girl with questions.

"You really didn't get a wink?" I asked.

"Not a one, but I was out until almost four," she admitted. "What's another few hours after call time? My record is a full thirty-six hours. I thought some days Henry was going to tie me to the bed to get me to sleep!"

Tommy raised his eyebrow.

"That's a hell of a marathon," I said. "I don't know of any places in Chelsea open to the small hours. Where'd you go?"

"The Turn Out, of course," she said, taking a heavy drag, stubbing out the half-burnt smoke into the bottom of her shoe and lighting a fresh one. "Been every single day or night since his killing. That's where I met him, you know."

"Henry?"

"Who else?"

"We heard through the grapevine that it was the kind of joint where people often tried to do things that were a little outside the law," Tommy said. "Do you know anything about that?"

"You mean to tell me a man who looks like *you* never colored outside the lines?"

I got the water in her sink to as high a temperature as I could, but if it was over body heat it was my imagination. I caught Tommy's eye, stared at the percolator, and then shook my head. We'd get a cup of joe after. "But Henry was really good at keeping people in 'em?" I asked.

"That boy loved a rule!" Frankie giggled. She reached up and unbuckled her shoe but left it on her foot. "He could be a real stick in the mud, but he always made you feel swell about being a little dirty. Never made it feel like he looked down on people who liked to toe the line, but I think he secretly did."

"Did you ever get muddy?" I asked.

"In these shoes?" She let out a peal of giggles.

"You should be saying 'in this coat'!" I laughed back, trying to keep it light. "It can't be real."

"Over two hundred little pipsqueakers sacrificed just for me!" she said. "Feel it." She held out an arm but didn't move toward me.

Instead, Tommy leaned over and grazed the pelt with his fingertips. "Very nice."

"Bergdorf's can't be beat."

"Frankie," I said. "Can I call you what Henry called you?"

"Sure, hon."

"Frankie, why was Henry living with you?"

"He liked strays," she said, taking a long drag on her cigarette. "And there are plenty in this neck of the woods. So he came to live with me. A stray that pays the full rent! What a lucky boy."

"If Henry never thumbed his nose at anyone, who could've been sour enough at him to hurt him?" I asked.

"My guess is Joe, even though he doesn't look like he'd hurt a fly," Frankie said. "And he hates me. That kitty's got claws."

"No one could hate you," Tommy flirted.

"Aren't you a doll!"

"Who's this Joe character?" I feigned ignorance.

"Henry's special friend." Frankie winked like a Stooge with a secret. "See, I know he broke some rules! But I never tattled."

"Why would he hate you?" I asked.

"Joe is a poet. A real one! Poor enough to be a real one, anyhow. Can't even afford twenty dollars a month for rent in the Village. He doesn't like that I live here. He thinks I should be uptown."

"Someone uptown keeping an eye on you?"

"The uptown folk are happy to keep me here," she shrugged. "I'm a bit messy."

"When you went to the club," I asked, "did you like to tease Henry?"

"The fellas were so jealous!" Frankie giggled again. "They'd throw down mountains of greenbacks trying to get a girl, and all she'd do is giggle and walk away. Sometimes Henry would step in to remind them of the rules. Then it always looked like I did the same trying to land Henry, and he would waltz out of the club at closing time with me, headin' the same direction!"

"So you made men at the club think boys could be bought but not the girls?"

"Oh, there's no way they thought that," Frankie scolded. "Henry told everyone the truth, he never lied."

The coffee was finally ready, and I pulled a dirty mug off a shelf, pouring in the brew without even thinking. I handed it to the daffy broad and looked her in the eyes. "Was there anyone particularly cheesed off at Henry? Someone real mad that Henry kept him from taking a girl for a good time?"

"Just the fella with the scar," Frankie said. "He should buy some Pan-Stik, no one would know."

"You're right," I agreed. "Any idea where we could find that fella with the scar?"

"At the docks," Frankie said.

"We checked the ports, there's too many people to go through without a name," Tommy said.

"Not the *ports*, the *docks*, you goose. The loading docks for the restaurant, out back. They go down below the sidewalk? He helps in the kitchen."

She took a swig of her filthy coffee and spilled half of it down her chinchilla coat. "Drat."

"Frankie, I'm going to leave you our card," I said, slipping one next to her on the couch. "You can call us anytime, okay?" We inched toward the door and away from the bubbling goof.

"I hope you catch whoever did this!" she called, waving her hand at the wrist. "Ta-ta!"

★ ★ ★

The sun was just starting to peek over tops of buildings as we fell back onto the sidewalk.

"Buy you breakfast?" Tommy grunted.

"Only if we go back to Chelsea," I said. "I might need another shower."

"Let's just go to the diner."

It was a slow and silent walk back north.

As we rounded the corner toward Miklos's spot for our second early-morning breakfast of the week, Tommy let out a sigh. "I could spit nails."

"There's no difference between ports and docks to most people," I said. "We'll get him. Now that we know."

"Not about the miscommunication, Dollface," Tommy said, pulling open the door. "I think Miss Frankie got her friend murdered."

Even though I couldn't get the stink of the apartment out of my nose, I was ravenous. I ordered a full array of everything—hash browns, bacon and sausage, two sunny side up eggs, toast, and coffee. It was everything I could think of to fill the gaping hole in my stomach.

Tommy just slathered some grape jelly on rye.

"That's disgusting," I said, trying to keep my potatoes in my mouth.

"I'm not that hungry."

"What's the difference between collaring the fella today or two days ago?" I asked.

"None difference," Tommy said, sipping his coffee out of a clean-enough mug. "I just don't like it. Don't like waiting when I shouldn't've had to."

"So what are you going to do about it?" I asked, finally swallowing. I waved down Miklos and ordered another round of potatoes and eggs, which showed up stat.

"I'm gonna keep an eye on the club as soon as we're done here," Tommy said, finally scooping up my second round of breakfast with his fork and downing it all. "See if I can't smoke him out."

"Good. I'm going to hoof it over to the office, get there before Betty," I said, checking my watch. It was about half past eight and she'd be there shortly after me if we didn't fall into step with each other on the way there. "See if there wasn't any forward progress on the box for Mr. Floristan. Then at one, I'm going to finally head on over to the zoo and sort out this missing banker. I'll watch my footing, don't worry."

Tommy threw a handful of bills down on the table and chugged the remnants of his coffee. "Be in touch, Dollface."

He swanned out the door.

★ ★ ★

I was only a quarter of the way up the block before I heard a piercing, "Viiiiiiiiiiiiiv!" come from behind me. Betty was gunning to be early for work, and I stopped in my tracks so she could jog on up.

"How'd the meeting go?" she asked, scrunching up her nose.

"Can you smell it on me?" I asked.

"You smell like damp laundry."

"Frankie. The roommate of the fella we saw get knifed. Squalor, Betty. *Squalor.* I've seen poor folk live in some conditions, but she had on a five-thousand-dollar chinchilla."

"Why would a rich girl ever want to act poor?" Betty asked.

"Beats me, but she had a real lead!" I said, explaining the mix-up.

"Tommy's gonna be on him like glue, huh?"

"All day," I said. We huffed up the stairs to the office and Betty was first with her keys.

"Coffee?"

"As much as you can give me," I said, shedding my layers. I went into the back office and pulled out my office chair, the wheels scraping against the wood floor. "I need to keep my pep up."

Betty yammered on about CiCi and C. Z. Guest and Mrs. Bouvier, and all sorts of fancy ladies who were starting to make the papers again now that the holy season of Christmas was behind us, and it was time again to raise holy hell. "Who's still got funds to give to the fundraisers after Christmas?" Betty asked.

"Not me," I said. "I don't even know if I should take this to the doctor." My ankle was smarting after all this morning's walking.

"Stick it up here," Betty said, sitting down and patting her lap. I did as the nurse told me. She untied my shoe and I slipped off my stocking and she poked my swelling like I was a steak.

"*YeOUCH.*"

"You aren't broken."

"But I'm battered."

"For sure. If you don't stay off your feet for a few days . . ."

"Will they have to cut it off?" I asked.

"Of course not," Betty rolled her eyes. "But you're not going to be a happy camper." She pulled a roll of tape out of her purse.

"Were you prepared to do an exam?"

"Mrs. K told me to," she shrugged. "It's fine, just let me fix you up as good as I can."

"Thanks, Betts."

"No problem," she said, slipping the medical supplies back into her bag. "Now leave me be, I have the work you actually pay me for to do."

I slid back into my office on my chair and promptly took a nap on the desk.

★ ★ ★

Betty's fingernails tapping at the office door woke me. "It's eleven thirty," she whispered. "I told Thelma I'd have lunch with her. That okay?"

I wiped some drool off my cheek and spotted a puddle on my desk blotter. "Of course," I said.

"Thanks, Miss Valentine." Betty winked at me and I heard her leave.

"Guess I'm on my own for nosh," I said to the office. I put back on all my sweaters and coat and followed Betty out, heading to the nice little restaurant close to the zoo.

Betty's tape job held up admirably against my sweating foot encased in a snow boot. The day had not warmed up appreciably since five o'clock in the morning, and even though I had a quart of coffee in my veins, my yawning told me I could use another. I was shivering my timbers as I got to the restaurant and plopped onto the same stool at the counter as yesterday, ordering a hot pastrami on rye with the coldest pickles the waitress could come up with. Once that was settled, my brain switched off. I could only do so much with what I had for each case, and now we were in the waiting game.

The man next to me at the counter coughed and I couldn't help but turn.

"Are you doing all right, miss?" he asked tentatively. He was still wearing his overcoat, but his leather gloves were on the counter—sitting on a file folder of paperwork—and his cuffs revealed his own flashy gold watch. His face was young, and his head of hair was full, and pitch black. He wasn't a bad lookin' fella, if a girl was fresh out of high school and looking to bag someone on the rise. "You had one of those hundred-yard stares."

I took a deep breath and let it out slowly. "I'm fine. Thank you for asking." I added a few sugar packets to my coffee for my nerves. Normally I drank it straight from the pot, but something in my insides was telling me I needed as much energy as I could get today, like I was going into shock.

"I really cannot quite stand these doldrum days of January," he continued. His conversation was stilted, but still he kept on talking. "I do not know if human beings are meant to stay in one place during the winter months. Our ancestors were nomads, and I feel as though we are meant to move south, somewhere where it is warmer with more sunshine. In the northern latitudes, it is much too dark. There is not a single thing to look forward to until Groundhog Day, and I do not get excited about oversized rodents."

Coming out of Tommy that would have been a joke, but this young man didn't have even a hint of a smile in his voice. I think he meant what he said about rodents.

"I'm surrounded by enough giant rats in my regular life that one more telling me the weather doesn't even register," I said. "I got cops arresting harmless vagrants from underneath my nose, men suspicious of their girls even though they don't have any right to be, thieves and working girls and murderers and black-mailers and all sorts of people asking for help or just wanting to be left the hell alone, and can't catch a moment's peace, from either me or the people meant to help 'em. I don't give a . . ." I stopped and broke into fits of tired giggles.

"Rat's ass?" the man offered, but quietly, like the curse word pained him to say.

"Bingo."

"But I must ask: are you all right?" The boy was nervous.

"I am, I just got up very, very early and my work hasn't been going as well as it normally does," I admitted.

"That's a shame, you seem extremely capable."

"Just a few more complications than I normally have," I admitted. The sandwich landed in front of me and smelled like slaw and hot black pepper. "Do you mind if I take a big, giant bite out of this?"

"Not in the least," he smiled. "I normally get the turkey club."

"A good choice," I admitted once I swallowed. "The bacon certainly does a lot of the heavy lifting in that one. But if pastrami is on the menu, pastrami I shall get."

"Interesting." The young man considered the sandwich. "I have never had it."

"You're in New York City and you have never had pastrami?!"

"I am not a terribly adventurous eater," he said. "My mother is committed to the boiled potato."

"If it keeps you fed."

"Yes, but I do feel as though I am missing out."

I flipped open the top of my second half of sandwich and stabbed the pile of meat with my fork. "I'll share." I handed him the speared brisket.

He turned a bit green.

"You didn't see me spit on it or anything," I said, pushing again. "If you don't want it, no skin off my nose."

The man was pensive, and I have never before seen a man spend so much time thinking about eating red meat.

"If I do not enjoy it, will it insult you if I spit it into my napkin?"

"Let me give you less, then." I used my knife to clear the fork, and speared him a little less.

"Thank you." He took my fork and put the meat into his mouth. He chewed a dozen times and swallowed. "That is . . . acceptable."

"Glad you like it." I put the top back on my second half and dug in.

"May I pay for your lunch?" he asked. He glanced up at the clock, and my eyes followed. It was five to one.

"I won't argue for you not to," I said. "That's very sweet of you."

"You were very kind to share your meal with a stranger." He threw a few bills on the counter. "I would like to stay and continue talking, but I have a meeting."

"Me too, come to think of it," I said. "Nice talkin' with you."

The man put on his gloves but no hat, picked up his file folder, and left out the front door.

"He's been coming here every day for a while," the waitress said. "Good tipper."

"Nice fella," I agreed. "Thanks for the chow."

"Don't mention it."

★ ★ ★

I scurried across the street, minding the cabs and oncoming traffic, and grabbed a map at the entrance to the zoo. It all seemed so convoluted, so I waved down a person with a broom to ask the way.

"Sea lions?"

He pointed dead ahead. "Keep your ears open," he grunted. "Can't miss 'em."

Sure enough, I was just past the restroom when I heard some throaty screaming and an enormous splash. A young man with no hat winced as the wave came near the side of the pool, close to the stone eagle next to which he stood.

"Hey!" I shouted to the man who had just paid for my lunch. "Are you . . ."

He didn't offer a paw, but he did nod slowly. "My name is Trevor."

"Well, bust my buttons."

Trevor began to explain. "That was the closest eatery in proximity to the meeting point at the Central Park Zoo," he said, even though I knew by my own decision to eat there that he was correct. "If one does not include street vendors, and I must admit that cleanliness limitations precluded them from my consideration."

"I try to put that out of my mind when I need a hot dog," I admitted. "By the way, I'm Viviana Valentine, and I'm a private investigator."

"Glad to meet you, Miss Valentine. I believe my former employer is your current client."

"Mr. Bowen is paying us a pretty penny to find you," I told him. "Were you expecting me?"

"Not you, per se," Trevor waggled his hand like a see-saw. "But someone."

"What if I'd been someone . . . meaner?"

"By that you mean . . ."

"Someone Bowen hired to rough you up."

"That is why I chose a public forum frequented by children," Trevor said. "And if anyone tried to body me a way, I can yell quite loudly. My father taught me how. It is how one communicates in a mine shaft."

"All solid deductions," I said.

"I can trust you?" Trevor asked.

"We've shared a sandwich, buddy. And I don't share my pastrami with just anyone."

"I can see why," Trevor said. "I may order one, one day."

"Now—your boss. Something is rotten there. I feel it. Peggy says so too."

"Yes, Margaret. She is very nice to me," the young man nodded. He clutched the folder closer to his chest. "She knows what is happening."

"Is that proof?" I nodded at what he was holding.

"As much as I could copy in the six weeks that I had."

"Copy?" I asked. "I'm not sure if you scrawling notes is admissible in court. They can be fudged."

"No. Thermofax." Trevor opened the file and slipped out a few pieces of shiny white paper with smudgy black writing. "It can be a bit difficult to read, but it is all there."

"Why, you sneaky devil," I said, punching him on the arm. He blushed. "Sorry. You got your boss to buy the rope he hung himself with?"

"He won't get the death penalty for theft and tax evasion." Trevor's brow furrowed.

"No, I'm sorry. I meant that you convinced Mr. Bowen to purchase the equipment you used to gather evidence, which will hopefully convict him in the court of law."

"Yes. I could not afford the machine myself, and there are also rules about taking paperwork from the office." Trever was very resolute on that.

"You are very smart, Mr. Penhaligon."

"It was a logical conclusion," the young man said. "And the office benefited from copies of each form and my organizational system, regardless."

"So, give me the gist of what we're looking at here," I said. He still hadn't given me the paperwork.

"Mr. Bowen and his co-conspirators are fraudulently inflating the value of small market capitalization stocks and heightened the appearance of demand by purchasing several companies' unsecured stock and controlling the volume and price of the assets."

I nodded like I knew what the hell he meant. But I did know one word, so I pounced on it. "And if we hand this over to the police, their white-collar crimes people will be able to assess this level of fraud?"

"I wrote a document describing it, step by step."

"It seems pretty complicated," I said.

"It is a complex machine," Trevor said indignantly. "But I know how it works."

"I believe you on that front. Mr. Penhaligon, may I please have the evidence?"

"No!"

"I promise you, I will not show it to Mr. Bowen," I said, holding up my hands like I was in a stick-up. "I just want to take it to the authorities."

"No."

"Mr. Penhaligon," I started. "There's a phone booth near the bus stop at 63rd and 5th, just outside the gates to the zoo. Would you like to come with me while I call authorities I believe you can trust? They can help you in the investigation against Mr. Bowen."

The young man thought for a moment. "That seems acceptable. Ladies first."

We marched like a strange little parade to the booth.

"Hon, my investigative partner and I went to your apartment," I asked as we skirted the edges of the pretzel stand. "Your parents weren't home. Peggy said you might've shipped them to Arizona, but I couldn't find any trail of that."

"We would like to go to California," he said. "I do not wish for them to be that far from the coast. They are from Wales. Not more than ten miles to the shore."

"Are they okay?"

"They're fine."

"You'll think I'm nuts, but I even checked at the Plaza to see if they were guests there."

"The Plaza?" Trevor chuckled. "No, no. They're at the Waldorf."

"But of course."

We got to the phone booth and I left Trevor outside as I closed the door and busted out laughing. I dropped in a nickel and spun for the operator. "Midtown North, please," I said.

"Is this an emergency?"

"No, I just need to have a chat with someone there."

"Don't we all."

The desk sergeant answered with a grunt. "I need Detective Jake Lawson, please. Tell him it's Viviana Valentine."

"Got it."

My pay phone beeped for another nickel and I fed it.

"Lawson."

"Hi, Detective. I'm standing in front of the Central Park Zoo right now and I have a fella here who has some evidence to a crime he'd like to submit to you."

"He do it?"

"No, and don't go treating him rough, neither," I said. Trevor was outside the booth and I took for granted he couldn't hear me. "He's a sweet soul. You're not the right guy for this case, but you're the only copper I know who I don't want to push in front of a bus."

"You always know what to say to a man," Lawson said. "Fine. I'll be there as soon as I can."

I motioned for Trevor to sit with me on the bus bench.

"Listen," I said. "I'm a PI, so cops and I don't have the greatest relationships. But this one is okay, and he'll help make sure all of that gets to the people who need to see it."

Trevor nodded. I knew he didn't like small talk, so we sat on the bench and waved on buses that stopped and expected us to take a ride. It was kind of nice, really, to sit next to a fella and not be expected to put on a song and dance routine, even if it was taking ages for Lawson to show his lousy mug.

An unmarked police car finally pulled up to the curb and the detective got out of the passenger seat, leaving his door wide open.

"This him?"

"What did I say about being nice?" I asked. "Mr. Penhaligon has hard evidence that his boss at Keller Bachmann, an investment firm, is committing some pretty major fraud."

"Is that true, young man?"

"Yes, sir."

"And it's all in that little folder there?"

"Yes, sir."

"Would you like me to get you a lawyer?"

"Yes, sir." Trevor turned to look at me. "May I call you if I need anything?"

"You won't need to, hon," I said, slipping him a card anyhow. "But of course."

Detective Lawson led the boy to the back seat of the car and shut the door after he sat. "This won't make me forget about the murder!" he shouted.

"Me either!"

Lawson got into his ride and peeled away.

"Phooey!" I shouted at the sidewalk and kicked a trash can with my good foot. "Now Bowen won't pay us."

NIGHT 11

Wednesday, January 10ᵗʰ, 1951

There was nothing to do but head back to the office and hope that Tommy had better news.

Between my early-morning wake-up call, my shouting ankle, and the weight of the world on my damn shoulders, I was moving down the avenue as slow as molasses in the dead of winter. Men bustling to wherever their butts needed to be jostled past me, knocking my shoulders, at least half a dozen times before I lost count and stopped caring at the indignity of being seen as autonomous as a curbside trash can. The sun was threatening to go down before I finally made it up the stairs and back to the office. Betty was standing in the middle of the room, wringing her hands.

"Oh, thank *God*," she said. "You're finally back. We got a call from Tommy."

"Is he okay?" My stomach dropped to my ankles.

"He's fine, but he wants you to come down to the club as soon as you can," Betty said. "He talked to that Norma girl before she started her morning shift. She knows exactly who you're talking about and said that she'd try to get him to have dinner with her, after her shift ends at five."

"That's in less than a half hour!"

"You better sprint, then, Viv," Betty shouted as I ran down the stairs. "I'll fix up your ankle at home!"

★　★　★

"Damnit, damnit, damnit, damn *it*," I puffed as I raced down the sidewalk as fast as my feet could go. It was ten or so blocks to the club—the short lengths, thank God—but I was still afraid I was going to miss the action. I skidded to a stop near the exact spot I'd witnessed Henrik Fiskar get killed ten nights before. Tommy was nowhere to be seen. A church bell on the wind bonged the hour.

Norma was coming out of the alley, her arm looped through the arm of a tallish man in a dark overcoat. I crouched and pawed through my purse, acting as if I wasn't watching their every move. They headed north, brushing past me, and Norma kicked out her heel as she walked by, spraying me with a bit of snow. I got the hint and stayed behind.

"Dollface!" Tommy was coming north up 9th and greeted me. "Where should we go to dinner?" I looped my own arm with his and we fell into step with Norma and our man, half a block behind.

Tommy bent to whisper in my ear. "Called Lawson," he said. "Surprised to hear from me. You rang?"

"About banker," I said. "Long story."

"Tried to give the gist here," Tommy said. "Need her to stay close."

"We'll get him," I said. Norma and our man strolled north past half a dozen or more perfect joints for a stakeout—diners and restaurants, a malt shop, and even the tobacconist who was standing in his horse stall, the scent of vanilla and smoke streaming from his long, black cigarette.

"Where is she going?" Tommy muttered.

"What makes you think she's choosing the place?" I asked. "He's probably dragging her to some no-name joint."

They tumbled into a low-lit bar behind a heavy oak door, the mystery man's meaty fist rolled up into the collar of Norma's coat, holding her close and directing her through. The door swung shut in our faces.

"Rats." Tommy kicked the sidewalk. "It ain't got windows and I don't feel like tussling with a drunk."

"Nothing's done here, ol' Tommy boy," I soothed. "And unless he goes out the back, he's not getting away."

"I hadn't thought about the back."

"Then you go wait there, and I'll wait here, and we'll do what we can do," I said. "And even if he scrams, Norma can tell us his name and where we might be able to find him later. If he ever lets her jacket go."

Trailing a man into an establishment *with* windows is harder, in my opinion, than waiting for him to come out of a place where he can't watch you back. I didn't have to pretend to look for a bus stop or fake file my nails. I just leaned against an electrical box and trained my eyes on the door.

The good news was Mr. Bowen's case was over, we had found his missing banker, and our client was hopefully going to the hoosegow, even if that meant there was no one to bill for all the trouble it had caused us. That just left Rachel, who I had to trail tomorrow, Mr. Floristan's mystery, and the murderer I was waiting on to show his busted-up face.

And I had to figure out how to soothe my landlady's son.

And plan a wedding.

And meet my in-laws.

And my lawyer.

And plan a honeymoon.

And live through renovations on my apartment.

All that 1951 held before me was starting to make my heart race when a fella came running out of the bar in front of me, overcoat flapping in the breeze, and a desperate Norma in her mussed up, fake-fur coat scrambling after.

"That's him!" she hollered, falling off her heels and making a spectacle. "He just told me he did it! Get him!"

Lucky for me, the fella was getting slowed by a group of working stiffs walking five abreast down the entire sidewalk, heading toward our very location, but he definitely heard Norma's screaming and was doing his damnedest to put distance between me and him. No one else was the wiser to what we were up to, and, assessing my ankle, there was no damn way I was going to catch up to him on my own two feet. Norma's shrieks were still ringing across the building fronts when I bent down, picked up a crusty hunk of dirty snow, packed it into a ball, and threw it as hard and as fast as I'd ever thrown anything, aiming at the back of our perp's head.

He never knew what hit him as he landed face first on the sidewalk, the back of his head now dripping with slushy, dirty snow. I took my time walking up to him and placed my foot on the back of his neck.

"Hot damn," Norma said, running up to join me. "Who's your daddy, girl? Vic Raschi?"

"Do you have anything to tie him up with?" I asked. "My scarf isn't gonna work. Too stretchy of a knit."

"Sure." Norma reached up her skirt and pulled off a black, frilly, ornamental silk garter, and yanked it apart at the seam to make it one long ribbon. "This'll do the trick. Trust me."

I looped the garter as many times as I could over the man's wrists, knotted it tight, and left him lying on the ground. "Would you mind running to the back of the bar and grabbing Tommy? He's in the alleyway."

"On it." Norma dashed off, tottering on her sky-high heels in the snow. She was a pip, that one.

I pulled the concussed man to a sitting position. His dark-colored overcoat was stained darker in some places, and he smelled like a slaughterhouse. He didn't even have the cash to get a new coat after he stuck Henrik Fiskar in the guts.

"I take no joy in this, you should know," I told him. One side of his face looked like chipped beef and his nose was bleeding, but I could still make out a nice, two-inch scar going from the right side of his mouth down his chin, making him look like half a ventriloquist's dummy. He was wriggling and trying to get into a stand, but his hurting face was making him wobble. With my hip, I knocked him down back on his butt. "I hate having to call the cops, and this is gonna be the second time today."

"You could let me go."

"You ruined my New Year's," I said. "I'm the one who found Henry, and he died in my hands."

"He was gettin' in between me and the girl," the man seethed.

"The girl wasn't for you to have," I said. "She decides who gets her, not Henry."

"But look at her," he began to move his head in the direction Norma left but thought better of it once he felt the shrieks of pain that would soon be taking over his whole body. That kind of fall stays with you. "And you don't know what she does for a living."

"I do, actually," I said. "And look me in the eyes."

I put my hands on his shoulders and bent at the waist to stare at him. His one eye was swollen pretty good, but he did his best. "She could sleep with every other man on *Earth* and not sleep with you," I said, snarling. "And it would still be her right."

The man snorted up blood and mucus and shot it out his maw in my direction. One quick step to the left and it missed me clear.

"Can't imagine why she didn't want to go out with you," I muttered.

"I heard all about your aim, Dollface," Tommy said, sidling up. "Need a hand?"

"He's starting to feel it," I said. "Couldn't run if he tried. Where's the detective?"

"I called the precinct from the phone in the bar," Tommy said. "Dispatch said he'd be here soon."

"That's nice."

"The cops aren't gonna believe me," Norma sniffled. "They never believe girls like me."

"That's on them, honey," I said turning. "If they want to discount good evidence because of the source, well, then they're no good for this city. But this fella left the murder weapon at the scene, and he can't afford gloves. There will be fingerprints."

"And two of Henry's friends sent us looking for this mug," Tommy said. "His girl roommate and a poet he knew, both of 'em said that a man with a facial scar was the most likely culprit."

Norma pulled me away from the man on the ground. "Henry lived with Francine Kensington-Smythe, right?" she asked.

"Didn't get the full name when I met her," I said. "But if you mean a real piece of work he called 'Frankie' in a fur that cost more than most people's salary, then yes."

"Good," Norma said, shoving her fists into her coat pockets. "Her daddy's one of the best lawyers in the state."

"How do you know all this?" Tommy asked. "I thought there were no names at the club."

"Not *officially*," Norma said, scoffing. "But everyone knows CiCi Kensington-Smythe. Herb Sabella caught all of yous guys on film in the last week. Or don't you read the papers?"

Detective Jake Lawson and a nameless flatfoot were just peeling out of their squad car when I turned around. "Long time no see, sweetheart," he said in my direction. "Who's the trussed-up turkey?"

"I . . . actually don't know his name," I said.

"I do," Norma piped up. "His name is Marvin Girardi. His friends call him Pretty Boy."

"Got some nice, identifying features there, Pretty Boy," Lawson said at the man now shivering on the cold ground. "You sure this is the fella?"

"All that blood soaked into his coat isn't his," I said. "If it was, he'd be on a gurney."

"Well, let's get him in the car." Lawson turned to Tommy as the flatfoot peeled our perp off the pavement. "Good one, Fortuna. We'll be in touch."

"Thank Viv, if you need to thank anyone," Tommy said, throwing his arm over my shoulder. "She's the one who got him with a thirty mile an hour snowball."

Detective Lawson screwed up his face and joined his compatriot getting the bloody man in the back of the squad car.

"Norma, are you okay?"

"No," she admitted, her whole body shivering with cold and nerves. "But I have to be."

"Can we buy you a nice meal before the start of your next shift?" I asked. "It's only about seven."

Norma checked her watch to confirm. "Yeah. You know what?" She let out a shout of a laugh. "I think that's the *least* you can do."

DAY 12

I woke up at Tommy's having slept like the dead. My fiancé was already up and making breakfast.

"We've got the works!" he hollered from the kitchen. "Bacon, eggs, toast. I had some tomatoes that were about to go, so I roasted 'em like the Limeys do. Smells interesting. Come eat before you shower."

"So what's on your docket for today?" I asked.

"I think I have a buyer for the Cadillac," Tommy said. "I know it's not a case, but it couldn't hurt to have a few extra thousand in your pocket."

"That's amazing! That's happening fast."

"It is," Tommy said. "But the real bad news is that the buyer is up in the Hudson Valley. It's going to take me all day to get the deal done and get back."

"So it goes," I said. "All I have to do today is tail Morty's girl."

"You still going to confront her?" Tommy asked, helping himself to more tomatoes. "These aren't bad."

"Yeah, they cut through the fat of the bacon," I said. "We should do this more often. But yes. I need to talk to her. I'm trusting my gut on this one."

"And you have some mighty fine guts, Dollface."

"Thank you."

Tommy tossed our dishes in the sink. "I'll wash these later. I'm heading out, lock up when you leave. Love you, Dollface." He was out the door like a flash, keys rattling in his pocket.

As usual, I took my time showering at Tommy's apartment with his building's industrial-sized hot water tank. I left the bathroom door open to heat the place, and his front windows were nice and foggy by the time I was done. Even though he said he would get 'em, I washed and dried all the dishes, tidied up, and was wrapped up and ready to go after just over an hour. It's only a few short minutes to the office, and I was there only a few minutes after ten in the morning. I could get used to these kinds of hours.

But my delay in arrival might have been the end of my secretary—Betty was bubbling like a percolator, for the second day in a row.

"Calm down, girl, you're going to give yourself a heart attack," I scolded, taking off my scarf.

"That's not how that works, you know!" She shrieked, hopping up and down. "But hurry up! Dottie got it!"

"The flu?"

"No, the puzzle!" She all but shoved the wooden box into my hands. "She left it open for you but said she didn't touch anything inside."

"But you did?"

"Of course I did, I'm a busybody."

"Oh God, at this point I just hope it's an ear and we've been dealing with the second coming of Van Gogh," I said. "I can't take another puzzle."

"Bad news then," my secretary said. "Unfold the paper first."

P/S

SBUDPLG ILYH RQH CHUR RQH VLA VLA

★   ★   ★

"What's your guess?" I asked.

"No clue, but I'll try my damnedest, as usual," Betty said.

I reached into the wooden crate and pulled out a fuzzy, black jewelry case. "This must've been the clunk." I opened it to reveal a silver-colored brooch, made from twisted and sculpted metal.

Betty looked at it approvingly. "Pretty. Modern. No stones or anything shiny. But pretty."

"I wonder if this is what was snitched?" I asked.

"Only time will tell. Any updates on the other two cases?"

"Oh, get a load of this."

The recounting of the previous day's adventures took until lunchtime, when I had to leave and go trail Rachel to the Rainbow Room. I rifled through the photographs I had gotten from Thelma and put a choice few in my purse before wrapping myself up to head out again into the freezing tundra of January.

"I know I said I'd go with you," Betty said, as I offered her own coat. "But would you be mad if I just stay here and work on the puzzle?"

"Of course not," I lied.

"If you make it home at a normal hour tonight, Oleks and I were planning on going out to Oyster Bay to check out his new digs," she said. "Try not to drink too much at lunch!"

I scurried east again through the park and found myself at the foot of Rockefeller Center.

"It's just a *restaurant*," I muttered to myself, and joined the throngs in the express elevators. A man in a gorgeous uniform pressed the button and we rocketed up to the sixty-fifth floor so fast I thought I was going to fall over.

Lines of round tables were ramped together on a gleaming parquet wood floor. Above them, a ceiling with a grand circular design rippled around a stunning chandelier, dripping in crystalline spheres, surrounded by wisps of cigarette smoke. The hostess greeted me at the door.

"Are you waiting for the rest of your party?" she asked.

"I'm early—may I have a seat at the bar?"

"Of course."

On one side of the room, a gleaming wooden bar rippled through the crowd, surrounded by polished mirrors and hanging glassware. I sat down at one far end, where I could watch the comings and goings.

"What will it be?" the bartender asked, moving aside a full ashtray.

"Whatever you make best," I said with a shrug.

"My favorite order." He set about adding ingredients and ice to his concoction, shaking it, and straining it into a waiting glass. He added a twist of orange and placed it in front of me.

"What'd it end up being?"

"No name," he said with a wink. "Just delicious."

One sip and I gave the waiting man a thumbs up. "You got that right."

"Miss." He nodded and went to tend another customer.

Rachel arrived right on cue and was stopped by the same hostess. She sat down on a leather upholstered banquette, by the door, and I took this as my time to shine. I waved down the bartender. "Watch my drink," I said. "I have to go greet someone who just walked in."

Rachel was sitting nervously on the bench and I gingerly sat next to her. "Excuse me, are you Rachel Blum?"

"Y—y—yes?" She appraised me up and down. Everything about her was glamorous—her dark brown hair pulled into a shiny French twist, the black astrakhan collar on a spectacular white wool day suit, her manicured nails holding the butter-soft strap on her creaseless handbag.

"My apologies, my fiancé is an acquaintance of Morty's," I said, not quite lying. "I told him—Morty, not my fiancé—I was having lunch here today, and he said that I might run into you."

"Oh!" She seemed hesitant to admit that Morty shouldn't have known her whereabouts. "That's so sweet."

"He described you as pretty as a picture, and he wasn't wrong!" I turned my hometown garishness up on the dial, and signaling to Rachel that I knew I wasn't up to snuff put her a bit more at ease. Here I was, just some ramshackle tourist, and she could stomach me for a few minutes.

"That's Morty for you," she said, grinning uncomfortably.

"I don't want to eat into your lunch date," I assured her. It was best to let her know that I wasn't trying to be friends, but I had to stall for time. If her mystery man showed his face, manners would say she had to introduce me. "But I just wanted to say hello and tell you just how much I love Morty. What a fella!"

"Yes, he is *something*." The word had an inflection that could mean a few things, and, judging by how her eyes ran the room, most of those things were not good, at least not right now.

A man about my own height in a dark suit was coming from the coat check room.

"Hi, Rach," he said. "*Wer ist dein Freund?*"

Rachel's eyes got large. "*Niemand, aber sie sagt, sie kennt Morty.*"

"I'm Viv!" I said, sticking out my hand. "Friend of Morty's!"

"Hi, I'm Benjamin Blum," the man said, taking my hand. "Rachel's brother."

"Well, how about that! Nice to meet ya," I said. "Don't want to eat into a family reunion, just wanted to say hello." I nodded at Rachel and retreated back to the bar, where I sat down and took a deep, pleasurable sip of my cocktail.

"That is amazing," I said, to no one in particular, but the bartender was all ears.

"Thanks!" he chirped. "Want another?"

"If I had one, I may not be able to walk out of here on my own power. How much do I owe you?" I asked, as soon as all the liquid was gone and just the ice was tinkling in my glass.

"Two dollars."

"For one drink?"

"But it was a hell of a drink," he shrugged.

"You're right." I left him a dollar tip on the bar and left. I slipped as close as I could back past Rachel and Benjamin, to see if I could eavesdrop a bit more.

"*Je suis tellement inquiète pour le mariage . . .* ," Rachel said, but shut her trap as she saw me near. I gave her another wave, rescued my coat from the check girl, ready to walk back to the office, lighter than I'd felt in ages.

★　★　★

"Good news," I said, opening the door to a grinning Betty. "The bartenders at the Rainbow Room are really nice."

"That's what you're leading with?" Betty threw a crumpled-up piece of paper at my head.

"Oh, right, silly me," I said, leaning against her desk and unfurling my scarf. "He's her brother."

"Should we call Morty up and tell him?" Betty asked.

"You know what? Yes. Let's do it right now. Dial for me and listen on the extension." I went to the back office and made myself comfortable, picking up the phone to listen in on Betty connecting via the operator. She connected us, there were a few quick rings, and then a pickup.

"This is Morty."

"Hi, Mr. Lobel, this is Viviana Valentine."

"Hello, Miss Valentine. I take it you have news for me."

"I do, and I think you'll be pleased to know that you don't have anything to be nervous about," I said. "The mystery man is her brother."

There was a long, dead silence on the other end of the line.

"Did we lose our connection?" I asked the ether.

"No," Morty continued. "It's just a bit of a shock."

"Well, she isn't two-timing you," I snapped. "This should be a relief."

"And it is, please do not get me wrong," our client sighed. "But Rachel hasn't heard from her brother in years. It's a long story."

"Mr. Lobel, I don't mean to be rude, but I'd like to hear it," I said firmly. "I don't like the position you put me and Tommy in. And if you don't tell me, I'll get my keister right back to that restaurant and ask her myself."

"It *was* lousy of me to ask this of you," he agreed. "Let me come in and explain, I'll be there in an hour."

He hung up.

"Well, I guess our afternoon is spent waiting," I said out to Betty in the front.

"Not necessarily," she said, coming on back. "I got the puzzle this morning."

"You're kidding!"

"Dead serious! It looked simple, so I just tried the first kind of puzzle he sent over," Betty said. "The P/S I thought just meant *postscript*, like he was giving us a little note after we got this far in the chase, but it was the cipher key. The letter P became the letter S and it all fell into place."

"How are you so smart?" I asked.

"Just lucky." Betty placed her steno pad with the solved puzzle in front of me. "Pyramid, five, one, zero, one, six, six. Can't be anything but a phone number."

"When you're right, you're right. Did you call it yet?"

"No, I managed an ounce of self-control and decided to wait for you," Betty admitted. "You want me to go direct dial it?"

"God, yes! I'll listen in."

Betty spun the rotary and voice picked up on the other end.

"Talcott's Answering Service, how may I help you?" A young girl's voice rang through the line.

"Hi, my name is Viviana Valentine . . ."

The girl cut me off.

"Oh, it's you!" she squealed. "I was hoping I'd be the one to get this call. Hold on."

Betty spoke through the phone line. "What the hell is going on?"

"No idea," I said.

The girl was back. "Our client told us if either you or Tommy Fortuna called in, we were to play this recording. Hold on while I set up the reel-to-reel."

"Excuse me?" No one was at the other end, but I heard some fumbling and cursing. After a few minutes, I heard the squeal of tape and then just a series of beeps.

Then there was a long silence.

"Betty, what the hell is going on?" I asked my secretary.

"It's Morse code, Viv, shush up, it's starting again."

Another long silence and I knew better than to open my trap.

"Third time's the charm," Betty said over the wire. "I think we can hang up."

I did so and walked out to the front.

"Do you . . . *know* Morse code?"

"I don't," Betty said, frowning. "But I'll call . . ."

"The library?" I said. "Ask them to read you the alphabet?"

"Know of any other way of getting it?"

"No, actually. Carry on, I'm just going to watch you."

After a few minutes of chatting and scribbling down the Morse alphabet on a spare sheet of paper, Betty was off to the races. The phone rang, and I picked it up, trying to save her from breaking her concentration.

"Fortuna and Valentine," I said into the receiver.

"Where's Betty?" Tommy shouted.

"Right next to me, but she's busy," I said. "And you don't have to yell, Tom, it's modern technology."

"The deal went faster than I thought, I'm about to get on the express train, should be back in an hour or so," he continued screaming.

"Good, because Morty's coming in to the office, too, he's got some explaining to do," I said.

"How was the lunch?"

"Strange," I admitted. "Hurry home."

"Will do—oh, and Dollface, you got full freight for the car."

His nickel was beeping. "What do you mean?"

"The buyer paid original sticker," Tommy said. "Four grand." The phone cut off and I was left sitting in the office, a few thousand dollars richer than I'd ever been in my life.

Betty looked up. "What's that?"

"Tommy. Should be back about the same time as Morty." I didn't feel like cluing her in on the sale of my car.

"Good. Everyone should hear what he has to say." She went back to scribbling.

"How much longer?"

"However long it takes me," she grunted.

I went back to sit at my own desk.

★ ★ ★

Tommy arrived first, blowing in with the wind and a fat, manila envelope stuck up under his armpit.

"They paid in *cash*?"

"Sure did." He handed it over. "Stow that someplace safe. As soon as possible."

"It makes me nervous just to see it," I said. "Who'd you sell the car to?"

"Ol' friend," he grinned. "Monty Bonito is feeling well after his injuries."

"How does Monty afford a four thousand dollar car?"

"He doesn't, but his employer does," Tommy smiled. "Not naming any names."

"No, don't. The less I know the better." I eyed the envelope. "You sure the greenbacks are real?"

"They're real." Tommy flumped into his chair. "So what happened today?"

"Betty's working on the latest mystery for Mr. Floristan," I said. "You know what's fishy?"

"What's that?" Tommy stretched, and six joints in his body let out deafening pops.

"Mr. Floristan has never once called to check back in on his case," I said. "Nervous fellas like that usually call every day."

"That *is* fishy."

"Maybe we'll have news for him soon."

"Hopefully," Tommy said, pinching the bridge of his nose. "And Morty?"

"Mystery man is her brother," I said. "Met up with them at the restaurant and weaseled my way into a little introduction session. Morty's going to have to explain how he knew where she was off to every Thursday, but that's no heat on us."

"Why's he coming here?"

"I demanded an explanation," I said indignantly. "I need to know why she's hiding her brother from him. Who cares about a standing family lunch date?"

"You're too nosy."

"I'm curious and I want to go on record to say that my gut feelings were dead-on accurate about this case, ol' Tommy boy."

"You're right."

Betty came in, red in the cheeks and gripping a pencil like she was trying to break its neck. "I hate his damn thing!"

"What damned thing?" Tommy asked.

"Morse code," she said, throwing her steno book on Tommy's desk, having it skid to a stop just before it went off the edge. "I can't do it!"

"Betty."

"Yes, Mr. Fortuna?"

"I was in the navy." He picked up his own pencil and started scratching away at the paper, turning dots and dashes into letters, like magic.

Betty's face unscrunched, but she folded her arms. "Right. Forgot about that."

"You didn't even hear it, how do you know where the stops are?" I asked.

"Practice. Shush."

A few more minutes and Tommy let out an expletive, handing me the notebook.

"*I'm always chasing rainbows, Watching clouds drifting by, My schemes are just like all my dreams, Ending in the sky,*" I hummed. "'You've found the end of the rainbow. Thank you for playing my game. In lieu of payment, please wear this brooch and think of me. Sincerely, Mr. Floristan.'"

"You're joking." Betty looked steamed.

"He was having a go of us?" I asked.

"Probably why he didn't call," Tommy shrugged. "Gimme that pin, I'll have to take it to a pawn shop and find out how much it's worth."

"Why, I'm so mad I could spit!" Betty yelled.

"I hate the tricksters," I said. "They happen about once a year."

"Some fella calls us to take photos of his wife and it turns out he *likes* us taking photos of his wife," Tommy said. "It's usually that kind of thing. But normally they don't leave anything of value."

"This might be out of a Cracker Jack box, ol' Tommy boy," I said, tossing him the box with the pin.

"Might be, but I'm not betting on it," Tommy said, examining the jewelry. "Our Victorian underwear salesman might have left us something nice."

"Underwear salesman?" Betty asked.

"Long story."

And thankfully, I didn't have to tell it because Morty was here for our after-hours chat.

NIGHT 12

Thursday, January 11ᵗʰ, 1951

He'd been hovering outside the door behind the pebbled-glass window, acting like we couldn't see him, for more than a minute, very much like a man who did not want to be where he was. To drive all the way in from Bensonhurst at this time of night—admittedly, against traffic but still not an easy schlep—meant he sure as hell hadn't given us all the details on his beloved when he contracted Tommy's services. And if he didn't, he was proving Tommy's rule just right: anyone who couldn't make an appointment probably didn't have the guts to hear the information they were asking us to find out.

Morty finally mustered up his courage, spun around in the hallway, and knocked lightly on the glass pane of the door. Betty showed him to the back, and I followed him in. He sat straight up on Tommy's penitent wooden chair and looked me right in the eyes.

"So," he sighed. "Rachel's brother is back."

"Why is she hiding him from you, Mort?" Tommy asked.

"Was he in the slammer?" I asked.

"No."

"*Should* he be in the slammer?" I asked again.

"It depends on who you ask."

"Oh, well, that's a horse of a different color then, isn't it?" I said.

"It's a painful . . ." He stopped. "I just . . ."

"Mr. Lobel . . ." I asked. "When did Rachel's family immigrate to America? Was it before the war started?"

"It was not," Mr. Lobel said, looking at me.

"Did most of them manage to make it out?" I asked.

"More than most families."

"Does Rachel . . . is Rachel worried that her brother being alive might stir up some emotion for you?" I asked. "Considering . . . considering what you survived?"

Mr. Lobel stared at his folded hands. "Rachel's family is from Holland. They were reasonably well-to-do, the family business was across Europe. Furniture business. They were planning on moving before it all started and left as soon as they could. Her brother had the hardest time leaving," he whispered. "Given his age and all sorts of other reasons. He barely made the ship. He *fought* to make the ship. She was very proud of him."

"I'm still not sure why she's afraid of you meeting him, sir."

"He was a grown man by the time they made it here, in his twenties. By '42, he was pressured . . ." Mr. Lobel stopped. "Some young men were pressured to enlist."

Betty was outside the office door and we heard her gasp. "And go *back*?"

"Just come on in, Betty," I said. "You'll hear it all eventually."

"Many did so happily, and I believe Benjamin did as well." Mr. Lobel shook his head. "At least at first."

"Mr. Lobel, does this have anything to do with the fact that Benjamin and Rachel speak three languages?" I asked and looked over at Tommy. "Remember what Rocío said about studying mathematics and speaking Spanish?"

"Right!" Betty said. "Oh, my goodness!"

"They speak six, actually." Morty sat up straight and looked proud. "Fluently."

"I heard English, German, and French myself . . . ," I said. "I've picked up the basics in most languages I've ever heard of, you know. Please, thank you, hello. I can tell most languages apart. Makes living in the city a lot easier."

"They also speak Italian, Russian, and Dutch."

"I think I read about a program . . . ," I started. "Boys trained at a camp near DC? Meant to be translators, do interrogation, try to break codes and communications . . ."

"Camp Ritchie. It was supposed to be hush-hush."

"Nothing was hush-hush," Betty said. "Despite how often we were warned loose lips sink ships."

"Lots of people who fled Europe were recruited," I explained to Betty and Tommy. "And a lot of them were Jewish fellas. I suppose the government thought they'd fight extra hard."

"But when Benjamin got back to Europe—he couldn't take it. It was terrifying. This is what Rachel told me."

"Did he . . . did he get *leave*?" I asked.

"No."

The word hung in the air of the office.

"No one could ever blame him," Tommy said. "*Ever.*"

"And I don't!" Mr. Lobel looked up with tears down his thin cheeks. "I could never! I *would* never! One shell-shocked man putting himself in harm's way was not going to free me any faster, or save *more* lives."

"If he didn't get leave, how did he get back to the States?" Betty asked.

"He didn't. He hid," Morty said. "In the woods. Off the land. For a very, very long time. I am proud of him for surviving."

I walked up to our client and kneeled before him, holding his hands. "Rachel needs to hear that from you. And I believe her brother needs to be at her wedding."

"Morty, you want a drink?" Tommy gave me the eye, and it was my time to leave, even though it wasn't officially quitting time. I hustled out of the office with Betty, whose mascara was working its way down her rosy cheeks.

"That poor man! The both of 'em!" Betty said.

"Mr. Lobel has an uphill battle in front of him," I said. "He might be fine with Benjamin, but his family may not as easily forgive, forget, or move on."

"His family isn't marrying her," Betty said.

"*Ehhhhh.*" I moaned and looked at my own left hand, even though my ring was covered with a puffy, white mitten. "You don't want to be the reason the person you love gets kicked out of their own family."

"You worried the other Mrs. Fortuna is going to make a scene?"

"Yes and no," I admitted. "I mean, Tommy's pretty resolute on marrying me, and I believe him. Let me be honest, I'm more worried about my own comfort. I hate walking on eggshells around people."

Betty let my discomfort sit in silence as we walked back to Chelsea.

"Speaking of . . . ," Betty said after a while. "You still want to come with me and Oleks to Long Island tonight? I promised him we'd go and scope out the neighborhood his uncle wants him to move to."

Oleks flung open the door. "Come on, Viv. Besides, Mom is making Spam and macaroni loaf tonight."

"Oh God, the last time we had that three months ago it threatened to make me kiss the porcelain throne," I said. "No more need be said, we'll get dinner on Long Island."

"I knew you'd understand." Oleks shuffled his big shoulders out of the doorway so Betty and I could slip into the house.

"Let me just grab some spending money." I was upstairs and down in less than a few minutes and met Betty on the sidewalk.

"There's a sixish out of Penn Station," Betty said, reading a slip of newspaper ripped from that day's print. "We can make it if we scurry. That boy better get his snack in a hurry."

"Let me detain you for just a moment." A thin voice rang out in the night, and I knew exactly who it was.

"Didn't Tommy say 'office only,' Herb?" I squared my shoulders and put myself between Betty and the reporter.

"Sure, sure," Herb waved me off. "But I heard you caught your killer."

"You can hear about it from the detective in charge," I said.

"Tell me all about this . . . Norma Ragazzo?"

"Who's that?" I feigned.

"Think of it! Maybe she could sell her story to the pictures and get out of those dumps. Girl on the streets, defies the odds. Risks life and limb and reputation for justice."

"You print anything like that and I'll . . ."

"What? You know it's not libel," Herb sneered.

"Who the *hell* are you?" Oleks barged out of the house and down the stairs.

"You two-timing Fortuna with a younger man, eh?"

"I will make you bleed," Oleks growled.

"Message received. Ta-ta!" Herb scampered back into the shadows and down the street.

"Who was *that*?" Betty asked.

"The man who put our picture in the paper the other day," I said. "We'll have to sort *him* out in the future."

We set off in silence. Betty and I retraced our steps, heading north along 9th Avenue, with Oleks impatiently waiting for us every few feet. His stride was practically twice the length of Betty's and he could've made the train station lickety-split if we hadn't been weighing him down, but I also knew that Oleks didn't keep a job during the school year and probably needed me to pay his train fare.

Betty and I were all out of breath—and Oleks fidgety and nervous—when we fell into the train's seats and set out into the wilds of Long Island. The conductor came by and collected my cash, raising an eyebrow at Oleks, who didn't even reach for his wallet.

"Thanks, Viv," the teen boy muttered when the conductor slipped us our punch tickets and went on collecting the cash of commuters.

"Don't mention it," I said. "You can pay me back when you're a big spy."

"Do you think I could?" Oleks asked.

"I've met a whole room of FBI agents," I told him. "You'd run circles around 'em. But try to go to college and not the army, at least until the mess is over in Korea."

"But then why will Uncle Sam need spies?" Betty asked. "When the war is over?"

Oleks gave me a look with a capital L. I should've known the boy whose parents fled Ukraine during the Holodomor could read the temperature of world politics.

"You know, you're right, Betty," he said nicely. "I'm sure once everything in Korea is mopped up, we'll go back to normal."

The entire train ride out east took a few hours with all the stops, and by the time we landed in town, Betty was already looking at the printed schedule on the wall of the train station to suss out how to go back into the city.

"We have to be back here by eleven thirty," she said, checking her watch. "Three hours to bum around and see what we can see."

"Which doesn't look like much," Oleks pouted. I hated to admit that he was right; we were near the ocean and I felt every single waft of wind that was coming in over the water. It smelled better than the Port of New York had, but that was a pretty low bar. There was a large parking lot, now empty of commuters' cars, as the last few people on the train with us got into Dodges and Chevys and headed toward home and a warm dinner. The yellow light of the sodium lamps made Betty look a little bit ill.

"What I *can* see is a main street with a little restaurant," I said, pointing toward some dimly lit sidewalks and a line of buildings, some short, squat, and brick and others short, squat, and covered with graying cedar shingles. "And that seems as good a place as any to get a feel for the place."

It was a bustling seafood restaurant, filled with the scent of butter, salt water, and beer.

"Okay, well, don't tell my mother, but this is my kind of joint," Oleks said as we sat down at the wooden table, sticking somewhat with malt vinegar and covered with a thousand layers of high-shine marine shellac. "Not saying I want to live here, but at least it's not stuffy."

"I do think they *actually* fish here," Betty said. "It may not be just rich people with boats."

"That's good."

"What do you all want?" I asked. "I think it's counter service."

"I'll eat anything," Oleks said.

"Same."

I took off my coat and hung it on a hook next to our table. "Be right back."

"So, what's good here?" I asked the girl behind the cash register.

"Everything," she smiled. "And I really do mean that, I'm not being an ass."

"Wonderful news!" I said, pulling my purse out of my pocket book. "Give me one each of your three favorite things, three orders of fries, and three beers."

"Can do," she said, handing me a receipt. "What kind of beer do you want?"

"Whatever's on tap."

"Fantastic." The girl rang me up. "Hoot and holler when you hear Janice shout 'twenty-six' into the dining room in just a few minutes."

"Which one's Janice?" I said, turning to squint at the faces in the bar.

"The one shouting numbers into the dining room."

"Right."

I returned to the table and, within a blink, our hands were raised like school children when a short lady bearing baskets of fried food entered from the kitchen.

Oleks was looking less grumpy as his French fries went down the hatch. He took a bite of the sizzling hot cod. "Oh, that's *really* good."

"If you ordered drinks, they're at the bar," the waitress grumped and went off to pick up her next round of food.

"Good to know," I said. "Oleks, I got you a beer." He was still seventeen but if I got the drinks, no one would care.

"You shouldn't have. But thanks."

I got to the bar, which was decorated with buoys, nets, and plastic lobsters. "Those three beers?" I asked, and three giant mugs of amber liquid were deposited in front of me.

"You . . . need any help with that?" A man with curly brown hair looked up from his own drink.

"Normally, I'd be indignant and say no, but I think the glasses each weigh five pounds, so . . . yes, please. If you don't mind."

"Not at all." The man picked up two mugs and followed me to the table.

"Wow!" Betty's eyes got huge, but following her line of sight, I suddenly didn't think it was for the drink. "Um, thanks, Viv, I'll get you back when we get home. And thank you . . . ?" She held out her hand to our mystery man and he put a beer in front of her to free up a paw to shake it.

"Mike. Michael. Michael Wolf. Dr. Michael Wolf," he stammered.

"Hi, Dr. Michael Wolf," she said, turning on the flirt. Oleks grinned and leaned against the wall, hoovering up fries and watching Betty turn into goo. "I'm Nurse Elizabeth Wagner. Why don't you join us?"

"Sure!" Dr. Michael Wolf almost knocked over three chairs and a waitress on the way to and from the bar to retrieve his drink. He and Betty started yammering, and I took a glance around the joint.

"Oleks," I said, turning to him and looking him in the eyes. "I'm not sure if you've noticed, but there's a girl behind the bar who hasn't taken her eyes off you."

"I noticed," Oleks said.

"Go get me another beer," I said, swigging mine back in one painful gulp. "Here's a buck."

"If it all goes well, it's going to be a while before I come back with that beer . . . ," he laughed.

"Just be back to the table by eleven fifteen so I can get you home," I said. "Your mother is going to be furious with me for keeping you out this late on a school night."

"It's fine," he said. "She'll just be happy to hear that I kind of like it."

"You might like it a *lot* in ten minutes," I said and he swatted me on the shoulder as he moved toward the bar.

There was nothing to do but eavesdrop on Betty, munch on cold French fries, and stare out the window, but the night passed wonderfully as I watched my two friends each slip into easy conversation with their companions. A half hour before we had to get back to the station, I gave Betty a little cough and Oleks a wave; at fifteen minutes, I put on my coat. We were at the station a few moments before the train heading back to Manhattan rumbled in, and both were in a quiet little daze as the fog rolled in off the sound.

"So, it's not hell?" I asked as we sat down in our chairs, both Betty and Oleks taking window seats.

"Mmm?" Oleks was caught in thought.

"Well, I won't tell your mother about all of *that*," I said.

He didn't seem to hear me as he leaned his head back against his chair and shut his eyes. Within a few minutes, Oleks was snoring.

"You're going to have to tell me something about that doctor, Betty," I said. "Or I'm going to fall asleep on this train."

"He has a practice in the city," she said, voice a little loopy. It might've been the beer—I'd never seen Betty put away anything more than a small glass of brandy.

"What kind of doctor?"

She gave me a wicked grin. "Podiatrist."

"Say no more."

Betty leaned her head against the frozen glass and watched as the scenery became less black and foresty and increasingly illuminated and filled with brick buildings. As we slid through Long Island City, I could see the buildings of lower Manhattan twinkle in the distance.

It felt great to be going back home.

THREE WEEKS LATER . . .

Thursday, February 1st, 1951

"There's a phone call for you both." Betty came into the back office, her hair in a kerchief. She was wearing what Mrs. K referred to as *hanchirky*, which I think meant "rags." Everything was a little bit stained, warped, and fraying, and I didn't have the heart to tell her there was a hole in the seat of her pants. It wasn't her usual office attire, of course, but she insisted—really, truly insisted—that she scrub the entire joint before she started her new job.

"Any idea who it is?" Tommy was not pleased that we were being left without a secretary and that Betty was insinuating that his rat's nest of an office needed a wash and dust-up, but he knew not to hold it against Betty. She was a great secretary. But an even better nurse. There was no reason for her to continue to stick around here with our low pay, when she could be cutting people's corns off in the office of her new beau, Dr. Michael Wolf, foot doctor.

"It's Norma," Betty responded. "She was hoping you could meet her at her Times Square job and go to lunch with her."

Tommy checked his watch. "Tell her no problem."

Betty nodded and returned to her post.

"Actually, let's cut out a bit early," Tommy said, picking up his hat. "I want to take that pin of yours to someone who might know what it is."

"Oh, but it's so *warm* in here," I said from my seat on the radiator. "And February is *horrible*."

"That's how I feel about January," Tommy said with a grouch. "And you had me outside on New Year's Eve."

"Fine." We bundled up, Tommy slipped the velvet jewelry box into his pocket, and we told Betty we'd be back later.

"It's probably some cheap little jobbie," I said. "Why would Mr. Floristan leave us something nice?"

"Because I have a queer feeling in my stomach about Mr. Floristan," Tommy said. "I'll bet we haven't seen the last of him."

"Well, we've certainly *seen* the last of him," I said. "I doubt Floristan will ever make another office visit. But I doubt we've *heard* the last of him. Our next secretary is going to have a fun time opening the mail for the foreseeable future. Encoded post-cards, letters, presents. Who knows what's going to show up?"

"Too right."

We found the pawnshop Tommy was looking for on 53rd near the fancy part of town between 5th and 6th.

"This'll be the fella." Tommy opened the door to a light tinkle of bells, and a man with a sleeve of tattoos up to his elbow greeted us at the front case.

"Looking for something special for the missus?" he asked, nodding at me. "Something to say 'I'm sorry,' 'She meant nothing,' or 'Thanks for the beautiful baby boy'?"

"Nothing like that," I said. "Yet."

"Besides, if there's ever a 'She meant nothing' scenario, I have a feeling you'll be reading about someone finding my head in the East River."

"Oh, don't be silly, honey, they'll never find it," I said, laying my hand on Tommy's shoulder.

The tattooed pawnbroker laughed. "Okay, you two, I give up."

I plucked the box from my fiancé's pocket. "We were wondering if you could tell us about whatever this is."

The man took the case, opened it, and grabbed a jeweler's loupe. "Hmm. This is a weird one."

"You're telling me," I said. "The finish is hand-hammered and not very shiny. The spiral shape is not perfect, either."

"It's handmade, every bit of it," the pawn man said. "Do you see how the pin part of the brooch . . ."

"Yeah, it's just wire that's wrapped around a section. And it secures in a looped bit of metal, not a standard safety-type pin clasp."

"How good are your eyes?"

"Not good enough to have found whatever you want to tell me, probably," I said. I was leaning on the case at this point, staring at the pin as if it was a holy relic. My body was tingling.

"The artist's name is scratched into the metal just . . . here." The pawnbroker picked up a pencil and pointed to a tiny little spot on the back of the pin.

"Calder?" I asked.

"Read it in one," the man said. "You heard of him?"

"No," I admitted. "But I'm not really one for fine things."

"Well, you've got a mighty fine thing right here." He slipped the piece back into its velvet box. "If you want to learn more, MoMA is right there." He nodded toward the street.

"What's MoMA?"

"Sweetie, you need to get out more," the pawnbroker scolded. "The Museum of Modern Art. You'll find at least half a dozen Calders inside."

"This pin is made by a man in a *museum*?"

"Yeah, and some people would be very happy to buy it off of you, if you wanted to sell it. I'm one of 'em. Peggy Guggenheim is another."

"Get out."

"Hold onto that, girl," the man behind the counter said. "It's only going to be worth more as the years go by. He doesn't sell a lot of his jewelry, it's mostly gifts for friends."

"Well, that's the weird bit about our client then," Tommy said. "Not an underwear salesman."

"No, definitely not."

The man behind the glass case gave us a look but carried on anyhow. "It's worth at least a grand, probably more. I can't believe I'm telling you this. I'm a pawnbroker. It's my job to fleece you."

"Well, if I ever have anything I need to hock, you're the first person I'll call," I said. "I'm Viviana Valentine, by the way. Private investigator."

"Well, if I ever need a gumshoe, I know who to call," he said. "Thanks for stopping by."

★　★　★

We exited to the sidewalk and Tommy wrapped his arm around my shoulder. "So, Dollface, how does it feel to be a few grand richer than you were at the start of the year?"

"Strange," I said. "It doesn't feel like I earned any of it."

"Sure you did," Tommy said. "Living with Tally Blackstone for a few months more than earned you that Cadillac, and getting all those puzzles solved sure was worth the brooch."

"You know, I didn't solve a single one of those ciphers," I pointed out. "I just found the people who could. Betty got two of them and Rocío, and her military contacts, did the second."

"Eh. Don't remind the girls of that," Tommy said. "But let's get a move on, we're going to be late to meet Norma."

Our eight-block scurry south got us to Monsieur Baiser's just as Norma was leaving the front entrance, knapsack in hand. She was steaming, her arms crossed in front of her, and kicking a black hill of slush like she wanted it dead.

"Come on, I'm completely starving," she said. She marched along at a good clip, barreling through men in suits who spun at the force of the short woman knocking into them, unaware that she was even there on the sidewalk in the first place. Tommy and I struggled to stay in her wake, even though we each had inches on her stride. We ended up at an enormous automat, the front doors chromed and as shiny as the entrance to a temple, but this one just served sandwiches, cakes, cookies, and anything else you could dream of having for lunch.

Tommy pulled on the gleaming metal door pull and herded the two of us in. Just inside the entrance was an older lady with a beehive hairdo sitting behind a brass cage. In front of her was a worn slab of marble. Tommy handed the lady at the counter a fiver, and she handed back a sack of a hundred nickels, which rested comfortably in the groove of the stone.

Tommy opened the sack, and Norma and I each took a handful of coins. "Go crazy," he said. "I'll grab us a table."

The entire restaurant was two tiers of homage to postwar efficiency. Upstairs and down were rows and rows of marble tables with cast-iron pedestals, wooden chairs, and girls in mint-green uniforms whisking away tubs of clanking dirty dishes, each with bright lipstick and a smile on their face despite how much cranberry sauce and cola was spilled down the front of their aprons.

We lined up for trays and separated at the walls of food. First stop was sandwiches, where two nickels got me a pastrami on pumpernickel with a whole mound of coleslaw right on top. Then a plate of dill pickles for another five cents, a slab of macaroni and cheese, and a wedge of apple pie. Topped off with a cup of coffee dispensed automatically from an ornate brass nozzle in the shape of a weird sea creature, and I had a whole buffet in front of me for less than fifty cents.

Norma and I reconvened at the table where Tommy sat, stomach gurgling. She'd managed to pick up baked beans and three different kinds of dessert with her coffee.

"Don't you want to eat anything that has a vitamin?" Tommy asked, staring at her coconut cream pie, cherry pie, and vanilla cake decorated with a single red icing rose.

"Nope!" Norma sat down and picked up a fork. "I know you bought lunch, but I'm going to start without you."

"Better hurry," I said, plopping down and picking up a pickle.

"Be right back."

I let Norma eat her baked beans in peace and didn't even bother with a question until Tommy returned with chicken salad on white and a glass of orange juice.

"So, what's the matter?" I asked as soon as Tommy plopped his keister in the chair next to Norma.

"Vice squad rolled through all the joints," she said. "The Turn Out has turned out the lights. And it's not like Marv was keeping a low profile with that stupid name for the peep show."

"Both of 'em?" I asked. "In the same *day*?"

"The coppers kindly let me do my last morning shift at the show," she said. "Turns out they watched the whole time before arresting Marv and chasing all the girls out. I'm lucky I even got a skirt on before I was out on the sidewalk."

"Jesus Christ," Tommy muttered.

"In his name, that's for sure." Norma was violently shoveling her coconut cream pie into her mouth, the flaky bits of candied coconut on top falling off her fork like snow.

"Any idea who called for the bust?" I asked. My guts knew the answer already and I put down my half a pastrami.

"The detective that picked up Pretty Boy, I think." Norma was unaware how far back Detective Lawson went with our office, and I set a little reminder in my brain to return to the office, call Midtown North, and give the investigator a little piece of my mind. "As soon as you and your fella were photographed in front of the dance club, they had no choice but to shut us down."

"I'm real sorry that happened," I said. "How long does a place usually stay open before the vice raids start?"

"They start almost as soon as the door is unlocked," Norma pointed out. "But I've never stayed at a joint for longer than a few months."

Tommy caught my eye and gave me a nod. I couldn't help but smile. "You know, Norma, our secretary is leaving tomorrow."

"Hmm?"

"The pay isn't probably as good as the clubs, but the hours are slightly shorter and more regular," I said. "How'd you like to answer some phones at our office for a little while? Just until you can go back to your other work."

"You really mean it?" Norma threw down her fork and got up to throw her arms around my neck. "I had no idea how I was going to pay the bills this month."

"Of course we mean it," Tommy said. "Can you answer a phone and make coffee?"

"Of course."

"Then there's nothing else you can't learn," he shrugged.

"Besides, taking that fella out for a drink when you knew he was the one who murdered Henry," I said. "That was braver than *anything.*"

Norma had tears streaking down her cheeks, taking most of her paint with 'em. "I was so scared to go into that bar, it didn't have any windows and I was sure he was going to do something stupid."

"The cops should be giving you a medal, not busting up your employment," I said, pounding my fist on the table.

"I'd prefer if they just left me and the other girls alone."

"Maybe one day," I said. "But you have us, whenever you need. And if you need a gig now, then we got a gig for you starting on Monday." I slipped her our business card so she could have the address.

"I don't know what to say."

"Say something to the lady at the counter," Tommy said, throwing down another few dollar bills. "Get us some nickels. We need more food to celebrate."

* * *

We spent hours chatting in the restaurant and getting to know our new secretary. She went home with a whole great big bag of leftovers, plus a bag of food from the shop next door, once she explained that her three roommates were also dancers for Marv at the club. Tommy and I went back to his apartment to listen to the wireless and sleep it all off.

I curled up on Tommy's sofa in my flannel pajamas, a hot toddy in my mitt, while Tommy fiddled in the kitchen trying to come up with a snack.

"I'm *filled* with apple pie," I moaned. "How can you think of eating?"

"I found the pizzicato I got earlier this week," he said, pulling out a canister of cookies filled with jam. "You can't turn these down."

"You're right." I grabbed an apricot jelly and set to munching it. "These are good."

"Not as good as my mother's," he mumbled through crumbs. "You want to meet her this weekend? I'm going up on Saturday."

"I . . ."

"Short notice, I know, but everyone's going to be there. Donna, Gina, Bianca. All the husbands and their rug rats."

"That's . . . a lot."

"Like pulling off a Band-Aid," Tommy said. "Just get it over with."

"And then we'll have to start planning the whole thing," I said, my insides getting nervous.

"Sure, but you know what?"

"What?"

"You have to go on vacation first." Tommy reached over to the coffee table and pulled a plane ticket out of a magazine. "One ticket to Los Angeles, round trip. You leave on Monday afternoon."

"Oh God!" I took the ticket, my hands shaking.

"What?" Tommy asked. "I thought you'd be happy!"

"I am!" I admitted, throwing my arms around his neck. "But I don't know what's scarier—meeting my mother-in-law, or getting on a plane!"

ACKNOWLEDGMENTS

First and foremost, I must thank David for keeping me sane and alive while writing this book and for keeping everything else going. Those few months sucked, but you made it work.

My editor, Faith Black Ross, for taking a chance on Viv and offering me a series of books in which to explore her personality and growth. I never thought I'd write more than one book, but you gave me a career.

Endless gratitude for my incomparable agent, Anne Tibbets, and Donald Maass. The entire team at Crooked Lane Books: Madeline Rathle, Rebecca Nelson, Dulce Botello, and Melissa Rechter. You do so much work and a sentence or two of praise does not seem enough.

A special thank you to cover designer Rui Ricardo, who made Viv tangible. And to my friends who have nudged me along the way: Andrew Rostan, Michelle Athy, Taverlee and Z Laskauskas, Will Wallace, Nekesa Afia, and Lauren and Dani and Val and Emmett and Lillah and Philip and Derik and Rob and everyone I've met through FBOL who has turned into a true friend and cheerleader—thank you. My aunts Teresa and Jeanne and Maria and cousins Tricia and Kelly. You are an amazing community and I owe you.

And my therapist, Suzanne. Sorry I cried so much.